Praise for the novels of Laura Caldwell

The Year of Living Famously

"Sharply observed, fresh and compelling,
The Year of Living Famously is a captivating look
into the cult of celebrity."
—Leslie Stella, author of *The Easy Hour* and *Fat Bald Jeff*

"A stylish, sassy novel that shows the dark side
that haunts the world of glamour and glitz.
Laura Caldwell paints a sensitive picture of two ordinary
lives thrown into turmoil by the pressures of fame."
—*USA TODAY* bestselling author Carole Matthews

A Clean Slate

"Told with great energy and charm,
A Clean Slate is for anyone who has ever fantasized about
starting over—in other words, this book is for everyone!"
—Jill A. Davis, author of *Girls' Poker Night*

"Weightier than the usual fare, Caldwell's winning second
novel puts an appealing heroine in a tough situation and
relays her struggles with empathy."
—*Booklist* (starred review)

Burning the Map

"This debut novel won us over with its exotic locales
(Rome and Greece); strong portrayal of the bonds between
girlfriends; cast of sexy foreign guys; and, most of all, its
touching story of a young woman at a crossroads in her life."
—*Barnes&Noble.com*
(Selected as one of "The Best of 2002")

"The author produces excellent settings and characters.
It is easy to identify with her protagonist, Casey.
We learn that maybe the rat race isn't all it's cracked up
to be. This is a very thought provoking book."
—*Heartland Reviews*

Laura Caldwell

The Night I Got Lucky

**RED
DRESS
INK**
TM

THE NIGHT I GOT LUCKY

A Red Dress Ink novel

ISBN 0-373-89531-3

www.RedDressInk.com

Printed in U.S.A.

Acknowledgments

Thank you so very much
to my editor, Margaret O'Neill Marbury,
my agent, Maureen Walters, and the crew at
Red Dress Ink—Donna Hayes, Dianne Moggy,
Laura Morris, Craig Swinwood, Katherine Orr,
Marleah Stout, Steph Campbell, Sarah Rundle,
Margie Miller and Tara Kelly. Thanks also to the
amazing friends who read my work and help me shape
it—Kris Verdeck, Kelly Harden, Ginger Heyman,
Ted MacNabola, Clare Toohey, Mary Jennings Dean,
Pam Caroll, Karen Uhlman, Jane Jacobi,
Trisha Woodson and Joan Posch.

Most of all, thank you to Jason Billups.

prologue

There was so much more security at the Sears Tower than there used to be. Of course, the last time she'd been to the indoor observation deck on the highest floor, she was a freshman in high school. She and her girlfriend had locked arms and whispered about the upcoming dance, more concerned with scoring some Boone's Farm wine than the panorama.

She was distracted today, too. She had a purpose.

She filed out of the elevator behind a group of gum-cracking, giggling kids, a few backpackers from Australia and two Japanese tourists gripping guide books like life preservers. She held the tiny object in her right hand, not wanting to lose it in her purse. If she could just get a second, just one second alone, hopefully she would be done with it.

A guide stood outside the elevator. She was a young black woman, wearing braided chains around her neck and skin-tight hot pants below her Sears Tower uniform shirt. She looked as if any minute she might grab a microphone and audition for *American Idol.* "This way," the guide trilled, drawing out the last word.

The observation deck took up the entire top level of the Sears Tower, and was surrounded by floor-to-ceiling windows. In the center were giant exhibits, touting the history of Chicago.

The groups scattered. She glanced over her shoulder at the guide and followed the Japanese tourists to the right. It was nearly the end of the workday, but because it was summer, the sunlight blazed inside from the west windows.

She wandered around the deck, from window to window. She pretended to be absorbed by the view of the Loop from the east, sight of Soldier Field from the south. But as she looped around again, she looked more closely this time, not at the vista of the city laid out before her, but at the center of the room. She hoped there was some access away from the observation deck other than just the elevator.

Finally, she saw what she was looking for—next to a display featuring Chicago architecture was a tall silver door with the sign reading Stairs. Emergency Use Only. But there was an alarm on the door that would sound if she opened it. She chewed at her bottom lip. She didn't want to scare anyone. She just had to get rid of it.

The door was behind a rope, but that barrier would be easy to get around. She leaned against a nearby window and waited.

The pop star guide passed by at one point. "Enjoying yourself?" the guide asked.

"Oh. Yes." She swung around and slipped a quarter in a telescope. She focused it in the direction of her Gold Coast apartment, wondering idly if she'd turned off her straightening iron this morning. The guide moved away.

She kept checking her watch. The observation deck

would soon close. She tried not to tap her foot nervously. Now that she was here, she wanted desperately to do this. But would she get the chance? A better question—could she pull it off?

Finally, about fifteen minutes later, two workers clad in navy blue coveralls and carrying toolboxes undid the rope that stood in front of the stairwell door. One selected a key from his tool belt and put it in the alarm box. The other re-hooked the rope behind him. The door swung open, and they moved through it. As soon as it started to shut, she leaped over the rope and caught the door with her hand. She stood there a moment, frozen, hoping the guide wouldn't come back. When she was sure the workers were gone, she slipped inside.

The door closed, and she blinked to let her eyes adjust. The stairway was dimly lit except for red exit signs, all pointing downward. But she went the other way. She went up.

As she stepped through the doorway and onto the roof of the Sears Tower, the wind whipped violently, nearly knocking her over. She caught the door before it slammed and wedged her purse in the frame so it wouldn't lock behind her. Her hair was whisked straight back from her face. Her black skirt, newly purchased from a boutique on Damen Avenue, flapped against her legs. It was adorable and expensive and wholly inappropriate for the task at hand.

She was now in the middle of the flat roof, flanked by two giant antennas. She avoided them and cautiously made her way toward the edge. She clenched her fist tighter around the object in her right hand. She felt as if any minute the wind might whip her off the building.

The roof was gravelly and painted white. It made her feel even less sure of her footing. Still clasping the little object, she inched closer to the side.

Over the rooftop, she could see Lake Michigan glittering blue. She could see the cars on Lake Shore Drive whizzing past that blue. Her breathing became more shallow as she neared the edge. Only a few feet now. A gust swooped around her, seemed to push her sideways.

"Oh, God. Oh, God," she said, but the wind was too loud to hear herself.

She froze then. *Do it,* she told herself. *You're so close.*

But she couldn't make herself walk any farther. She stood for a few moments until a burst of wind nearly picked her off her feet. Shaking, she hitched up her new skirt slightly, dropped to her knees and began to crawl. The graveled surface cut into her skin, made her knees sting with pain. The skin on her right knuckles scratched as she crawled on her fist.

The rim of the roof came nearer until at last she was there. Her body trembled as she peered over the edge. The cars on Franklin Avenue looked like shiny colored beetles, the people as teeny as gnats.

Balancing on her left hand, she lifted her right hand and, slowly unclenching her fist, dropped it.

chapter one

My name is Billy. Not *B-I-L-L-I-E*, like Billie Holiday—which would be a smooth-voiced, sensuous woman's name—but *B-I-L-L-Y*, like a chubby little boy in a baseball uniform. Fact is my father wanted the boy in the uniform. He wanted boxers and brawlers and hunters. What he got was three daughters.

He gave us male names. (My mother claims to have been nearly comatose from the kind of potent childbirth drugs they don't use anymore.) He named us Dustin, Hadley and Billy. What he thought this would accomplish, I'm not certain. Possibly he hoped for some genetic, postpartum miracle, brought on by the names, which would produce male offspring overnight. It almost worked with my sisters. Dustin and Hadley are tall, lean women who run corporations during the week and marathons on the weekend. They drink scotch, and they own at least two sets of golf clubs each. They're the type to say to their respective husbands, "I don't care what the drapes look like, just don't spend more than ten thousand dollars."

I thought about Dustin and Hadley as I sat in a meeting for a new business pitch. Roslyn Jorno, my boss at the PR agency of Harper Frankwell, stood at the head of the conference table. Roslyn was a small woman who almost always dressed in dove-gray. She didn't look happy today, and we all knew that couldn't be good. Roslyn lived for her work (in fact, it was rumored that she actually *lived* at our offices on Michigan Avenue), so when she was unhappy, the rest of us were soon to be miserable, too.

"This isn't going to work, people," she said, pointing to a board behind her. On it was a list of suggested headlines we might obtain for our client, Grenier's Stud Finder, whose product used NASA-like technology to find wall studs. The headlines read: "Ladies Can Find Studs at Chicago Hardware Show," "Studs Aren't Hard To Come By Anymore," and "Find the Stud That's Right For You."

"'Ladies can find studs'?" Roslyn said mockingly.

I shot a glance at Alexa Villa seated next to me. Alexa, an annoyingly beautiful woman with dark hair and fair skin, had come up with that first headline.

"And 'find the stud that's right for you'?" Roslyn said. "Are we selling sex or hardware?" She crossed her arms and stared pointedly at me.

Apparently, she didn't like my work so much either. I had to admit I'd written the other headlines.

"I believe that was Billy's," said Alexa Villa seated next to me.

"Elegant, people! I want elegant. Understand?" Roslyn always preached elegance, which killed me. We crafted publicity campaigns for everything from power tools to pharmaceutical drugs to local news shows, but none of those products or clients was particularly elegant. It wasn't as if we were pushing the symphony orchestra.

Even though I rarely saw them, I thought of my sisters then because I was sure Dustin and Hadley not only owned stud finders with laser technology but knew how to use them. Yet Dustin and Hadley were both the epitome of elegance, the kind of women whose angular frames looked stylish in jeans and a man's T-shirt while they wielded a power saw.

I, on the other hand, would take off a limb if I tried to use a power saw. I wouldn't know a putter from a hockey stick, and the mere whiff of scotch makes me flinch.

"Elegant," said Evan across the table. "Very interesting." As if he hadn't heard this thirty-three thousand times before. "You're absolutely right, Roz."

Since Evan had made vice president, he'd been calling Roslyn "Roz," something no one else had ever attempted, and, Evan being Evan, he got away with it. I couldn't help but grin when he turned his head and winked at me. Although I'd been married for two years, I had a little crush on Evan. Okay, more than a little. My friend Tess liked to call it the Everlasting Crush.

"Billy," Roslyn said, "you do know that most of our target demographic is male, right?"

I glared at Alexa, then cleared my throat, and sat taller. "Of course, but the point is to grab attention. And these headlines, if we could talk the press into them, would grab anyone's attention, male or female."

"Well, let's not alienate our male audience, okay?"

I hated Roslyn's habit of speaking in questions. It made me want to do the same thing. It made me want to ask, *Wouldn't it help all of us if you got laid?*

"No problem," I said instead. I batted away the thought that it would probably help if *I* got laid once in a while.

"And Billy," Roslyn said, "you realize this campaign is important for a number of reasons, right?"

If it were possible, I would have crawled under the table. Lately, Roslyn had been making ominous threats (always posed as queries, of course) that not only might I miss the VP promotion I'd been waiting for since the Mesozoic Era, but I might be demoted (or worse) if my productivity didn't improve. And now this loosely veiled threat in front of the team let everyone know my ass was on the line. I saw Alexa suppressing a grin. Evan, God love him, looked miserable for me. The rest of the group shifted uncomfortably in their chairs. Should I quit now? I wanted to. I *desperately* wanted to. But the truth was I'd been putting out my feelers for months and the industry was in a lockdown. No one was hiring.

"I understand completely," I said. With the last shred of dignity I had in my body, I looked right at her. There was a painful silence during which Roslyn and I stared at each other. No one muttered a word. William, the guy to my right, shuffled some papers. Alexa cleared her throat.

In my mind, a montage of photos from my career at Harper Frankwell flashed before me—first as an eager intern rising quickly to assistant and then account exec and so on. It seemed I was a natural at the job, and I adored it. I loved writing press releases, creatively shading words and drawing out sentences to make our clients appear more worldly or accomplished or cutting edge. I loved pitching those clients to the press, subtly hounding producers and editors until the victorious moment when they caved and agreed to cover us. It seemed right to everyone, including myself, that I was heading straight for a vice presidency. I'd been told by Jack Varner, my old boss, that it was a formality, merely a matter of months. But then Jack found God, or something approximating God, and followed that deity to California where he was now training to become an instructor of Bikram yoga. In came Roslyn and out went my thoughts of professional glory.

In the boardroom now, Roslyn and I still stared at each other. I could feel a bead of sweat collect under the waistband of my pants. I could feel the glances that the team members shot from one of us to the other.

Finally, Roslyn dropped her eyes to the pad of paper in front of her. She crossed something out, probably my future, and called the meeting to an end.

Evan waited for me outside the doorway.

"Don't worry about it," he said as we walked down the hall. He gave me a thump on the arm worthy of a linebacker.

In the PR world, which is populated by so many women and gay men, Evan was the token straight guy. The token straight guy who happened to have thick yellow-blond hair, mint-green eyes and dimples that creased his cheeks when he smiled. The linebacker pats were for the best, I knew. I couldn't be tempted by someone who thought of me only as buddy material.

"Seriously, don't listen to her bullshit," Evan said. "Just do your normal stellar job, and maybe this will be the campaign that gets you the VP."

"Right," I said. I prayed he was correct. I prayed that Roslyn's threats were really just tough love maneuvers designed to motivate me.

We reached Evan's office, the one he got when he was named VP. The wall behind his desk was covered with an eclectic combination of Renee Magritte prints, Notre Dame football posters and framed handbills from the band, Hello Dave.

"It's been a long time since I've seen those guys." I pointed to a Hello Dave poster announcing a show at the Aragon.

Before Chris and I got married, Evan and I used to see Hello Dave together. We would drink way too much and dance until way too late. The music made my heart thump with happiness; it made my body feel light and free. The music seemed to separate me from myself in the most wonderful way. It made me bold enough to bat my eyes and drop some not so subtle hints, hoping Evan would make a pass. He never did. The next morning, we'd huddle around the pretzel tin in the company kitchen, deconstructing the set list, the people we'd run into, the women who'd given Evan their numbers. But then, I met Chris and my crush on Evan disappeared. Eventually, I stopped attending Hello Dave shows.

"They've got a gig this Saturday," Evan said, sounding excited. "Yeah, it's at Park West. You've got to come."

"Maybe." But I knew I wouldn't go. My crush had returned sometime in the past year—residing back in my subconscious—and thinking about Hello Dave reminded me how hot and bothered Evan could make me. No need to torture myself, and besides, Chris and I were supposed to have dinner with my mother in Barrington.

"Oh, c'mon. For old time's sake." He smiled, and those dimples pleated his smooth golden skin.

"Who're you bringing?"

"Shelly."

"A new one?"

"Yep, and she's hot. God, you should see her. You wouldn't frickin' believe how hot this girl is." This was how Evan talked to me—again, like a fellow linebacker.

Strangely, many people in my life seemed to think I was a man, or asexual in some way. This now included Evan, and even my husband. We had gone from having sex at least twice a week prewedding to, if I was very lucky, twice a month postwedding.

"Who loves ya, girl?" Evan said as I neared the door.

I answered as usual. A listless, "You do." Because Evan didn't really love me, except as a close friend. That was enough, I knew logically—I was married, after all—but this little ritual often depressed me.

"You got it," he said.

"Billy, honey, how did the new business meeting go?"

My mother knew entirely too much about my life. I'd mentioned once that such meetings usually took place on Monday mornings, and now here she was calling me, at precisely 11:00 on Monday.

"Not so great." I put on my headset and clicked on the Internet. If I gave my mother's daily phone calls my undivided attention, I'd never get any work done.

"What happened?" she asked. "Didn't Roslyn like your stud finder ideas?"

Damn, had I told her about the Grenier's campaign? That would add an extra ten minutes to this call.

"You should ask Dustin or Hadley about it," she continued. "They probably know about those tools."

This immediately saddened me. It was true that Dustin and Hadley knew something about hardware, but it was also true that they both avoided our mother, claiming busyness and time changes. My mom was only mentioning their names now to see if I'd spoken to them, to learn about the two daughters she didn't know very well anymore.

"I got an e-mail from Hadley last week," I said.

My eyes shot to the black-framed photo next to my computer monitor. In the picture, my mom and I, the short women in the family, are flanked by Dustin and Hadley, who rise over us, looking like twins. It was taken in San Francisco, right after Dustin moved there and a few months before Hadley was transferred to the London office of the investment bank she worked for. That was four years ago. I'd seen Dustin three times since then—once at her wedding, once at mine and once when I was out West for business. I'd only seen Hadley the one time at Dustin's wedding. Hadley and her husband, Nigel, hadn't been able to make it to mine. There was no great rift, no great drama, except for the little fact of what had happened twenty-five years ago—our father took off. None of us had seen him again. None of us had been the same since. It had wounded us each separately and we'd never been able to truly help one another. And so over time, Dustin and Hadley had drifted farther and farther away.

"What was in the e-mail?" my mother asked, her voice forlorn.

"Hadley is really crazy right now," I said, hoping to assuage the melancholy in her voice. "The bank might be bought out, and so she's in meetings all the time."

Roslyn stopped by my cube and waved one of my press releases. "Can I see you?" she said in a loud whisper.

I put on a serious face and nodded. I pointed at the phone and mouthed, "Client. One minute."

Roslyn sighed, gestured toward her office, then left.

"Is Hadley still trying to get pregnant?" my mom said. If it was possible, her voice became more heartbreaking. She knew little about Hadley's procreative attempts, and since Hadley had sworn never to move back to the States. ("Why should I?" she'd said. "It's more civilized here and people aren't so nosy.") We'd probably never see the result of those attempts, even if she were successful.

"I think so," I said.

"Ah, well, I'm sure she'll be calling to tell me soon."

"I'm sure, Mom."

I opened my e-mail program. *You have 67 new messages,* it said. "Shit," I muttered.

"What's that, Billy?"

"Nothing." It was hard to cut her off, even when I had no time to talk. Somehow, I'd become my mom's only daily social outlet. She had sisters who lived on the North Shore, but they hadn't had much contact since my mom married my dad so many years ago. My aunts had foreseen what an utter schmuck he'd be, and my mother was too embarrassed to give them the satisfaction of admitting they were right. And since her second husband, Jan, died three years ago, she'd almost secluded herself, rarely visiting with the few friends she had in Barrington.

"What are you doing today, Mom?" I asked. "You should get out of the house."

"I know," she said simply. "I'll try." My mom kept saying how she wanted to move on—she wanted to get over Jan's death and get on with her life, but her motivation seemed to have disappeared.

"So anyway, sweetie," she said, changing the subject, "are you still seeing that therapist?"

I groaned and began reading my e-mail in earnest—one from Evan reminding me about the Hello Dave show on Friday night, one from my husband asking me to buy his flax-seed oil when I stopped at the grocery store on my way home. "Yes," I said. "I'm seeing her tonight, actually."

"And what will you discuss? You and Chris, I assume. How is he?"

"He's fine, mom, and I'm sorry but I've got to go."

"Maybe you can talk to her about your father, too. I was

able to let that go when I married Jan. But you still need to work on that."

"I know, Mom, I will. Love you. Bye now."

"Bye, baby doll. And don't forget to talk to that therapist about work, too. I think you're angry."

My mother was right. I did have some anger socked away. It had started small, somewhere in my rib cage. I'd trapped it there for a while, ignoring that tiny but festering wound, because I didn't want to be one of those people who hadn't a single good thing to say about their life. Yet that pocket of anger had grown over the past few years, despite my best intentions. I expected certain rewards from my life, I had worked to achieve certain milestones, and yet I'd missed the meeting when recognition and happiness were passed out.

The vice presidency was one issue. I'd earned it.

My mother was another. I loved the woman so much. She had raised three girls on her own, for years taking in stride the ridicule of a small Illinois town that gleefully watched as her rich husband escaped to the glitz of the west coast; a town that somehow enjoyed the carnage my father left in his wake. Much later, she finally moved to another suburb and found some peace with Jan, but he'd suffered a stroke while standing at the barbeque on a warm September day. Now she was alone again. Alone, and way too invested in my life. She needed one of her own.

On the other end of the parental spectrum was my father. I'd never gotten over him leaving. At seven, I was the youngest, and for some reason I'd always assumed it was his disappointment in me that had pushed him to flee. I wanted desperately to get over that notion. To be done with him.

My husband was the remaining piece of the anger puzzle. My clichéd attempts at seduction were too painful to recount—feel free to insert stereotypical woman wearing lingerie waiting with cold dinner image—and so I'd given up trying to entice him, trying to figure out what was wrong with him. With us. With me. We were roommates now. Roommates who occasionally, *very occasionally,* scratched an itch.

When I was in one of these black moods, there were two things that would help—throwing myself into work or hitting a bar and seeing some good, loud live music. The Hello Dave show was coming up, but Chris didn't like seeing bands as much as I did, and we'd committed long ago to visiting my mom. I hated to disappoint her. So work would have to be it.

I went and spoke to Roslyn about my press release. When I came back, I opened the computer file that read *Odette Lamden.* Odette was a local chef who occasionally went on the news shows as their cooking expert. Odette's restaurant, Comfort Food, was one of my favorites, because it served just that—comfort food, stuff like mac and cheese (with four cheeses), overly buttered mashed potatoes, bread pudding, gooey with caramel, and fudge sundaes as big as your head. I'd met Odette on a TV set one day when I'd gone to visit a publicist who'd enlisted us to handle extra work. Two days later, Odette hired me, or I should say hired Harper Frankwell, to publicize her cookbook, also called *Comfort Food.* Her own publisher had done little to promote it, and she wanted to get the word out there. It was the type of client I loved—someone who needed help with a product I truly liked.

But Roslyn had been less than thrilled. "It's not even ten thousand dollars worth of work," she'd said, scrunching her mouth disapprovingly. This was Roslyn's main complaint with me, and why she asserted I wasn't ready for a vice presidency—I wasn't pulling in any big fish, and I was wasting the firm's time on the small stuff. "It could turn into something big," I said.

"Doubtful," Roslyn answered.

"I think we owe it to the community to help certain people once in a while. People who can't afford big campaigns."

"We owe it to this company to make money, don't we?" Roslyn looked down at her desk, my cue to leave.

I understood her protests, but I believed in the smaller clients I brought in. There was something rewarding about helping shed a little media light on products and people you believed in. And Odette and I had such fun working on her cookbook. I'd stop by the restaurant after she closed early on Sunday nights, and we'd huddle in her colorful office, eating leftovers and brainstorming about how to get her on *Oprah*. Odette, a forty-five-year-old black woman, whose family originally hailed from New Orleans, had become a friend as well as a client during this process. I wanted to get her book the best possible PR, no matter what Roslyn said.

But I wouldn't think about Roslyn now. I wanted to work on a press release for *Comfort Food,* one that would land Odette interviews with newspapers and spots on radio shows. I started writing. *Sick of the Atkins Diet? How about the South Beach Diet? Tired of eating boiled chicken breasts and dressing-less salad? Renowned Chicago chef, Odette Lambden, owner of the acclaimed restaurant, Comfort Food, introduces a cookbook to soothe us all.*

Once I'd begun, I barely noticed the beige walls of my cubicle that had seemed tighter and more constricting lately. I ignored the ring of my phone, the beep from the bottom of the computer announcing an instant message. Instead, I tapped away at the keyboard, waxing poetic about Odette's book. I reread sentences, mulled over words and dialed up certain sections. This was what I loved about my job—generating excitement about a product or person, the imaginative use of words to reflect a given tone. The ability to create.

I was just rereading the press release for grammatical errors, feeling pleased with myself, content with my job, when Alexa appeared, leaning on the frame of my cube.

"Hey, Billy," she said. Alexa always said, "hey," never "hello" or "hi." She looked like a prep school princess, but she didn't always talk like one.

Alexa was one of those timeless women who could have passed for any age between twenty and thirty. Although I assumed she was twenty-seven or so, about five years younger than me, she possessed a haughtiness and a coolness that made her seem older. I supposed it was this confidence that had swept Alexa through the ranks at Harper Frankwell; unfortunately, with her cutthroat attitude and with her nipping on my heels, I couldn't appreciate it. My fear was that she would make vice president before I did, causing me to die of shame and jealousy.

My contented mood waned. *"Hey,"* I said back, drawing out the word.

Alexa gave me her patented you-are-such-a-fool smirk. "What are you going to do about the stud finder headlines?"

"What am *I* going to do?" This was a team project, after all, and she was on the damned team.

"Well, Roslyn seemed to want you to handle it, so I just want to respect that and ask you where you're going to start." She smirked again.

"It's supposed to be a team thing, Alexa. And let's make sure we take credit for our work, okay?"

I usually got along great with other women, but since the day Alexa had started, wearing her black cashmere twinsets and high, patent leather pumps, she had irked me. Her arrogant condescension got old quick. I'd tried to show her who was boss, so to speak, but I wasn't really her boss—just ahead of her in the food chain—and Alexa couldn't be shamed into submission. If anything the pressure made her more confident. If I had liked her even a little, I might have grudgingly approved of her don't-mess-with-me attitude.

"Oh, I'm not suggesting that you handle this project on your own," she said, laughing a little. "God, no."

See what I mean?

"What then?" I said, my voice flattening.

"Well…" She trailed off and crossed her arms. She was wearing the sleeveless part of one of her usual black cashmere twinsets. Since it was May, the cardigan would be thrown over her chair, waiting for the moment when the booming air-conditioning system kicked in, but meanwhile her movements showed off lean, sculpted arms. Alexa and I were around the same height—five-four—and we were both relatively thin, but her body was more toned, her skin more smooth, her black hair as shiny and pencil straight as my sisters'.

"I know this project is important for you, Billy," she said, the condescension as thick as fog.

I crossed my arms now. "What do you mean?"

She laughed again. I was beginning to think that if she laughed once more, I might launch Odette's cookbook at her head.

"Well, you know," she said coyly. "You're not getting any younger and you're certainly not getting promoted…" She shrugged.

And you're not getting any cuter and you're not getting married, I wanted to say. Instead, I remained silent, fixing her with a steely stare.

"So anyway," Alexa went on, "I was thinking, why don't

you try rewriting the headlines, then e-mail them to me, and I'll go over them for you."

"You'll 'go over them' for me? That's so nice of you."

"I thought so."

The truth was, I'd rather do the headlines on my own—I actually liked that kind of work. It was the meetings and the busy paperwork I disdained. But I wouldn't let Alexa get away with a monumental buck-passing.

"Fine," I said, "but I'd like you to make the media list." In our world, making the media list—the roll call of different targets for a PR blitz—was a bottom-of-the-barrel job, something an intern usually did.

Alexa let out a little puff of exasperated air and seemed to be ready to protest, but I knew she wouldn't. She was smarter than that. She had passed off work to me, but she'd have to handle something on this project or Roslyn would figure it out eventually.

"Fine," Alexa said, mimicking me.

I uncrossed my arms and swung back to my desk. I wished desperately I was a vice president right now. Not for the professional splendor of it all, but because if I was a VP, I would have an office and if I had an office, I would have a door. And if I had a door, I would slam it hard in Alexa's darling little face.

chapter two

Chris was at our condo when I got there, which was surprising. He'd already gotten his big promotion—partnership at one of the city's top law firms—but he worked harder now than he did before.

As I dumped my bag on the wood floor of our foyer, I saw that he *was* working, sitting in front of the computer, which we'd set up on the dining room table. (We rarely had people for dinner anyway, and we usually ate on our own or in front of the TV.)

"Hi, Bill," he said, when he heard me come inside. He didn't turn his tall frame from the computer. His big hands kept clacking awkwardly at the keyboard.

"Hello, Marlowe." Marlowe is Chris's middle name, after the playwright Christopher Marlowe. His parents, a couple of academics from the University of Chicago, are staunch proponents of the theory that Marlowe was the real author of Shakespeare's plays.

I patted Chris absently on the shoulder, a pat very similar to the one Evan had given me that day. "I got your flaxseed."

"Thanks."

"How was work?" I asked. "What's going on with that health care merger?"

"Nothing much."

I ruffled his short brown hair.

And that was about it. That was the extent of our marital affection. Not so different than any other day.

I went into the kitchen and put Chris's flaxseed oil in the stainless steel fridge. When we'd bought this place shortly before our wedding, we'd filled it with top-of-the-line appliances, gleaming granite countertops and shiny hardwood floors. It was as promising as our relationship. Now, God knows why, the only things luminous were our furnishings.

"I'm going to see Blinda," I called to Chris.

This made him twist around from the computer. "You're still seeing her?"

"Yes."

"I thought you said the therapy wasn't doing much."

"It's not."

"So—"

"So, I'm giving it a shot."

He nodded. "Well, that's good."

"How about coming with me?"

"Billy, you know…" He turned back to the computer, and I couldn't hear the rest of his words.

Chris didn't believe in therapists. He believed, like his parents, that William Shakespeare was a myth, but he didn't believe in therapists.

Blinda's office was on LaSalle, only a few blocks from our condo. I'd never noticed the place until one day while I was walking back from the gym. The building was a brick three-flat that appeared to house luxury apartments, like so many on the block, but that day I saw a small black sign with gold letters in the window of the basement unit. Blinda Bright, M.S.W. the sign read. For Appointments Call 312.555.9090.

I'm not sure why I stopped and stared at that sign for as long as I did. It was nearly April, a capricious time in Chicago, and although it had been a lovely sixty degrees the day before, it was in the forties. Despite my optimistically light coat and the fact that I'd begun to shiver, I stood in front of that brick building, staring at the gold lettering and the gold light that glowed from behind the curtains. M.S.W. meant masters in social work, right? So this Blinda person must be some kind of therapist. I committed the number to memory.

I had considered therapy for a while. I knew I was messed up about my father, I knew Chris had pulled away from me after we got married and I knew it was wrong that I coveted my coworker. Over the past few months, I'd collected referrals from friends, and I had five therapists I could try. But it was that sign in the basement window that, for some reason, made me realize now was the time and she was the one I should call.

At the initial appointment with Blinda, I decided to attack one issue at a time. I explained that the main reason I'd come to see her was, as I put it, "to get over the abandonment issues I have with my father." I thought this sounded rather intellectual and valid. Wasn't there a reverse Oedipus complex or something? But Blinda didn't approach it quite like that.

"He just took off, huh?" she said, shaking her head like she was pissed off. I told her what I knew about my father and how he'd left our house one morning and never came back.

"At first he told us that he had business in L.A.," I said. "He was an importer of goods from Germany, and he had a brother who ran things from overseas."

"What kind of goods?"

"Tiles, pots, earthenware."

"Ah." She sounded disappointed.

"Anyway, he said he had to go to Los Angeles for business, only he never came back. My mom spent lots of money looking for him and trying to enforce child support decrees, but he kept disappearing."

"Bastard," Blinda said under her voice.

I blinked a few times, studying her. Where were the sage comments about the father/daughter Oedipus complex or whatever it was?

"Right," I said. "Well, my mother eventually realized she had spent more money trying to find him than she'd likely ever get from alimony, so finally she just had to make do. Before he left, we had a great house with white columns. I always thought it looked like a wedding cake. We lived in this little town about an hour and a half northwest of Chicago."

Blinda smiled at the image.

"But she couldn't afford it anymore, so we moved into an apartment behind the old hospital. My mom had one bedroom and my sisters had another, and they put a cot for me in the half room by the washing machine."

Blinda nodded for me to continue. I hadn't talked about this for so long—maybe never—and now I felt like I couldn't stop. I told her about how we went from being one of the richest families in town to one of the poorest. I told her about how Dustin and Hadley were taunted at school about our deadbeat dad and how they became tough little girls, always getting into fights, coming home to proudly display black eyes and bloody noses. I explained that my mom got a job working as a receptionist at an auto plant, and that Dustin and Hadley had to get scholarships and put themselves through college. I told her about Jan and how it was he who put me through school and who took my mom out of that apartment behind the old hospital, out of that town and into the beautiful house in Barrington where she still lived.

Blinda chuckled at that point, although I didn't think I'd said anything particularly funny. She caught my inquisitive look. "Sorry," she said. "It's just ironic that your father considered himself such a man's man, enough to give you girls male names, and then your mother marries someone named Jan—a rather womanly sounding name—and he makes her happy again."

I laughed then, too. I think that's when I knew for certain that Blinda was going to be different from the therapists I'd heard about.

This was our sixth visit, although I felt in some ways as if I'd been seeing Blinda forever. I knew to hang my sweater on the antique brass rack inside the door. I knew to pour myself a cup of the jasmine-scented tea from the cracked Asian pot on her sideboard. I knew that I could just start talking whenever I wanted, that Blinda was always there with a nod of her blond head or an empathetic cluck of her tongue. I knew the routine, but I didn't necessarily feel any better for it.

"It's not that much to ask for," I said now.

"You want your husband to pay attention to you, is that right?" Blinda asked. I had moved from the topic of my father to my other issues—failing marriage, heartbroken mother with no life of her own, inappropriate crush on Evan, inability to get promoted.

"Well, yeah," I said. I shifted around on her woolly red and orange love seat that looked like it was purchased in a Marrakech marketplace. On either end sat bamboo tables with lit yellow candles and boxes of recycled tissue. Those boxes were always different, replaced, each time I came. It seemed I was Blinda's only client who didn't cry constantly. I was the only angry, irritated one. "Yeah, I want Chris to look at me like he used to when we were dating, but I want more than just that," I said.

"What else?" She leaned forward, her straight, blond hair swinging. I could not figure out Blinda. She looked like an aging beach bum, someone who would smoke a lot of pot and live in her parents' basement, and yet hanging on her wall were a plethora of framed diplomas, photos of Hindu Temples and two pictures of her with a robed, bespectacled man who looked very much like the Dalai Lama.

I sighed. I'd told her all this already. "I want to get the vice presidency. I want my mom to get her own life. I want to get over my dad. And I want Evan to want me."

She raised her eyebrows at that last one.

"Not that I'd do anything with Evan," I said. "It would just be nice if he had a thing for me."

"I see," Blinda said. "Billy, what have you actually done to get these things you desire for yourself?"

"Everything!"

She raised her eyebrows again.

"It's true! I've been campaigning for the VP job forever. I've asked Chris to go to therapy with me, but he won't. I'm talking to you about my mom and dad. I mean, I feel like I've been trying."

"At the risk of repeating myself, I'll tell you to look inside for your happiness." She put her hands together in a prayer position and put them against her T-shirt clad chest. On it was written something in French.

I stopped short of rolling my eyes. "I have."

Blinda studied me. "If you get those things you want, would you be happy then?"

"Yes," I said without hesitation. "Absolutely."

"You're sure?"

"Yes. As I said, I don't think I'm asking for that much."

She crossed her legs and rearranged her colorful, flowy skirt. "Billy, I'm going out of town for a while."

I opened and closed my mouth, surprised at the shift in topic and the concept of Blinda leaving. "Where are you going?"

"Africa. I'm going to visit the village where I lived when I was in the Peace Corps." She smiled beatifically, and I got an image of blond Blinda surrounded by native villagers doing tribal dances, praying for water. Immediately, I felt chagrined at my list of "needs."

"I'd like to give you something," Blinda continued. She stood up and crossed the room to an old wood hutch with glass doors. Opening one of them, she reached inside. When she turned around, she held a small green object in her hand. "Here you go."

The object was made of a glittery, jadelike material, and it was shaped like a frog on a lily pad. The frog's hind legs were rounded little haunches, his eyes tiny jade spheres. His mouth was a long slash that ran under the eyes.

"Well, uh…thank you." What was I supposed to do with it?

"In ancient Chinese culture, this icon was thought to bring good fortune to the owner."

"Right. Great." But what I was thinking was, *Of all the New Age crap…*.

"I'll let you know when I'm back in the city, but in the meantime, keep this. I hope it brings what you wish for."

"Thanks, Blinda." I glanced at the ivory clock on the cof-

fee table. My hour was up. I'd now have to cut her a check
for a hundred dollars, and all I had to show for it was a crappy
piece of green rock.

"What's that?" Chris said. He was in bed already with a little light reading—a book called *The Second Carthaginian War.*

"A frog." I put in on my nightstand next to my clock and
set the clock for seven-fifteen. "Blinda gave it to me."

"Why?"

"I'm not entirely sure."

Chris laughed. "Sounds like a top-of-the-line therapist."

I put a hand on my hip and gave him a look.

"Sorry," he said, still laughing.

I looked at the frog again. It seemed so little and Asian
and out of place on my contemporary maple nightstand,
next to my sleek black clock that played ocean and rainfor-
est sounds in addition to the radio. And then I couldn't help
but laugh, too.

"Come to bed," Chris said with a smile, and I wondered
if tonight was going to be one of those few nights we spent
in each other's arms. There used to be many of them.

I remembered the evening I'd met him at a northside pizza
place. We'd been set up by Tess, my high school girlfriend,
and her husband, Tim, who worked with Chris. Chris was
adorable that night in his navy suit and tie, his brown leather
loafers shiny and uncreased as if he'd just bought them. He
was eager to meet me, unlike Evan, who never seemed to notice me, and unlike the other guys I met, who had to be oh-
so-cool all the damn time. We bonded at first over two small,
strange things—our birthdays were only one day apart and
our parents had given us weird names.

"Billy's not so bad," Chris had said. "Think about my middle name. I mean Marlowe, for Christ's sake. It's so pompous,

but it really means something to them. If you meet my parents, don't ask them about it. They will never shut up."

I smiled, wondering if he really thought I'd meet his parents one day. "Well, if you ever meet my sisters, don't challenge them to anything. They're fiercely competitive, and they play to win." I told him about my previous boyfriend, a guy named Walter with the ghastly nickname of Wat, who made the mistake of telling Dustin that he was an ace chess player. The two times they met each other, Dustin and Wat huddled over the chessboard. And both times she won.

Chris and I talked all about our families, barely noticing Tess and Tim, who sat across the table with pleased smiles. When we left the restaurant, he walked me the eight blocks home, even though it was the opposite direction of his place.

It was seamless. It was as if we were dating right from that night. I loved his big hands, his tall lanky body. I loved how he tilted his head a little to the side when I talked, like he was fascinated with my words. We went to Cubs games—Chris's passion, despite the fact that he'd grown up on the south side. We saw quirky foreign films at the Landmark Theatre, then went to the bookstore across the street. We spent weekends at his apartment on Eugenie Terrace, where the decor had no apparent theme. The place had books all over and a huge comfortable chair under the windows where I sat and read while Chris cooked. I liked how he used odd little vegetables I'd never heard of before. I liked how he went across town to a gourmet delicatessen to buy a cheese his mom recommended. And I liked what happened when we went to bed at night.

But after we were married—or was it during the planning of the wedding?—Chris gradually stopped listening intently the way he always had. When I spoke, he barely looked up from his computer or his book. He agreed with my suggestions without contributing. He stayed on his side of the bed. When I brought it up, he said he didn't know what I meant. He was busy, I was busy, and that was all there was to it.

But it seemed Chris was in the mood tonight.

"I'll be right there," I said, giving him a smile. With a spark in my step, I went into the master bath—white and gray granite in there with maple cabinets—quickly brushed my teeth and gave myself a spritz of perfume. I opened the door and began undoing the buttons of my blouse in what I hoped was a sexy way, but I could tell I'd already lost him. His nose was buried in the Carthaginian War again, the covers pulled up to his chin.

When I slid in bed he squeezed my hand for a brief moment. "Love you," he said absently, not taking his eyes away from his book.

"You, too," I said, which was true. I still loved my husband. I turned over and looked at the frog one more time before I shut off the light.

chapter three

There were people in my bedroom, and they were talking. Laughing. Too much laughter.

I squeezed my eyes shut. I burrowed under the blankets. More chortling, more talking. The woman's voice sounded vaguely familiar, then the man's voice became more clear. I heard the words "traffic" and then "coming up." And then I remembered who these people were—Eric and Kathy. They were DJs, and they were on my radio, which meant it was time to get up.

I have always wanted to be the kind of person who awoke refreshed and lovely at the first hint of daylight. I'd even thought I'd become such a person after years of work, but alas, I still felt like a college kid who needed to sleep until noon. Chris was worse than me. He required two alarm clocks and three snooze button hits before he'd rouse from the bed. As a result, I was usually showered and out the door before he got up.

Eric and Kathy were laughing again, talking about some

reality show. I rolled over and shut off the radio. And then I flinched. What was that thing on my nightstand? I opened my eyes more fully. The frog from Blinda, that was all. It seemed bigger this morning, more green. The spherical eyes gleamed, the haunches appeared ready to leap, and that slash of a mouth was turned up at the edges. The thing was smiling.

I turned the frog around so it wasn't looking at me and dragged myself out of bed and through the dark bedroom. I stopped at the window and pulled back the tan linen drapes. Outside, it was hazy wet and gray, the air thick with fog. The tree trunks bore a deep charcoal sheen. Chicago looked like a misty Scottish bog.

In the bathroom, the lights blazed on like a fast-food joint. I glanced in the mirror, running my hands through my dark hair, unruly now from sleep—parts curly, parts flat, parts electric and standing on end. This was my typical morning do. But I looked different somehow. I leaned closer to the mirror. Eyes still blue, lashes still long. I stepped back and surveyed the rest of myself—one shoulder was slightly higher than the other, same as always. My hips were still too broad for my taste, my breasts a little too small. Nothing had changed.

"Get going," I muttered to myself. Enough vanity. I turned on the shower and on second thought, flicked on the steam component. When we moved in, we expanded the shower, installing four different showerheads and a steam function. It was one of my favorite spots in the house.

The steam kicked on, making the stall as misty as the weather outside. I took a deep breath and let the heat seep into my body. I soaked my hair, picking up a bottle of shampoo. And then I heard a creak. A footfall came next. Then a shuffling sound. The door of the shower was yanked open, and I yelped, clutching the shampoo bottle to my chest.

"It's me, hon." Chris stepped fully inside the shower, the steam parting for him.

"What are you doing?"

"I thought I'd join you."

"Oh." It was all I could think of to say. We'd never been in that shower together, despite the fact that I'd had a number of fantasies about how to use the tiled bench.

"Let me do that for you." Chris took the shampoo from my hand. He turned me around and began soaping my hair, massaging my head gently with those large hands of his. He went on like this for a few minutes, then he whispered, "Close your eyes," and he tilted my head under the water to rinse it.

When he was done, Chris drew my head back and kissed my neck. He nibbled on my earlobes. The water beat down on my belly now, and I heard myself moan softly. The steam was thick. I don't know if I could have seen Chris if I opened my eyes, but I could feel him. He stood behind me, and I felt his broad, wet chest against my back, his lean legs behind mine. And then I could feel something else. Chris might not have been in the mood last night, but he certainly was this morning.

Afterwards, we stood nuzzling in the steamy bathroom.

"I've missed that," Chris said.

"You have?"

"Yeah. Hell, yeah."

I used a towel to dab some water from his forehead. "Me, too."

"C'mere." He pulled me by the hand, back to our bed, its gray-green sheets twisted and rumpled.

"We'll get the bed all wet," I said.

"Who cares?"

"Not me." I hopped into bed and threw off the towel. Chris and I nestled into the still warm sheets, and, nose to nose, started talking like we hadn't in years.

"What's going on at work?" Chris said. "What's the status of getting you into a VP office?"

The reminder of my failure to be promoted should have disheartened me, but I was too content and snug with my husband to be affected. I happily filled Chris in on all the work gossip and on Alexa's condescending attitude.

"That little bitch," Chris murmured, and I snuggled closer, pleased to have someone on my side.

"And did you and Evan get that press release done?" Chris asked.

I paused a moment. Chris had no idea about my crush on Evan, at least I didn't think so, but the mention of Evan's name from my husband's lips startled me.

"Um, yeah. We did."

"How is Evan?"

"He's fine. Good." I searched my mind for another topic, but finding none, I elaborated about Evan. "He's got his promotion, and he's bringing in business, so Roslyn loves him."

"And is Roslyn still tough as nails?"

"Oh, yes."

"Not like you, Treetop. You're soft and sweet." Treetop was Chris's nickname for me, based on my maiden name, Tremont. I hadn't heard him use it in a long time.

I shifted closer to him, and Chris kissed the tip of my nose. It was an intimate gesture, in some ways more intimate than what had gone on in the shower, and the sweetness of it nearly made me cry.

He grinned at me, really looking at me like he used to, and I smiled back.

"So enough about me," I said. "What's going on at the firm? Any news?"

"Well, you know that health care merger?"

I nodded. I didn't remind him that when I asked about it last night he hadn't seemed willing to talk about it.

"It's a complete mess," Chris said. "I've got to go to court this morning." He lifted himself up and glanced over me to my alarm clock. "But I've got time."

This made me flip around. The angry red lights of my clock said 9:04 a.m. And that damned frog—somehow it was turned around and facing me again. No matter, I was late. *Really* late.

"Shit, Chris," I said, leaping out of bed. "I've got to go."

He groaned. "Another ten minutes."

"No!" I laughed. "You've got to be in court, and you know how Roslyn is about me being on time." I'd been reprimanded more than once about my inability to get in before nine.

I tore open the closet doors and rifled through my pants. I threw on a pair of wide-legged chocolate-brown trousers, trusty old favorites. I grabbed an ivory silk blouse and buttoned it up as fast as possible. I added a chunky silver necklace and grabbed my makeup bag and my purse.

"Okay," I said to Chris, who was still lazing in bed, "I'm out of here."

"Give me a kiss."

I halted my frantic scrambling. "Of course." I leaned over the bed. Chris sat up and stroked my face with his hand. Then slowly, slowly, he kissed me.

"What's gotten into you this morning?" I asked.

He laughed. "I don't know. Something good."

I had to agree.

"Sorry," I muttered to anyone who might be listening as I hustled out of the elevator and down the beige-carpeted hall to my beige-walled cube. A look at my watch told me it was 9:39. Not good.

"Hi there, Billy," the receptionist said as I sped past her.

"Hi, Carolyn."

"Billy, I have messages for you!" she yelled after me.

That stopped me. Carolyn took messages for no one but the VPs and the higher-ups. The rest of us had to make do with voice mail. The only reason Carolyn might have a message for me is if Roslyn wanted to talk to me. Roslyn, who no doubt wanted to kick my ass, or my career, for being late again.

I took a few tentative steps toward her and held out my hand. There were three slips, which couldn't be good. Possibly the owner also wanted to fire me.

"There you go," Carolyn said. "Have a nice day."

Was she mocking me?

I flipped through the messages as I retreated from her desk. Two were from clients. It was curious that she'd taken those. Maybe there was some kind of emergency. The last one was from Roslyn.

Please see me, was all it said.

I felt something quake inside me. Not at all good.

But what really made my stomach rattle was the sight of my cubicle. It was empty. Completely empty.

The photo of me with my mom and my sisters was gone. Odette's cookbook, my haphazard stacks of press releases, a stage bill from a musical Chris and I saw during our first year together—all gone. I cleared my throat. I tried to think of a logical reason why this might be happening. Had I missed a memo about a move? I looked around. No, the other cubicles were still full of people and their possessions. There could be no other reason other than the obvious one—I'd been fired.

I considered simply going home. Roslyn had made her message pretty clear. Why should I now sit in her office so she could run down the list of reasons that Harper Frankwell was letting me go? But the more I stood there, gazing at the empty beige walls, the more incensed I became.

I marched up the hallway toward her office. I was clomping my feet so hard my toes began to cry for mercy in my stylishly pointed shoes; I almost welcomed the pain.

"Hey, Billy," Alexa said, passing me, wearing another black cashmere top. Obviously she hadn't heard the news of my firing yet, because she walked by quickly, not even bothering to gloat.

I didn't say anything in return. I kept my focus on Roslyn's office at the end of the hall. Then something distracted me.

I stopped and turned slightly to my left toward one of the VP offices—one of the better ones—which had been empty for a few months. I stepped closer and peered inside. Obviously someone had been promoted; the place was occupied now. Two broad windows faced Michigan Avenue, so it was warm and white with the morning sun. There was a pine credenza, left behind by the previous occupant, one with fleurs-de-lis and scrolls carved deep in its sides.

And atop the credenza sat the photo of my mom and sisters, right next to Odette's cookbook.

I opened and closed my eyes a few times, still trying to focus on the credenza. Was this some kind of freak joke? I glanced at the desk and saw my Northwestern Wildcats cup filled with my pens. There was my orange notebook, the square leather box where I kept my CDs, the yellow mug I bought years ago at Old Town Art Fair.

Startled, I stepped back outside the office. And there, on

the wall next to the door, was a gold nameplate that read *Billy Rendall, Vice President.*

"Oh, my..." I said, my breath coming fast. It had happened! That was why Roslyn wanted to see me—she'd finally given me the job!

"Billy." It was Roslyn's voice. I turned to see her head sticking out of her office. "Can I see you?"

"Absolutely!" I trotted down the hall, beaming at everyone I passed. This was the validation I'd been waiting for— the official proclamation of my worth. And how sweet of Roslyn to move all my things!

When I reached her office, she was seated and signing letters, her assistant standing near her desk. I beamed some more, ready to hear rounds of congratulations. But Roslyn barely looked up.

"Billy," she said, sounding distracted. "Are you free for lunch with Lydia?"

"Lydia Frankwell?" I had never been invited to break bread with the firm's owner.

"Of course."

"Any special occasion?" Aha, I thought, they were going to officially announce my vice presidency at lunch. Again, such a thoughtful gesture!

"No, no. We just need to go over a few things, mostly the budget for the Teaken Furniture account. We'll have salads brought to the conference room."

"Oh...okay." Should I raise the fact that I'd seemingly been promoted overnight?

Roslyn's assistant gave me a benign, fleeting smile that seemed to say, *Morning. Nothing new here.*

"Lydia is flying in from Manhattan, so we'll do a late lunch," Roslyn said. "I'll see you at 1:30, all right? I've got to get these letters out. You know how it is."

"Sure, okay."

My walk down the hallway was slower this time. I expected someone to jump out of the shadows at any minute and yell, "Surprise! Congrats!" but everyone was going about their work as if this were any other day. As if I had always been a vice president.

The leather chair behind my new desk was the color of red wine. I sank into it, but it was too low, too cushy. I spent ten minutes trying to adjust the damn thing, but even when I'd raised it, I felt like a little kid in a big La-Z-Boy. It was too deep, my feet barely touched the floor. I found a Chicago Yellow Pages, the shape and weight of an anvil, and put that under my feet. I took my camel sweater off the hook behind the door and balled it up behind my back. Now what?

I turned on my computer. Everything looked the same there. I clicked on my e-mail account, scanning a note from an old college friend who was coming to town. There was also an e-mail from Odette suggesting new ideas for how to promote her book. I made notes on a pad of paper, reading Odette's e-mail slowly. The last line said, *If you don't have time to call, don't worry, just have your assistant, Lizbeth, give me a buzz.*

I put my pen down and sat back in my big chair. Who the hell was Lizbeth?

I looked at the phone—a sleek black model with typed speed-dial names. One of them said "Lizbeth." I stared at that a second, then slowly lifted my index finger and brought it down on the button.

"Hiya, Billy!" A chipper voice shot through my phone. "What do you need?"

"Uh…" I considered my possible responses. A lobotomy. A *clue*. "Lizbeth?" I said, the word alien on my tongue.

"Yeah?"

"You're my assistant, right?"

A peal of girlish laughter. "Of course."

I sat back in my chair.

"Billy?" I heard through the phone.

"Yes. Uh… Lizbeth, what day is it?"

"May 5th."

That sounded right to me. "And it's Tuesday, right?"

"Yeah. Is something wrong?"

What could be wrong? I'd had fabulous sex with my husband that morning, and I'd been promoted overnight. The only problem was I didn't seem to know anything about that promotion. Then I got an idea. I knew who could help me.

"No, everything is fine," I said. "Have you seen Evan today?"

Evan looked up from his desk, his green eyes sparkling, his dimples crinkling. "Hey there! I'm glad to see you."

He came around the desk and hugged me tight.

"Whoa," I said, pushing him back a little. Evan and I might hug when we saw each other out at night (me being the one holding him a tad too closely) but we never embraced at work. It wasn't that kind of office.

"God, it's weird, but I missed you," he said.

"You missed me since yesterday?" Wasn't it yesterday that I'd gone to the team meeting, that I'd been humiliated by Roslyn, that he'd mentioned the Hello Dave show?

"Yeah." His hand, still on my arm, felt almost like a caress.

"I've got to ask you something." I slipped away and closed the door.

"Sure." He gestured to one of the chairs that faced his desk and went back to his own.

"What's going on around here?" I said, taking a seat.

"You look sexy today," he said.

"Do I?" I took a quick look at my brown pants, my ivory blouse. I'd worn the outfit to work no less than fifty times.

"You do." His eyes dragged down my body, then back up again. "God, what is it about you today?"

"I don't know." *Maybe it's the fact that I just got steamed an hour ago?* "Look, Ev, focus for me, okay? What in the hell is happening around here?"

"What do you mean?"

"Why do I have a VP office?"

He laughed. "Because you're a VP, baby. Get used to it."

"Why did it happen so quick?"

"What do you mean? You deserved it for a long time."

"I know," I said, irritated. "But why did they just move me in there overnight?"

"What are you talking about? You've been VP for a while."

"A while? How long?"

He ran a hand through his blond hair—the kind of gesture that normally made me sigh with desire. "I can't remember." He scratched his head. "Huh. That's strange. Well, anyway, it doesn't matter. Are you tense?"

"What?"

"You seem like you're tense. Let me give you a neck rub." In a flash, he was around his desk and behind me, his hands massaging my neck.

My eyes drifted shut for a moment, then snapped open. "What are you doing?"

"Helping you work out the kinks." His voice was low, thick, the kind of voice I was sure he used with his girlfriends in bed.

"Okay, okay." I stood up and spun around. "Is this a joke? Seriously, this is unbelievably cruel if it is."

"What are you talking about?"

"My VP office! And—" I pointed at him, unable to find the words "—*you,* acting like *this.*"

"Sorry." A confused expression. "That was inappropriate, wasn't it?"

"Uh…yeah."

"Geez, what is with me?" He shook his head. "Are you all right? Is it tension in your lower back? Here, let me work on that." He moved forward, his muscled arm slipping around my hips.

"All right, I'm out of here," I said. With a nervous laugh I headed for the door.

"Want to get lunch?" Evan said, looking like a child left behind on the playground.

"I've got plans." Odd. It was the response he usually gave me.

Back in my office, I climbed into the chair, and with my feet on the phone book, let my eyes sweep the room. All my stuff was there—no doubt about it—and everyone seemed to think I was a vice president. But it felt surreal, having it just happen like that. I wanted a party, maybe a cake with *Congrats Billy!* on it in pink frosting. I wanted someone to say, "You deserve it."

I needed my mom. She would ramble and rave; she would make me believe this was real and I had earned it. I slid the phone closer and perused the speed dial buttons. There it was. *Mom.*

Two rings went by, then three. I knew her machine would pick up on the next ring, and I'd hear the message, "Sorry we can't come to the phone. We'll call you back." My mother hadn't changed the message since Jan died, and so it still sounded as if he were running around town with her, about to head home and check voice mail.

The answering machine clicked on, and surprisingly I heard something new. Tinkling piano music in the background, then my mother's chipper, "Hello! I'm not here right now. I'd love to phone you back. Just leave your number. Ta ta!"

Ta-freakin'-ta? She sounded like Joan Collins on *Dynasty.* "Mom, it's me," I said. "Nice message. Give me a call as soon as you get in."

I put the phone back on the receiver. What to do now? Work, I supposed, but it seemed I might have a different role now, one I was unclear about.

"Hello, Miss Billy."

I looked up and saw Gerald, the elderly black man who ran the mail office at Harper Frankwell and personally delivered everyone's mail each morning.

I greeted him, and waited to see if he commented on my new office.

"Have a lovely day now." He handed me a stack of mail. He turned and left, whistling an aimless tune.

I flipped through the envelopes—letters from clients, one from a TV station in Dallas, where we'd been trying to get coverage for a new product. And then there was a shiny lacquered postcard. The photo on the front showed a multi-spired white building. I flipped it over and looked at the printed words on top. *The Duomo,* it said. *Milan.*

Below that, in my mom's tiny, perfect penmanship, there were three lines: *The collections are surprisingly tedious! The Trussardi stuff—particularly stale. Love, Mom.*

I flipped it back and looked at the front. I turned it again and read the lines a few more times. It appeared that overnight my mother had transported herself, *by herself,* to Milan and the fashion district. My mother adored fashion. She was always decked out in the latest, and she'd always talked about going with Jan to the shows in Milan, but when he died, so did that dream. Until now. If this postcard was legit, my mother had a real life, something I'd been hoping for her for so long. And if it was true, then she'd gotten over Jan, and in a much shorter time than it took her to recover from the loss of my father.

With that thought, I noticed something different inside myself. Deep inside me, where there was usually a space for wonderings about where my father was and worries that his abandonment might somehow have been my fault—or his disappointment in me—was empty now. Those wonderings and worries were gone. I could remember the pain, the longing, the sadness that used to reside there, but I didn't feel it any longer. Like reminiscing about a distant love affair, the emotions had vanished.

I took a breath. There seemed to be more room in my lungs now, more room in my head, too. The hours with Blinda must have taken hold. I'd broken the reverse Oedipal thing, and I was free of him.

I smiled to myself in my new office. I felt lighter, happier. Not only had I gotten over my dad, but I'd had a wonderful morning with my husband, I'd been promoted and Evan had flirted with me. Even my mother had begun her own fabulous life. I had no idea how it happened, but in one night I'd gotten incredibly lucky.

I thought of my visit with Blinda last night and the frog she'd given me. Could they have anything to do with this? Intuitively, I answered *yes!* but that seemed entirely illogical. Yet either way, it didn't matter. I'd gotten everything I'd wished for. And I was going to enjoy it.

chapter four

When Evan made VP, I had pumped him for every bit of information he possessed about the perks of the promotion. He'd gotten a new computer and cell phone, ditto for new office furniture, and there were no longer limits on client lunches and entertainment, the way there were for the non-VPs.

I rubbed my hands together at my desk now. Time to spend some company money. Then it occurred to me—maybe I had already done that, somewhere in the yawning chasm between my today and my yesterday.

I hit Lizbeth's button again.

"What's up, Billy?" she said cheerily.

I still hadn't seen the girl, and I supposed I'd better "meet" her now so that I didn't run into her in the hallway and give a blank stare. "Can you stop by my office for a second?"

A moment later, a woman in her early-twenties appeared in my doorway. Her sandy brown hair was worn in artful waves about her very round face. She had wide, startled eyes and a rosebud mouth shellacked with cotton-candy pink gloss.

What's going on?" she said, taking one of my visitor's chairs.

"When I made vice president…well, maybe I should say, do you remember when I made vice president?"

"I got hired right after, so I don't remember the exact day, but yeah." She looked at me oddly.

"Sure, right. And when was that? I mean when did you get hired?"

She laughed wryly, as if this were an easy question, but then she scrunched up her shiny mouth and looked at the ceiling. "Gosh, when was that?" She looked back at me with a stumped expression. "I can't remember."

Just like Evan, I thought. Everyone seemed to assume I'd been in this position forever, but I knew different. It made me feel as if I were playacting. It made everything unreal.

"Billy?" Lizbeth said. "Did you want something?"

I shook away my thoughts about the strangeness of it all. No sense fighting a good thing, I told myself. "What I really wanted to ask you was if you remember some information I got about furniture and technology stipends."

"Yeah, I think it was in that packet of material from Ms. Frankwell."

"Great, great. And where do I—I mean *we*…keep that?"

"You told me to file it at my desk, remember?"

I made a big show of snapping my fingers. "Right! That's right. Could you grab that for me?"

A few seconds later and she was back with a stapled set of papers, headed *New Vice President Information Packet*.

"Thank you, Lizbeth. And can you find out for me where the firm buys our computer equipment?"

I leafed through the packet while Lizbeth trotted off down the hallway. The terms were the same that Evan had received. Perfect.

Lizbeth soon buzzed me with the name of a computer

dealer we used. Five minutes after that, I was on the phone with one of the salesmen and browsing their Web site for different computers and monitors. I finally settled on a sleek, flat-screen monitor and a top-of-the-line computer that had tons of memory and would allow me to burn my own CDs and download lots of music. Not that I knew how to do that. Not that I even owned one of those cute MP3 players. But then maybe that was different now, too. I'd gotten what I wanted overnight, and I'd always wished I could be one of those iPod people. It might all just flow from my hands as soon as I got the new computer.

When that was done, I buzzed Lizbeth. "I'm going to look for new office furniture," I said. "I'll be back soon."

"Don't forget about your 1:30 lunch meeting."

I looked at my watch. It was 12:00. "No problem." I clicked the intercom off, and sat staring at my watch for another minute. It had a large mother-of-pearl face and a burnt orange leather strap. My mother had given it to me for Christmas last year, and she'd selected it carefully. Was she now selecting dresses and skirts from a runway in Milan?

I knew where the company-approved furniture store was because I'd been there with Evan. Outside our building, I fought the tourists for a cab and headed to the intersection of Ohio and Franklin.

The showroom was a loft space with brick walls and high ceilings. I found a salesman and told him I needed a new desk and chair, explaining that I already had a pine credenza I planned to keep.

The salesman, a short, balding man in a suit, clearly saw a purchase ready to happen. He practically clicked his heels together before whisking me around the showroom, pointing out various styles of desks.

"You know, maybe I should just focus on the chairs," I said after a few minutes. Who knew how ridiculously expensive desks could be? And my stipend wasn't that large.

The smile on the salesman's face dimmed a little, but he gave me a pert nod and began showing me chairs. All of them seemed to be black leather—black leather with chrome bases, black distressed leather, shiny black leather with buttons.

"These are all so—" I searched my mind for the word "—typical," I said at last. I thought of the wine-colored chair in my office. It was entirely too huge but at least it was a little different. Maybe I should stick with that.

But then I saw it. Across the showroom, next to a mod, curved desk was a small, butter-yellow leather chair. I quickly made my way and sank into it. The chair hugged me like an old, comfortable sweater, yet it was stylish and sleek.

I glanced at the price tag. One hundred dollars more than my furniture stipend, but I could pay that out of my own pocket. "I'll take it."

When I got back to the office, I called Chris. "I have some news."

"What?" He actually sounded excited.

"How about dinner tonight and I'll tell you?"

I waited for him to "cry swamp," as I called it—*I'm so swamped with this merger, I'm swamped with my billing statements, I'm swamped with this deposition.* But to my surprise, he said, "Absolutely."

"How about Spring at six?" Spring was a restaurant in Bucktown where Chris and I first started talking about getting married. We'd been giddy that night with our plans for our future. For some reason, we'd never been back.

"Perfect," I said.

"I'll make the reservation."

Just then Lizbeth buzzed me. "Your meeting is about to start."

I grabbed my purse from under my desk, patted powder on my face and swiped lipstick across my mouth. Ready. I ditched my purse again and looked at my watch. One-thirty exactly. I felt a rush of nervousness. I'd insisted for years that I was cut out to be a VP, but I wasn't sure what to expect from the role.

In the conference room, a long thin space with an oval glass table, Roslyn was studying a file and silently munching on a plain green salad.

"Hi, Billy," she said, glancing up. "You prefer Caesar, don't you?"

"Um…yes, I do." Had I ever told Roslyn that? I couldn't ever remember discussing my favorite books or movies with Roslyn, much less salads.

I moved to the sideboard and picked up a Caesar. A second later, Lydia Frankwell swept into the conference room, filling the place with the scent of Chanel No. 5. She was a very well-preserved woman somewhere in the age range of fifty to seventy. Twenty years ago, she'd started the firm with Bradley Harper. Rumor had it that she and Mr. Harper had been having an affair while at their previous firm, an affair that continued when they started Harper Frankwell. Mr. Harper died eight years ago, right before I'd joined the firm, leaving Ms. Frankwell at the helm. I'd always found her a bit flighty. Not that she wasn't business savvy, but she seemed more of a figurehead, a yes-man who schmoozed clients around the country while Jack, and now Roslyn, ran the real show.

"Roslyn. Billy," Lydia said. I watched her, ready for a *Congratulations on your promotion!* but nothing came.

Roslyn murmured a greeting. I paused a moment, debating the use of first names versus my usual "Ms. Frankwell." I must have paused too long, because both she and Roslyn looked at me strangely.

"Afternoon, Lydia," I blurted out. I held my breath.

Roslyn looked back at her file. Lydia gave me a serene smile that barely lifted the corners of her heavily BOTOX-enhanced eyes, then headed for the remaining salad. I sighed internally as I took a seat.

"All right," Roslyn said when Lydia was seated as well. "Let's discuss Teaken Furniture."

"Mmm, good," Lydia said. I was unclear whether she meant the salad on which she was now munching or the Teaken Furniture account. It was an account we'd had forever, and one I'd inherited from Evan. They were an old-school Chicago furniture business who'd been running the same advertisements for years. There was really nothing new about their products, and therefore very little that we could get decent PR on, but the owner was friends with Lydia and so we worked with them year after year, begging magazines to write about their Frank Lloyd Wright look-alike chairs and their design team.

Roslyn launched into a discussion of the Teaken budget for the next six months. Lydia asked a question or two. I tried to do the same, but I found myself with little to contribute. It wasn't just that I was new to budgets and these types of meetings. I was, quite simply, bored.

This surprised me. I'd always spied on Evan in such meetings, walking by the open door at frequent intervals, trying to eavesdrop. It seemed so glamorous—meeting with the owner, coming up with the budget for some large account—but now I could barely keep my eyes open.

"Okay, that's done, isn't it?" Roslyn said at last. "Lydia, anything you need?"

"Hmm?" Lydia said. She was fiddling with a paper napkin. "Oh. Well, I should mention that I'm going to be in New York again for most of the next month. If there's anything you have to discuss with me—personnel issues or such—we should do it now." She made it sound as if she were going to the Antarctic instead of the Ritz-Carlton in Manhattan.

Roslyn frowned at her for a second, then gave a slight shrug. "Well, there is Carolyn."

Lydia lifted her eyebrows, or at least it seemed she was trying. "Who?"

"Our receptionist," Roslyn said, as if talking to a five-year-old. "She's been here for two years and keeps asking for a raise. Frankly, I think she deserves it."

"Fine," Lydia said. "Anything from you, Billy?"

I was about to say no. I'd been a VP for all of five hours, so what personnel or other issues could I possibly have? But then I thought of one. Alexa. I saw her smug face. I heard her voice say, *Oh, I'm not suggesting that you handle this on your own... God, no.* I heard her condescending laugh over and over.

So I said her name. "Alexa Villa."

Roslyn frowned. I was about to do a U-turn and say there was really nothing wrong with Alexa, it was just a mistake, but Lydia sat straighter. "Ms. Villa, yes," she said. "Tell me about her."

"It's just..." How to put this? I hadn't officially formulated anything about Alexa in my head, I'd just stewed internally about it for years.

"Yes?" Lydia said with an encouraging nod. "Go ahead."

And it all began to spill from my mouth.

I told Roslyn and Lydia exactly what I thought—that Alexa was constantly pushing off work on other people, that

she didn't respect authority, that she was rude and patronizing and very difficult to work with.

Roslyn looked a little troubled, and I wondered if I'd
overstepped my new boundaries. I pushed salad around on
my plate. The conference room was silent.

"I might be mistaken," I said, about to take it all back and
head for the hills. No need to screw up my new position by
bringing up Alexa.

But then Roslyn spoke again. "I suppose I have noticed
some of that. I just didn't realize it was so bad."

"Has this been documented?" Lydia asked.

"We've had a couple of issues with her," Roslyn said. "A
few years ago, there was a complaint from a client about a
comment she made."

"Mmm-hmm," Lydia murmured.

"And then of course there was the incident with Miss
Martha's."

"Good Lord, that's right," Lydia said.

Miss Martha's was a famous Chicago bakery, and they'd
enlisted us to promote the fact that they'd been chosen
by the *Today Show* for having the best chocolate chip
cookies in the country. Alexa was in charge of approv-
ing and sending out the press kits to media all over the
United States. The title of the kit was supposed to be,
"Miss Martha Sacks the Competition!" but Alexa failed
to check the final copy properly, and the kits went out
reading, "Miss Martha Sucks the Competition!" Needless
to say, Miss Martha was no longer a client of Harper
Frankwell.

"That was a grave error," Roslyn said, "but I believe she's
improved greatly since then."

"Has she brought in business?" Lydia asked.

"No," Roslyn said, "but—"

"Well, you know the policy," Lydia said. "It's been in place since Bradley was here." She gave a wistful smile at his memory. "If there are two written warnings in someone's personnel file, that person can be terminated."

I froze at the word "terminated." Fire Alexa? I really just wanted her to get a corporate slap on the wrist, maybe a little demotion.

"Billy, you're her immediate superior for the team," Lydia continued. "If you truly believe she's undermining our employees' ability to do good work, then something should be done. Isn't that right, Roslyn?"

Roslyn still had that slightly troubled look, but she nodded. "It's your decision, Billy. But if you decide to do anything, that's your responsibility, too. You'll have to be the one to tell her."

"Me?" I gulped. I had never handled *any* personnel issues before, much less fired someone. "Oh, I don't know…I just—"

"Billy, it's your responsibility," Roslyn repeated.

I felt power surge through me. It scared me, and yet I loved it. "All right," I said. "I'll consider it."

I went back to my office and mulled it over. I thought about how impossible Alexa was to work with. If I found her so difficult, others must too, and if that was the case, then wouldn't it be easier for everyone if she wasn't here? The firm wasn't overloaded right now. We could spare her until we found someone else.

I went down the hall and spoke to our Human Resources director. Alexa, she told me, was entitled to severance due to the number of years she'd been at the firm. There was no employment contract, but according to our guidelines, it could be anything from two weeks severance to three months. Since she was being terminated for cause, it was my decision, she said. A rush went through my body.

I thought about Alexa blaming her bad work on others

and the way she taunted me with not being promoted. "Two weeks," I said with what I hoped was an authoritative tone.

An hour later, the power surging even stronger through my veins, I phoned Alexa and asked her to come see me.

"Hey," Alexa said, appearing in my doorway. She crossed her arms casually and leaned on the frame, but her expression was suspicious.

I said hello, and asked her to sit. My body was nearly twitching with nervousness, excitement and shock at what I was about to do.

Alexa glanced around my office as she slipped into a chair. "Nice place," she said. She shook her head a little, her face saying, *I can't believe you're a VP.* That look irritated me—like everything about Alexa—but I could hardly believe it myself.

"I need to talk to you about something." My words faltered then. How, exactly, did you go about firing someone? I'd read the company HR manual. I knew the few key phrases I was supposed to say and how to explain what would happen to her benefits and such, but with her sitting in front of me, I couldn't think of how to start.

"Is it the Channel 7 News account?" she said. "You probably need help with the budget recommendations. You're not exactly proficient with that." Her mouth twisted into a smirk I was all too familiar with. "I'd be happy to review the figures for you."

And with that, the words rushed into my brain, all waiting like soldiers in perfect formation, ready to march. "It's not the news account," I said. "It's you."

Alexa tossed her hair over her shoulder, her eyes wary. She said nothing.

"You see," I continued, "your attitude has become a problem."

"Is that right?" Still, the smirk rested comfortably on her mouth.

"Yes, that's right." My voice became stronger. "You tend to be condescending. You push projects off on other people. And your attitude makes it very hard to work with you."

"Really? Well, I'll try to improve on it, okay? Thanks for the chat." She began to stand.

"Alexa, please sit down." My voice was still strong.

She sank back into the chair and sighed as if she were barely tolerating me.

"Alexa, I have to tell you that we're letting you go." My skin tingled with the words. I was *firing* her.

The perma-smirk disappeared. "What?"

"Yes, I'm sorry, but as you know, you already have two warnings in your personnel file." I made a show of looking at the piece of paper where this was documented. "First, there was the comment you made to the president of Ryder Sports Network when you said—" I glanced at the paper again " '—go fuck yourself.' "

"He grabbed my ass."

I blinked. I hadn't known about that. I would have said the same thing. "Yes, well…" I nearly faltered. "I'm sure you could have handled it better."

Alexa's eyes were steely now.

"And then there was Miss Martha," I said.

"Clara was the one who was supposed to check the last copy."

"Clara was working under you, correct?"

Alexa said nothing.

"So, that was your responsibility," I continued, the rush surging back. "Due to these past problems and those I mentioned with your attitude, we're letting you go."

"What?"

"You'll get two weeks severance."

"That's it? That's insulting."

"I'm sure you'll find another position during—"

"I want to talk to Roslyn," she interrupted.

"I'm sorry, Alexa, but the decision has been made. It's done." The words sounded strong, confident, managerial.

"You're *not* sorry." The anger in her voice startled me.

She was right. My whole body was humming from the experience, so I kept talking, filling her in on the termination of her benefits, how she would have twenty-four hours to clean out her desk. She sat rigid, looking at me with what I could only assume was intense hatred. I talked faster and faster. Finally, I asked her to sign the severance agreement.

"You know what, Billy?" Alexa said when I'd finished with my spiel.

"What's that?"

She rattled off a string of Spanish words.

"Excuse me?" I said politely.

"It's a Mexican saying."

"Well, however you need to deal with it. Now if you'll sign the agreement." I pushed it across my desk.

She ignored the pen I held out. I noticed that my hand shook a little, my body still humming.

"Don't you want to know what it means?" she said.

If it will get you the hell out of here, I wanted to say, but I remembered the warnings in the personnel manual about how to properly terminate an employee. "Sure."

"It means, essentially, what goes around comes around." She stood, shaking her shoulders back. "And I'm not signing that thing."

"Holy shit," Evan said, sticking his blond head in my office, "I just heard."

"What do you think?" I whispered.

He perched on the edge of my desk. I could smell his cologne, an earthy, sporty fragrance that always made me a little weak. "Impressive," he said.

"Is that a good thing or bad?"

He shrugged. "Lots of people didn't like her."

"What about you?"

His eyes twinkled. "I think she's hot as hell."

I scoffed. "Any other helpful opinions?"

Another shrug. "I thought she was pretty good, but you worked with her more. It was a ballsy move, Rendall."

"Well, you know me."

He cocked his head. He gave me a sexy, appraising stare with those mint-green eyes. "I'm not so sure. It's like you're a different person today."

I cleared my throat. "Yeah, I know what you mean."

I didn't want to give Alexa any more opportunities to put Mexican hexes on me, so I told Evan I had a doctor's appointment and slipped out of the office. I walked down Michigan Avenue, enjoying the sun now peeking from between the clouds. Due to the earlier rain, the air was humid, but because it was suddenly seventy degrees, it felt balmy.

What to do now? I had time before I had to meet Chris. I thought about going home, but as I crossed the street, I caught a glimpse of myself in a storefront window. Evan might have been impressed today with the trusty old brown pants and the ivory blouse, but I needed something better for a dinner with my husband to celebrate my promotion. I increased my pace and headed straight for Bloomingdale's. Once inside, I ignored the glittering makeup counters and took the escalator to one of the designer floors, where I never usually let myself shop. But I'd gotten a raise with my promotion (I'd checked on that with the Human Resources person at the same time I got Alexa's file) and I could afford a fabulous, celebratory outfit.

A saleswoman asked if she could help me. Usually, I turned the salespeople away, afraid of being pressured into a big purchase I didn't need, but I was in the buying mood, so I said, "Yes, please."

Soon, I was in the dressing room, trying on A-line skirts and sliplike dresses and spring sweaters the colors of Easter eggs. I decided on a slim marigold dress with velvety straps and a lace-up back. It was much brighter, much more chic than the clothes I usually wore, and it was perfect.

"I'll wear it out," I told the saleswoman.

Spring, the restaurant where I was to meet Chris, was on North Avenue in a building that had once been a Turkish bath. Outside, it still had the original stone face and columns. But inside, where it was decorated with Zenlike grasses and smooth wood tables, it was hard to imagine overweight men in towels being bathed and pounded upon by other men.

I went down the short staircase and saw Chris, sitting at the softly lit bar, a bottle of champagne in a bucket before him.

He slid off his stool. "You look gorgeous."

"Thank you. So do you." His hair was wet around the ears, and he smelled like shaving cream. He'd clearly showered at the gym before our date, a detail which touched me.

"You got the vice presidency, didn't you?" he said with a grin.

At last, someone who didn't assume I'd had the VP gig forever. Apparently, that strange assumption was held only by the people at work.

"I did!" I said. "I got it!"

He pulled me into a hug and swung me around. People were staring, but I didn't care.

"I knew it!" Chris said. "That's why I got the champagne."

Our table wasn't ready, so we settled onto bar stools and started on the champagne.

"Here's the thing," I said to Chris. "Everyone at work was acting like I'd been a VP for a while." I told him about how my stuff had suddenly appeared in my new office and how no one remembered when I'd actually gotten the promotion.

"They were putting you on," Chris said.

"I don't think so."

"Of course they were."

"It's just that everything is different today." *Like you,* I thought. But instead I told him about my mom and the postcard from Milan.

"That's great," he said. "She needed a vacation."

"I know, but don't you see? It all happened overnight, after I got that frog yesterday from Blinda."

"The frog?" Chris made a face that said, *c'mon.*

"I know it sounds ridiculous, but it's true."

"It just feels like that." His eyes twinkled as he gazed at me. "I'm so proud of you."

Hearing that meant the world. "Thanks, sweetie."

He squeezed my knee. "I can't wait to get out of here so I can get you into bed again."

I kissed his cheek, but then I had to ask. "Chris. Why today?"

"Hmm? What do you mean?"

"I mean, we've been having…." I wasn't sure how to say it. "We've been having troubles. You've been distant, and I guess I have too, lately. So why today? Why did you want to fool around and talk in bed and get champagne for me?"

He took a swallow from his glass. "You're my wife."

"I've been your wife for two years, and things haven't been good."

Silence.

"Was it something I did?" I said. "Is that why you've been so sweet to me today?"

"I don't know what you mean." He looked confused for a second. It was like he'd known exactly what I'd meant at some point, but now he couldn't find that memory in his head.

"Or was it something I said?" I asked.

"What does it matter?" He took the glass from my hand and drew me closer to him with one arm, looking in my eyes with an intensity that warmed me from the inside. To be back in his graces, to feel his devotion again, was irresistible. "Doesn't it feel right between us?" he asked.

"Of course." I kissed him.

"I love you, Treetop."

"You too, Marlowe."

A woman dressed in a stylish tuxedo jacket appeared at our side. "We can seat you now. Sorry for the wait."

"Ready?" Chris asked me. He stood up and held out his hand.

I let the questions fall away then. I reached out and placed my hand in his.

chapter five

The next day, I left the office around 4:00 p.m. I walked the crowded streets of Michigan Avenue and made my way up the steps of the Art Institute. At the top, I stopped for my traditional pat of the stone lion on the left.

I'd spent most of the last eight hours trying to pretend that my new job was exactly the way it had always been—everyone at work seemed to think so—but it was hard to keep up the facade when I had no idea what I was doing. Much to my chagrin, I found that budgeting was a big part of my new position as vice president. For each account I oversaw, I had to design the budget. When I was a mere account supervisor, I used to toss my hair and complain that I simply didn't have enough money, but now that I was making decisions on how much to charge a client (and therefore how much money we had to work with), I realized how tricky it was. If you decided a client needed too large a budget, they might balk and take their business elsewhere, yet if you reduced it, you might not have enough money to execute the campaign properly. By the time 4:00 rolled around, my head was aching and my eyes were exhausted from crunching numbers.

Inside the Institute, I flashed my annual pass at the ticket taker and wandered the cool marble hallways. I gazed at the Etruscan pitchers made of bronze and the metal armor that seemed too tiny to hold a knight. I stared at the Cassatt and strolled through a Manet exhibition.

Meandering through the Art Institute was an old trick of mine, something I'd discovered when I first started working. I loved the unhurried reverence of the place. And by taking in the beauty and the antiquity, it reminded me how small my purported troubles were, how insignificant. I was able to laugh (or at least chuckle grudgingly) at my so-called problems and forget what ailed me.

But it wasn't working today. There was no way to overlook what had happened—the massive shift in all facets of my life that had occurred with no transition, no official proclamations and very little recognition of the change by anyone. It was almost like being a car accident victim, someone who had glanced down to switch the dashboard radio station and looked back up to find a tractor-trailer stalled in their path. Life can change in an instant—we all know that—but in my case, I seemed to be the *only* one to know the change had happened.

Finally, staring at a miniature portrait of a woman with ruby-red lips, I decided to just get on with it. Embrace the new life, the new job.

And so I slipped my silver cell phone from my purse and called Evan, still at his desk, and asked him if he'd discuss budgeting with me over a cup of coffee. I couldn't talk to him in the office, for fear that someone would overhear us and I'd look ill-suited for the job.

"No coffee," Evan said. "I need a beer. Sounds like you do, too."

"Fine. Wrightwood Tap, I presume."

"Baby, I love how you know me." It wasn't hard to guess that Evan would want to go to Wrightwood Tap, a DePaul University hangout. Evan had attended DePaul for his undergrad degree, and the Tap was still his favorite watering hole. It probably didn't hurt that the place was always full of female coeds, sipping beers and hiking up their very low-waisted jeans.

At five o'clock, I met him at the bar, and we found a tall open table by the front windows. The place had a center rectangular bar, scarred wood floors and laminated menus boasting the usual bar fare.

We ordered beers—a Corona for me, Old Style for Evan. Despite being a VP and living in a slick, north side condo, Evan was still very south side in his beer tastes. "It's in the genes," he always said. Personally, I felt that Evan was holding tight to something that would make him similar, in some small way, to his father. Tommy O'Reilly, Evan's dad, was a career plumber who wanted his only son to learn the business and eventually take it over. Instead, Evan got a scholarship to DePaul and went into PR. He endured constant barbs from his father about how he must be a "fairy" to do such a job, but Evan still went back to the south side on Sundays to watch football or baseball with his dad. And he still drank Old Style.

"So what's happening, hot stuff?" Evan asked as our beers were delivered.

"It's the budgeting. I don't know how to do it. I mean, math has never been my forte, and now I'm crunching numbers all the time. I never know if the numbers I'm throwing out there are legit or if they're totally off. And how do you decide on an initial figure? It's so random. And—"

"Whoa, whoa, slow down. It's no big deal. You'll get the hang of it."

"It *is* a big deal."

"Why?"

"Hello? Because I'll get fired if I can't do this job correctly."

"So, you're afraid someone will do to you what you did to Alexa?"

I silently fiddled with the label of my beer bottle. I'd been trying not to think about Alexa all day. I'd avoided her now empty cubicle. I'd sent her file back to HR. But I couldn't stop seeing her shocked face when I'd told her, and I couldn't stop hearing the sound of those lyrically vindictive Spanish words.

"Thanks for the reminder," I said at last.

Evan shrugged innocently.

"All right, yes," I said, "I'm afraid I'll get fired or demoted or whatever. You know how hard I worked to get here, Ev."

"Sure, I do, but no one's going to fire you." He reached across the table and patted my hand. Actually, it was more than a pat. It was something like a rub. His hand was very warm.

I felt a crazy desire to grasp his hand, but instead, I pulled away and made a show of glancing at the menu. "C'mon, Roslyn will demote me or fire me in a heartbeat if I don't pull my weight."

"No, she won't."

"What do you mean? Remember Chad from two years ago? She fired him after he'd made VP. And she just okayed me to fire Alexa, so she obviously doesn't have a problem with axing people."

"Yeah, but that was Chad and Alexa. She'd never fire you."

"Why not?"

"Because…" Evan's mint-green eyes squinted for a second, as if searching for something in a bright room in his mind. "She just wouldn't. You're supposed to be a VP. So it doesn't matter what you do."

I was reminded of Chris last night, when I raised the topic of why we were suddenly getting along so well, telling me it didn't matter. I got a flash of that green frog on my night-stand.

"Look, Ev, just help me out, okay? Tell me how to do this." I pulled a manila envelope from my bag, the one holding Odette's account, which was up for rebudgeting. I wanted to be able to do so much for her, but I knew she had limited funds to pay us.

"Anything for you." Evan dragged his stool around so we sat side by side. Our arms touched as he pulled Odette's file from the envelope.

"Okay," he said, holding out the old budget. As he did this, he put his other hand very lightly on the side of my thigh. It seemed an innocent enough gesture, but I could feel the warmth of his hand on my leg, and for a moment, my Ev-erlasting Crush turned on with full force.

Evan began talking about the different figures on the page, about the results we'd gotten for Odette thus far and what that meant in terms of revising her budget. I tried to focus, but the numbers swam. His hand now felt heavy and hot. I had a brief flash of longing for that hand to move higher.

A moment later, he took his hand away to search for something in the file, but I could still sense it, as if he'd left a handprint, one that seared through my skirt, into my skin. Even after I'd thanked him, paid for our beers and began walking home, I could still feel it.

I called my sister Hadley the next morning.

"Billy! How are you?" she said, voice booming through the phone. In London it was the end of the day, but she sounded as chipper as if she'd just arrived at her office after ten hours of sleep. The truth was, Hadley was one of those people who required only five hours a night.

"I'm great, Hads. How are you?" I took a seat on a bar stool in our kitchen, my morning Diet Coke in front of me.

"It's insane around here. You know how it goes."

"Sure," I said. But really, I had no idea what it was like to be a top asset manager at an investment bank, nor did Hadley ever tell me. Although we e-mailed occasionally, this was the first time I'd spoken to her on the phone in months.

"What about you?" Hadley asked.

"Well, I just made vice president."

"That's amazing!" Hadley might not have come home for my wedding, but she appreciated corporate ladder-climbing.

"Yeah, thanks. Hey, have you been in touch with Mom? I got a postcard that said she's in Milan."

"I saw her last night."

"You did?" I tried to keep the shock from my voice. Not only was my mother at the fashion shows in Milan, but she'd traveled to London, too? "Is she okay?"

"She's great," Hadley said. "She was so nice about the—" she cleared her throat "—baby stuff." The "baby stuff" was what Hadley called her infertility problems.

"How's that going?"

"It's not. I think maybe I waited too long." Her voice was lower now, and it made me sad.

"God, I'm sorry, Hadley. This must be so hard."

"Oh, it's okay. Nigel mentioned to Mom that we might look into getting a surrogate, since I seem to be the problem, and when Mom heard that, she offered to do it."

I cracked up at the image of my nearly sixty-year-old mother with a ripe, pregnant belly, but it didn't surprise me that she'd offered to do something scientifically impossible.

My mother would do (or at least attempt to do) anything for us. Particularly since my father had left. At the fleeting thought of my dad, I waited for the usual pang to hit my psyche, the feeling of utter disappointment, a sick wondering of *why*. But nothing happened. I made myself think of him again. Wonderfully, nothing.

"So when is Mom heading home?" I asked.

"Not sure. She's back in Milan as far as I know. Hold on." Hadley began talking to someone in her office, rattling off stock prices and call orders.

"Hads," I said, "I'll let you go, but do you know where Mom is staying?"

"The Grand Hotel. You want the number?"

I grabbed the pad of paper sitting on our granite bartop and jotted the phone number.

"Congrats about the promotion, Billy," Hadley said. "You deserve it."

"Thanks." But her words somehow failed to register.

As I dialed the Grand Hotel, Chris came into the kitchen, looking handsome in an olive suit and gold tie. I expected him to dash past me with a kiss on the cheek as usual—especially after we'd fooled around half the night, both of us only getting a few hours of sleep—but he stopped and hugged me from behind, nuzzling my shoulder.

"Good morning," I said slowly, thinking that if I could start out every day with a hug and a nuzzle from my husband, I'd be a very satisfied girl.

Chris growled. "Come back to bed."

I giggled and pointed at the phone. "I'm trying to find my mom. What do you have going on today?"

Chris nibbled my earlobe, mumbling, "Nothing important," before he disentangled himself and began taking eggs and turkey bacon from the fridge.

"What are you doing?" I said as the phone rang at my mother's hotel.

"Making breakfast for you."

I sat there, surprised. "That's sweet, but I don't eat breakfast. I don't like it."

"You just think that." Chris slipped off his suit coat and turned up his shirtsleeves.

"No, I really don't like breakfast. And you know it, too." I could eat a big lunch with clients, I could inhale a fat bowl of pasta from Merlo for dinner, I could consume a large buttered popcorn at the movies, but I could not eat breakfast. There was something repulsive about eating first thing in the morning. It was as if my stomach hadn't yet woken up with the rest of my body.

Chris shook his head and gave me a knowing smile as he went about cracking eggs.

I was about to reassert how much I didn't want breakfast, but cooking for me was such a kind gesture, so Chris-of-old, that I hesitated, and then a cultured male voice answered with a string of melodic Italian words, two of which were "Grand Hotel."

"Katherine Lovell," I said.

"One moment," the man said, switching to English. "I'll connect you."

I listened to the tinny ringing of a phone while I watched my husband sauté onions and some kind of exotic mushrooms. I put my hand over the phone. "Chris, honey, seriously," I said, shaking my head at his culinary goings-on, but he only winked and waved me away.

"Pronto?" my mother's voice called into the phone.

"Mom, it's me!" I sounded like a seven-year-old.

"Baby doll! How are you?"

"I'm great. How are *you?*"

"Oh, just wonderful."

"What are you doing there?" I asked.

"Well, the shows are almost over. I was *so* disappointed at first. I mean, honestly, I missed most of the shows, and do you know how hard it is to get in to the rest? If I hadn't met Claudia, I'd still be sitting at the hotel bar. But then I did get in, and yuck! The Trussardi stuff was just plain boring. Finally, yesterday, Claudia and I found the most to-die-for suits in this delicious celadon-green from Trevi."

"Who's Claudia?"

"Just someone I met over here. She and her husband have taken me under their wing. I swear, they've got me out to shows every day and some party or another every night."

"Oh," I said inanely. I felt a pang of jealously toward this Claudia.

"So anyway, this celadon is just perfect. I've ordered that, and we're going to the Cavalli and Strenesse shows today. Fingers crossed!" My mother prattled on about a pink coat she'd seen at a Pucci show and a white suit with a fur collar by Lancetti and a party that night on the Canals, while I tried to follow it all and still absorb the fact that my normally reclusive mother had a very hectic social schedule in Milan, of all places.

"Oops, baby doll, I just heard a knock on my door, so that will be Claudia. I've got to run, but I'm coming home Monday. I'll call you, okay? Kisses!"

And she was gone.

I stared at the phone, realizing that I hadn't even gotten to tell her about my promotion. I looked up then, just as Chris slid in front of me a frittata so big it could have fed an army barrack.

"Thanks, hon," I said weakly and picked up my fork.

★ ★ ★

The rest of the week raced by as I tried to master my job. I made notes from Evan's budget lesson and kept them minimized on my new computer as I tackled other, bigger accounts. The work was as slow and painful as a trip to the DMV. There really was no magic formula, just my own somewhat subjective determinations on how much it should cost to get a baby clothes manufacturer—or an interior designer or a pharmaceutical company—the publicity they needed. My new chair had been delivered, thank God, because I was in my office and on my ass all the time now. Before, I had excuses to leave frequently—visiting the printer to okay the press kits, meeting with a reporter from the *Trib*—but now such tasks were handled by lower members of the team. I was there to simply oversee it all.

And then there were the personnel issues that had become part of my life. Someone or another was always sticking their head in my office, asking for a chat. Sometimes these talks were truly about work issues—did I have any thoughts on how to get a psychologist on *Oprah?* Did I know anyone at *Cosmo* who we could approach about a story? Could I help them with a pitch or a press release? I relished those discussions, because they allowed me to use my old skills, my creative thinking. But more often than not, people wanted to talk about how irritated they were with the new assistant or how they were redoing their bathroom at home and could I find it in my heart to give them Friday off without docking their vacation days?

At first, it was interesting that people saw me as a go-to figure. I liked helping them sort through problems, and I liked the new deference my coworkers gave me. There was a respect in their words, a shy smile on their faces when they said, "Hi, Billy, got a second?"

Eventually, though, I realized that although they could have approached Roslyn or Evan or one of the other VPs, they were trying me out, hoping for the benevolence of someone slightly newer to the job. And the respect they gave me, well I assumed it came with the position, sort of like my new chair, but then I had a talk with Lizbeth on Friday afternoon. She'd been so chatty and kind when I realized I was a VP, but the rest of the week she was skittish with me, wary. I'd noticed it, but didn't have the time to worry or wonder until that Friday when she came into my office.

"Hi," she said, tentatively standing. I recalled my first day as VP when she'd immediately slouched on my visitor's chair.

"Hi," I said, raising my eyes away from yet another budget. "What's up?"

Keeping her head down, she moved quickly past my desk, and her hands slipped through some papers on my credenza. "I'm just looking for the Teaken Furniture file."

"Oh, I think it's there." I swung around in my new chair. It was easy now that the chair fit like a glove, and I had no phone book beneath my feet. But as I did so, Lizbeth shied away like a fawn too close to the highway.

"Something wrong?" I asked.

She shook her head. "No. Thanks for looking. But you know I can do that. It's my job, and I *am* performing. I do everything I was hired to do."

I blinked a few times. "Lizbeth, what's wrong?"

"Nothing. I really like working for you."

I frowned. "Can you close the door and sit down, please?"

She did so quietly. Instead of slouching in a chair like that first day, she sat straight, knees together, hands clasped on her legs. Her eyes were downcast, and her body language reminded me of a geisha I'd seen on a PBS documentary.

"What's going on?" I said.

"What do you mean?"

"You're acting strange."

Her eyes shot up to meet my face, then back down again. "Just doing my job."

"Why do you keep saying that?"

"What do you mean?"

"Okay, enough. Tell me what's going on."

She began to chew on one of her glossed lips, and I could see the pink coming off onto her white teeth. "Billy, it's just that I've wanted to do PR since college, okay? I had to work as a secretary at an accounting firm and then an ad agency before I got hired here. I love it. I really do." She looked up at me with plaintive eyes. "I can't afford to lose this job."

"Lizbeth, what makes you think you're going to lose your job?" I leaned forward on my desk.

"Well, Alexa got fired, and everyone's been talking, wondering who's next."

I sat back, deflated. Alexa. So that was why everyone was so deferential. "Lizbeth, you're not going to get fired."

"I'm not?"

"No. No one is."

She let out a breath and grinned a little. "Well, that's good." Then her smiled disappeared. "But then why…"

"Why what?"

"Why did Alexa have to go? I mean, I thought she was really good at what she did, and she was always taking time to explain things to me when no one else would."

"She did?" That shocked me. I assumed Alexa had pushed her work off on everyone else, just like she'd done with me.

"Oh, yeah, she would stay late and tell me what the team was working on, and why we were going after one type of media and not another. She was great, you know?"

I grimaced.

Lizbeth caught it. "Well, maybe not. I mean, clearly she did something wrong."

She was groveling again, and I held up a hand. "Lizbeth, it's okay. I promise you—no one else is going to lose their job."

She left, practically bowing on her way out. I got up and shut the door, then sat quietly, thinking that Alexa hadn't really done anything wrong, except piss off the wrong person. Me. I'd used my new position to get what I wanted, making the good of the team the excuse, not really caring whether my truth was reality. And now I'd gained an unwanted respect as the company hatchet man.

My intercom buzzed. "Billy?" Evan's voice rang through my office.

I pushed it. "Hi," I said softly.

"What's wrong?"

I sighed. "Nothing."

"Well, I'm leaving, but I just wanted to remind you about the Hello Dave show tomorrow night. You coming?"

"Chris and I are going to my mom's." But then I remembered that my mother wouldn't be home from Milan until Monday. "Actually, Evan, I think we might be able to make it."

"Excellent. It's been a while since you've seen them, and it's been a long week. You need to cut loose."

He was absolutely right. I needed some good loud music in a good loud bar with a good strong drink. "We'll see you tomorrow night."

chapter six

On Saturday night, I was the only one getting ready for the Hello Dave show. Chris had gone to work that morning, with promises to be back by 5:00, but the office had sucked him in and refused to spit him back out. None of this was unusual. Chris nearly always worked Saturdays, and he often stayed until an ungodly hour. But what *was* unusual was the way he handled it. Instead of "crying swamp" in a crabby, quick phone call, he sent a vase of yellow lilies to the house. *Sorry about the show, Treetop,* the card said. *You go, and I'll make it up to you later.* It made my eyes well.

I took forever to get ready, just like the old days when hitting the bars every Saturday night was vital rather than optional. I straightened my hair with an iron and flipped up the ends, admiring the dark sheen it now had. I made up my eyes dark and smoky, then emulated Lizbeth and applied lip gloss with a trowel. I dressed in black pants, strappy sandals and a flimsy aqua top I'd bought for my honeymoon. I threw my dark jean jacket over the ensemble and tossed my tiny Gucci bag over my shoulder. I put my nose in the lilies one last time, inhaling their perfume, thinking how lucky I was to have Chris, and then, smiling to myself, I was out on Dearborn hailing a cab.

At the Park West, Evan, who knew everyone in town, had put us on the guest list, so I picked up my free ticket and slapped an all-access sticker on my thigh. He was waiting at the bar inside the main doors, and he waved a hand over his head. People pushed their way around him, everyone trying to secure drinks while the opening band was still on, but Evan looked unruffled. He still did this every Saturday. Meanwhile, the crowd daunted me. The smell of cigarette smoke permeated the air. The women who elbowed me were so young, yet their expressions world-weary.

When I reached Evan, he gave me a tight hug, then looked behind me. "Where's Chris?"

"Duty calls. Making the world safe for democracy."

"I'm glad I'm not a lawyer."

"Me, too. Where's your date?"

He gave a sheepish look.

"You broke up with her already?"

"Had to be done. Guess it's just me and you tonight."

I was shoved from behind, and my hands flew up to protect myself. They landed on Evan's chest. A very firm, broad chest, I couldn't help noticing. "Sorry," I muttered.

He held my arm and stared down at me. "I'm not."

I chuckled uneasily. "How about a drink?"

Evan turned to the bar and with one movement, he was at the front, conferring with the bartender.

"Here you go," Evan said, putting a drink in my hand a moment later. The glass was icy cold.

"What's in it?"

"Stoli orange."

"And some soda?" I said hopefully.

"A splash."

I took a sip. The drink bit into my tongue, sharp with a hint of citrusy-sweet. "This is dangerous."

Evan lifted his eyebrows and smiled crookedly.

Inside, the theater was buzzing. A largely ignored warm-up band sang earnestly, while people milled around, jockeying for position, waiting for the main act. Our access passes got us to the VIP area at the front of the stage, but it was still packed. Evan put his arm around me and pulled me toward the stage. That arm felt bigger than Chris's, somehow more urgent, and, like the vodka, much more dangerous.

Soon, Hello Dave took the stage, and the crowd surged, yelling and clapping. Evan put that arm around me again, ostensibly to protect me. I let the crowd push me into him, breathing the light scent of his cologne. The lead singer yelled thanks to the crowd, then immediately broke into "Golden," a finger-snapping, hip-swaying song that reminded me of a sunny, summer afternoon.

Evan threw his head back and hollered. It was something that had initially attracted me to him—his absolute abandon in the face of live music. Chris was more of a step-clap, step-clap kind of guy, eyes firmly on the stage (although he was the sweetest of slow dancers, holding me tight, swaying perfectly to the music). But it was undeniable that Evan could *move,* and it was infectious. I took a gulp of my vodka—so I wouldn't spill it, I told myself—then allowed myself to be taken away. I closed my eyes, and my body charted its own course with the music. I felt beads of sweat along my hairline and the small of my back, but I kept dancing, swaying, and as I did, years melted away. I was no longer a thirty-two-year-old married woman who had steadily clawed her way to a position of power. I was young, I was free, I was somehow perfect at that moment.

At some point, Evan picked his way out of the crowd and back. "Drinks," he mouthed, holding two more vodkas. That arm slipped around me again, and we moved together to the music. I hoped the band would play forever. I wanted to drink vodka and stand near the heat of Evan's body and dance and dance and dance eternally.

"We have to do this more often," Evan said. He spoke into my ear so he could be heard above the music, and his breath sent a tingle down my neck, into my back.

I nodded, not trusting myself. My hips kept moving in time with his.

"You've been great!" yelled the lead singer. "Thank you!" He bounded into the final song, "Biminy," and the crowd became more frenzied.

Evan gulped the rest of his drink, then slipped behind me. He put a hand on my hip, a light hand, nothing insistent, but now our movements were perfectly in sync. I could feel that chest, those legs behind me, as if we were one person. "This is perfect," he said in my ear. Again, that hot breath, that tingle down my spine.

He said something else, but the music became louder. I couldn't make out his words. I could only feel the heat of his breath, his body behind mine. He muttered something else into my ear, and right then, I got the overwhelming urge to press my face into his. I tilted my cheek a fraction toward him. His mouth touched my jaw, his lips warm and soft on my skin. I began to turn into his lips, the air leaving my chest in one swoop. But I never reached them.

The music ended with a cymbal's clash. The room went quiet for a second before the crowd broke into applause. It was that pocket of silence that broke the spell.

I took a step away, and clapped like crazy to hide how flustered I felt. Evan did the same. "Thank you," I said to him, when the band left the stage. "This was amazing."

And then, before he could say anything, I ran for the safety of a taxi.

I didn't realize how sauced I was from the vodka until I was in my own kitchen, blinking at the half-light and feeling slightly stumbly. I didn't want to go to bed yet. How could I climb under the sheets with my husband when I'd almost kissed another man a moment ago?

Food. That's what I needed. Something to soak up the vodka, along with the memories of Evan's body near mine. I opened the refrigerator and scanned the contents. Not a hell of a lot.

I picked up a lone pear and examined it. It looked a bit sad, and it certainly wouldn't have the soaking-up properties I was searching for. As I bent lower to return it to the shelf, something touched my back.

"Oh!" I said, spinning around, crashing into the fridge.

And there was Chris. His hair was combed straight, and he wore a white button down shirt turned up at the cuffs. "Hi, Treetop," he said.

"You scared me!"

He laughed. "That seems to be happening a lot this week."

"What are you doing up?"

"Why don't you come and see?"

Chris took my hand and led me away from the fridge. I heard it fall closed behind me with a muted thump. Meanwhile, my heart thumped faster inside my chest. Was he waiting up for me because he sensed what I'd almost done with Evan?

Chris led me into our living room. "What do you think?" he asked, his hand outstretched.

On the hardwood floor, he'd set up a picnic. A green flannel blanket was laid flat, and on top sat his grandmother's silver candelabra with six lit candles. They were burned halfway down, and I wondered how long Chris had been waiting. Two cushions, taken from the couch, had been placed on the blanket along with a champagne bucket and plates of food.

"Oh, Chris," I said. I felt a rush of awe. When we'd been dating, we used to have picnics frequently, both inside the house, as well as out. Tim and Tess made fun of us, calling us insufferable romantics, but it had become a tradition of sorts. A tradition that had fallen by the wayside since we were married.

"We haven't had one in a while," Chris said, "and I knew you'd be hungry."

"How did you know that?"

"Because whenever you see Hello Dave with Evan, you're always starving."

I nodded, unable to say anything, unable to admit I was usually trying to fill myself with food to cover up the desire in my body.

"C'mon," Chris said, pulling me down onto the blanket. He took the bottle of champagne from the bucket and poured me a foaming glass.

"I had a bit to drink at the show. I don't know if I should have any more."

"Who cares?" Chris said, his voice sounding more lighthearted than I'd heard in years.

I gave a little laugh and accepted the glass. "Right. Who cares?" I took a sip, the bubbles tickling my mouth.

Chris lifted a plate with toast squares, something dark on them. "Would you like caviar?"

"You got me caviar?" My guilt was replaced with gratitude and adoration. "Chris, you are so good to me."

"You deserve it. And I got you this amazing cheese." He picked up a small white piece and put it in my mouth. The texture was firm, but it had a creamy taste. "It's Campo de Montalban," he said.

"Delicious. You went to Pastoral?"

He nodded.

"After working all day?"

"I wanted to treat you."

Chris took the champagne glass from my hand and placed it to the side. He leaned over and whispered in my ear. "I want to treat you with more than just the caviar."

The feel of his words in my ear gave me a flash of Evan. "Chris…" I said, not sure what else I wanted to say. *I almost kissed another man. I wanted to kiss another man. I am a horrible person, but I'd still like some more of that cheese.*

"Don't talk," Chris said, and he began to kiss my neck.

"But…"

"Later." His mouth moved down to my collarbone.

I sighed and let my thoughts swim away. I raised my arms and put them around my husband.

Late on Sunday morning, I curled up on my favorite chair, the one that had been at Chris's apartment when I first met him. It was large enough to fit two people and made of a soft suedelike fabric with big, flat arms. One of those arms now held my morning Diet Coke, the other the Sunday papers.

Some people feel depressed on Sunday, with the workweek looming, but Sunday has always been my favorite day. The phone rarely rings, the streets outside our condo are quiet, and on this particular Sunday, a nearly-white May sun had pushed its way through the windows, streaking across the hardwood floor, making me feel like a fat, contented cat. Chris's midnight picnic and the hour we'd spent rolling on the flannel blanket had satisfied me, made me languid.

Chris was still asleep, so I had the place to myself. I took another sip of my Diet Coke and began reading the papers. I came to an article about a British psychoanalyst who asserted that human beings had to learn to enjoy the things they normally disliked. I sipped my drink and thought about that a moment. I wondered if Blinda would agree. After all, it was she who told me to *look inside* for happiness, while I'd argued that the issue wasn't being happy with what I had, but getting what I deserved. Somehow, some way, this last week I'd gotten exactly what I wanted, and I wasn't about to pretend that I wasn't glad for it. I wouldn't pretend that I'd rather have tugged my reluctant psyche to a point where I was happy with the old me. I liked the new life. It was just the *way* it had happened that was so startling, so, well…mystical. My thoughts streaked to the green frog, who was, right now, sitting precociously on my nightstand.

The phone rang, surprisingly, taking me away from my musings. It was Tess.

"Shouldn't you be at church?" I said. Tess wasn't very religious herself, but she took her two kids to mass every Sunday. *Puts the fear of God in them,* she always said. *And they need it, because they certainly aren't scared of me.*

"I made Tim take them," she said. "I couldn't handle it."

"What's up?"

She groaned. "I need a girl's night. Are you free for dinner tonight?"

"Sure. Want me to come out there?" Tess lived in Wilmette, and it was usually me who made the drive when we got together.

"No, I need a night downtown. Tim will watch the kids."

At seven o'clock, I kissed Chris and left him in front of the computer. I walked through Lincoln Park toward Mon Ami Gabi, the French café where Tess and I planned to meet. The sun was staying later now, the sky a soft, deepening powder blue. The May air was warm, with a fresh, thick breeze coming off the lake, promising summer, soon.

Tess was already at the restaurant, seated at a cozy table by the windows. She was a willowy blonde who wore little makeup and tucked her simple bob behind her ears. I pointed at the large bottle of San Pellegrino in front of her. Normally, a bottle of wine would have held that place on the table. "You're not!" I said.

She nodded, her expression chagrined. "I am."

"Oh, my God, another baby? Congrats!"

Tess stood and hugged me weakly.

"Are you feeling okay?" I said as we took our seats.

"No, I'm not! This wasn't supposed to happen, and now it's no wine, no Advil, no brie, no hot baths. Pregnancy takes away everything that makes me happy."

"It was the Advil that really pushed you over the edge, right?"

She scowled. "Don't laugh!"

"I'm sorry, but it's kind of funny."

Her scowl deepened.

"Okay, Tess, it's not funny, but it's great! You love being a mom, and you're awesome at it. You and Tim will be great with this one, too."

She smiled a little. "I suppose you're right. But Tim is getting snipped after this one." She made a sadistic scissoring motion with her hand.

I sipped a white Bordeaux while we talked about her kids, Joy and Sammy, and the fact that Tess was depressed at the thought of getting "as big as a house." Tess stared at my wine with undisguised greed. When our salads were delivered, Tess said, "Enough about me. Tell me what's up with you."

"I got the vice presidency."

"What? And you let me sit here for twenty minutes talking about Sammy's poops and my water weight? Congrats! When did it happen?"

"That's the strange thing." I told her about Blinda and the frog and about how, on Tuesday morning, I'd woken up to Chris's affections and gone to work to find out I was a VP.

"It's just a coincidence," Tess said. "Your husband wanted some sex, good for you. And there just wasn't an official announcement. That happens sometimes."

"It was more than that. It was like everyone just assumed I'd been VP for a while, and I would always be a VP, even if I screwed up."

"That's just how you perceived it."

"I don't think so. And there's more." I told her about my mom's postcard from Milan and how I seemed to have inexplicably gotten over my father's abandonment.

"Well, thank God," Tess said. "I mean really. You've been carrying that baggage around way, way too long, and let me tell you it wasn't a pretty Hermès bag. It was a nasty nylon backpack that didn't suit you. This is all good news, so why don't you seem pleased?"

"No, I am, I am." I took another bite of my salad greens. "There's one more thing that's happened." I swallowed. "Evan."

"Meow." Tess had met Evan on numerous occasions and had found him as delicious as I did. "How is the Everlasting Crush?"

"He's been flirting with me," I said.

Her eyes widened. "What?"

"Yeah. You see what I mean? Everything happened in the span of twenty-four hours. I got everything I wanted."

"I still think it's a coincidence, but either way, you've got to tell me what's been going on with Evan."

"Well, last night…"

"What? What happened last night?"

I looked around the restaurant, at the soft light from the wall sconces and the patrons tucked into banquette tables. I turned back to Tess. "I almost kissed him."

"Holy shit. Waiter!" She gestured frantically with one arm. When he reached us, she said, "I'll need a glass of wine. Whatever she's having." She looked back at me. "I can have *one* glass, and my God, this story sounds like I'm going to need it."

I laughed. "You won't get flack from me."

I'd always thought the pregnancy ban on even a drop of alcohol a tad too strict. My mother, for instance, didn't realize she was pregnant with Dustin until she was almost four months along, having spent those months smoking and drinking Campari with my father in jazz clubs around Chicago. She drank while carrying Hadley, too. It wasn't until she was carrying me that doctors cautioned pregnant women against alcohol. Her abstinence during the pregnancy with me was a problem, as I saw it. Dustin and Hadley were clearly smarter than I was, more ambitious and accomplished. Would I have been the same if my mother had stopped teetotaling and kept boozing?

Tess made me wait until her wine arrived before I could tell her about the Hello Dave show. I left nothing out, giving the tiniest of details, just like we used to when we were in high school and didn't have jobs or husbands or kids to take our time away.

"And so that's it," I said. "I took off like the place was on fire. I had to walk five blocks to find a cab, and when I got home... Oh, you won't believe it."

"What?" Tess took the last sip of her wine. She glared at the glass, as if angered at it for holding such a small amount.

"Chris was waiting up for me. With champagne."

"No."

"And caviar."

"No!" she said again. "God, Billy, did you tell him about Evan?"

I shook my head. "I started to, but I couldn't. The picnic was so sweet of Chris. So *seductive*. I don't think I've ever been turned on by two men within the same hour. And there really wasn't anything to tell."

She raised her eyebrows as if to say, *maybe, maybe not*. "You know me. I usually don't give advice, but I've got to say something." She reached across the table and squeezed my hand. "I'm not sure what's going on with you, or why all these things have happened, but I do know something. You've got to be careful here, Billy. *Real* careful."

I quickly switched topics, and Tess and I talked for another hour about this and that, everything and nothing. But in the back of my head, I couldn't seem to shake her words. *Be careful here, Billy. Real careful.*

chapter seven

The next day, at exactly eleven o'clock, my office phone rang.

"Hi, baby doll," my mother said.

My heart bounced like a tennis ball. My mother was back from Milan and calling me at eleven on a Monday, just as she always did. It was like normal! "Mom, I miss you."

"You too, sweetie." But she sounded distracted. There was static behind her words, as if she was in a windy tunnel. "I'm on the plane coming home. We land in an hour or two."

"Do you want me to pick you up? I could get out early." The airport pickup was something my mother always desired, something I rarely did, but I wanted to see her badly.

"Oh, no. You keep working."

"Well, I could come out tonight, and we could make dinner." There was nothing that made my mother happier than the thought of having one of her girls home with a pot simmering on the stove. The sad fact was this dream rarely became a reality.

"How about tomorrow night, sweetie? We can go out."

"Out?" I said.

"I'll meet you at Milrose. That way it'll be right off the highway for you."

I was shocked into momentary silence. Milrose was a restaurant and brewery in Barrington, and it was, just as my mother had said, right off the highway I would take from Chicago. I had suggested dinner there numerous times before, but my mother said the bar was too crowded and the food too pricey, so we always got together at her house.

"Do you want me to pick you up?" I said.

"No, no. I'll see you there tomorrow. 7:00?"

"Okay. I won't bring Chris, so we can have some girl time."

The static grew louder, and then she was gone.

Later that morning, Evan stuck his head in my office. "How'd you feel yesterday?" His eyes twinkled mischievously.

"I assume you're referring to the vodka, but I can hold my own." I said this in a pompous voice, while I fiddled with a few pens, sticking them in the mug on my desktop.

"Since when?"

"You haven't gone out with me for a while. You're really too much of an amateur, so I had to move onto different pastures."

"Oh, different pastures, huh?" He stepped into the office and leaned against the wall, one leg crossed, toe on the ground. He wore gray pants and a light blue shirt. "I thought your other pasture was at home in front of the TV with your husband."

"Nope, that's not the case." And it wasn't. Although he was right about the TV, he wasn't right about Chris. Until the last week, we hadn't spent much time together at all.

Evan made another joke about my "pastures," and we bantered, just like we'd done many times before, but I noticed his words were more flirty than usual, his jaunty lean against the wall more practiced. And Evan was giving me "the eyes"—a pointed stare I'd seen him give other women when the conversation was light but he was imagining something much heavier.

"How about lunch?" Evan said. "I was thinking RL."

Although Evan and I frequently had lunch together, it was usually at Subway or the salad place downstairs. RL, on the other hand, the very chic Ralph Lauren café, was Evan's official first date spot.

"We don't need anything fancy," I said.

"I want to treat you."

"Why?"

He uncrossed the leg and moved until he was standing in front of my desk. He leaned forward, hands on the desk, and a lock of blond hair fell across his eyes. "Why do you think, Billy?"

The sound of my name coming from his mouth made me shiver. I could remember vividly the feel of his breath in my ear Saturday night. "I'm not sure. Why don't you spell it out for me?" I couldn't help it. I leaned forward too, and now our faces were only a few inches apart.

We stared into each other's eyes. I found it hard to get air in my chest. I had a crazy desire to press into his lips.

Finally, he spoke. "Because of your promotion. We never got to celebrate." His words were mundane, but his voice husky, as if imparting an erotic secret.

"Uh-huh," I said, my lungs still struggling to work.

"Well?" Evan said. He smiled with one side of his face, the dimple there denting his skin adorably.

I made myself sit back in my chair. Once the nearness of him was gone, I was left feeling cold and silly. "I think I'd better pass."

"Why?"

I murmured excuses about meetings and projects, but the truth was plain—I couldn't trust myself around Evan.

As I ate a carry-out Caesar salad, Lizbeth came into my office. She was more comfortable around me since our talk last week, yet still not truly relaxed. As a result, I tried hard to be engaging and kind, but managerial and bosslike. This attitude also helped to convince myself that I really was a VP.

"What's up today?" I said through a bite of salad.

"Some papers for you to sign. Oh, and the HR department wants to know if you got the signed severance agreement from Alexa."

I swallowed hard on a rough piece of lettuce. The guilt of firing Alexa was still eating at me. I'd gotten a taste of power, and she was the first one in my line of fire. "You haven't seen anything come through the mail?"

Lizbeth shook her head. "Let's hope she doesn't sue the company. Roslyn would be *so* pissed."

"Is that a possibility?"

"That's what HR said."

I pushed my salad away, feeling queasy. I'd wrongfully fired a colleague—just because I could—I'd given her a pittance of a severance, and now I might have landed the company in litigation. "Maybe I can help her get a job," I mused aloud. But even as I said it, I knew it would be tough. I'd been keeping an eye on the city's PR firms for over a year, and the industry was as dry as ash.

"Whatever you want to do," Lizbeth said. "Here's her info if you want to call her." She handed me a sheet listing Alexa's name, address and other identifying information.

I looked it over, staring at Alexa's address. She lived on

West Division. Probably in one of those new loft condos. Of course, Alexa might have a hard time affording the new loft condo with her ten days of severance pay. The guilt rose higher in my chest.

"I'll work on it," I told Lizbeth.

I immediately called HR and asked if I could get Alexa a longer severance. No go, the HR director told me. It was the company's policy not to change a severance once set, especially if the employee had been terminated for cause as Alexa had. She reminded me that we needed the signed severance agreement.

My guilt felt like it was scraping away my insides.

I sat silently at my desk until I knew what to do. After work, I'd stop by Alexa's place, and bring her flowers or something suitably apologetic. I'd tell her I was sorry for the way things had gone down, and I'd tell her that I would help her in any way I could. And then I'd get her to put pen to paper.

I pulled my salad toward me and at the same time pushed Alexa from my mind. It would be all right, I told myself. For both of us.

At six o'clock, I sat in the back of a cab traveling west on Division. In my lap was an enormous fern. I'd spent an inordinate amount of time at the florist, debating hydrangeas versus orchids, tulips versus sunflowers. Nothing seemed right. Finally, I settled on a huge fern in a yellow ceramic holder. The flowers had seemed too romantic, but the fern, I'd decided, had a hail-fellow-well-met effect and said, *I'm sorry I fired you and gave you a shitty severance, but you'll be just fine.*

I couldn't see in front of me, due to the fern, but out the side window, I watched as the cab passed the entrance to the highway and continued west. Ashland went by in a blur, the hip shops and cafés of Wicker Park starting to show themselves. Of course, Alexa would live somewhere trendy. She was probably from a waspy family in Kenilworth but considered herself "slumming" in the now-posh confines of Wicker Park. She began to annoy me again, if only in my head. I saw those cashmere twinsets and her smug grin. I remembered her uncanny ability to get me to do her work.

Suddenly, the fern seemed obscene. She had deserved to be fired, and she certainly didn't need my help. She probably wouldn't even want it.

I shoved the fern onto the seat next to me. It would look good in *my* house, next to Chris's big chair. I wanted to tell the cabbie to turn around.

I had just leaned forward and angled my head through the fiberglass window to speak to the driver when I noticed that we'd passed Damen. The cab kept moving. The trendy stores of Wicker Park gave way to Hispanic grocery stores and run-down bars.

"Excuse me," I said to the cabbie. "Have we gone too far?"

"Nope. Another eight blocks."

I sat back and watched the neighborhood grow steadily more sketchy. The cars were no longer of the Lexus or Mercedes variety, but appeared to be taken from a *Starsky & Hutch* rerun. People ambled on the street and sat on front stoops as if there was nowhere in the world to go.

Finally, the cab pulled to the curb and pointed across the street. "There's your address."

I checked it with the one I'd written down at the office. It was right. But how could this be? The building was cement block. The yard was made of dirt, with not a green bush or tree in sight. Some of the windows were boarded up. Others had sheets hanging in front of them.

"Want me to wait?" the cabbie said. "This isn't such a hot neighborhood."

"Thank you," I said distractedly, still staring at the building. "That would be great."

I hefted the fern up the sidewalk, glancing around nervously. This had to be a massive mistake. There was no way Alexa lived here.

But there was her last name—*Villa*—right on the buzzer box for apartment 3A. I pushed it. Nothing. I pushed again, relief filling me. No one home! I should have had the damn fern delivered.

But then the door clicked, followed by a faint buzz. The box crackled and a voice said something that sounded like, "Come on," but could have been, "Up yours."

Inside, the hallway smelled of cigarette smoke and spicy cooking. The doors to the apartments were made of cheap brown press board. I took the stairs as fast as possible, grateful for the Yellow Cab waiting outside. I'd drop off the fern, then I'd get the hell out of here.

The fern was heavy as lead, and by the third landing, I was huffing like I'd just run the Chicago Marathon. I knocked tentatively on the door for 3A.

It was opened immediately by a girl of about nine or ten with black curly hair and dark, saucerlike eyes. She smiled at me shyly.

"Is Alexa here?" I asked, trying to catch my breath and shift the fern to my other hip.

She looked behind her, then gazed up at me again.

I repeated myself.

Again, no response, just a bashful grin. Behind her, I saw a living room, its stained brown carpeting littered with toys. An ancient couch in a gray plaid fabric sat before an old TV with rabbit-ear antennae.

Just then, someone stepped into the living room. Alexa. "Who is it, Lucia?"

She saw me, and her face grew cold. Her eyes narrowed. "What are *you* doing here?"

I stood frozen in the doorway. This was no hip loft condo, and Alexa wasn't wearing cashmere. Instead, she had on tight blue workout pants, frayed at the hem, and a faded, black-and-white striped T-shirt that looked about ten years old. Was this her place? Was the girl her daughter?

"What are you doing here?" she repeated, her voice growing somewhat louder.

I thrust the fern forward. "This is for you."

Now I couldn't see her. All I knew was that she wasn't taking the fern. My arms began to quiver. I set it on the floor. "I wanted to see how you were," I said.

"Little late for that." She crossed her arms.

The girl giggled. A woman of about forty-five crossed the room, carrying a smaller child. She stopped and glanced at me, then said something in Spanish.

"No one," Alexa answered in English, never taking her gaze from me.

I cleared my throat. "Alexa, look…"

Just then another woman came into the living room. She looked remarkably like a tired, older Alexa, with white streaks through her long black hair.

"*Hola,*" she said to me.

"Hello."

She turned to Alexa and they spoke in rapid Spanish, but still Alexa didn't take her eyes from me.

There came a pounding on the stairs. I turned to see two boys in their early teens charging up the stairway. I moved, just in time for them to push past me into the apartment, barely giving me a look.

"I suppose you're looking for this," Alexa said, striding across the room and lifting a white sheaf of papers from the counter. The severance agreement.

"Well, ah...it would be nice if I could get that."

Alexa crossed the room again, her walk slow and purposeful, until she was in the doorway near me. "Let's go outside."

We descended the stairs in silence. I was relieved beyond belief to see the cab still waiting. I gave him a cheery wave, hoping to convince him to stay a little longer. Two men watched us from a stoop to our right.

"You got a pen?" Alexa said, not looking me in the face. There was a proud raise to her chin, but her eyes looked almost misty. That expression broke my heart.

"You know what, Alexa," I said. "Just forget it. It's too small a severance, and I'm sorry for that. I'm sorry for *everything*. And if you want to file suit against the company you should do that." I could hear the entire HR department screaming *Stop!* in my head. I ignored them and continued on. "I also wanted to see if I could help you get another job."

She scoffed. "You fired me, and now you're here to help me?"

I had to admit, it sounded ridiculous.

"I'm not going to sue Harper, and I am going to sign this," she said, shaking the agreement. "You know why? Because I support that family in there. And even though this is a pathetic severance, I need the money *now.*"

"Was that your little girl?"

She crossed her arms. A breeze blew a stray hair from her face, and despite myself, I noticed how beautiful she was. "She's my niece," Alexa said. "There's another niece and nephew in there, too, as well as my stepsister and brother."

"And was one of those women your mom?" The thought of Alexa still living with her mother was inconceivable.

She nodded. "And my aunt." She turned to me again. "I'm the breadwinner for this family. For all these people. That is, until you fired me."

"So you're not from Kenilworth?" I asked in a jokey tone. As soon as I said it, I wanted to ask the guys on the stoop for their handgun and shoot myself.

Alexa sighed and shook her head.

"Well, seriously, what about those black cashmere sweaters?" I said.

"What about them?"

"How do you afford all of them if you're supporting everyone here?"

"I bought three of them at TJ Maxx. I rotate." She dipped her head, as if embarrassed by this, but it was me who felt like a monumental ass.

"Oh," I said.

"Are you going to give me a pen?" Alexa gestured to my purse.

"Sure. Yeah, okay." Flustered, I rummaged through it, scrabbling my fingers until I came up with an old Bic.

Alexa snatched it, signed the agreement and handed it to me. "Show's over," she said. "Time for you to go."

As if on cue, the cabbie honked.

"Alexa, look," I said. "I am truly sorry. If there's anything I can do…"

She looked up the street. Her gaze was tired and sad. She moved to the front door and opened it with a key. "I think you've done enough," she said. She stepped inside and slammed the door.

chapter eight

When Chris got home from work that night, I was sitting in his big chair, only a small lamp illuminating the room. I was distraught about Alexa.

"Honey, what are you doing?" Chris said. His voice was cheerful.

"Nothing."

He switched on the overhead light, making me blink.

"What's up?" He sat on the arm of the chair.

I looked at him, not sure where to start.

"What is it? Talk to me."

Those words almost made me weep with relief. For the past two years, as Chris and I had grown steadily apart, I'd handled my emotional troubles on my own, wrestling in my mind in the dark of our bedroom, coming to my own decisions. But now here was my husband, attentive and wanting to talk. I didn't care what had happened to suddenly bring him back. I didn't care whether it was the frog or some freak shift in the universe. I was just happy he was there.

I reached out and touched his hand. "It's Alexa."

"I thought you got rid of her."

"I did." Now, I felt like weeping for a different reason. "I've destituted her whole family."

"Is destituted a word?"

"Chris!"

"Sorry, hon, but this is silly. You didn't harm her family."

"I think I did."

"What happened?"

I told Chris about the severance agreement and my visit to her apartment. "I thought she was from money," I said. "She always acted so superior and dressed the part. But according to her, she supports all these people, in this tiny apartment." I looked around our place and thought of all the relative riches we had—granite countertops, marble bathroom, enough space to avoid each other for years if we wanted.

"But Billy, it doesn't matter if she's rich or poor, you fired her for legitimate reasons."

I sniffled. "That's just the thing. I didn't like her, but I don't know that she needed to be fired. I think I just liked the power trip I got from being a VP. It was a convenience to get rid of her."

"That's not true," Chris said. I grimaced at how good and honorable he apparently thought I was. It made me ashamed.

"I rationalized the decision," I said. "I wanted her out, and so I came up with reasons why she should go. And because she'd gotten in a bit of trouble before it was easy to convince everyone. But I didn't do the right thing. I certainly wasn't thinking of the company. I was thinking of me." I dropped my head in my hands.

"Move over," Chris said, nudging me gently with his knee. He slid onto the big chair, pulling me onto his lap, embracing me. I squeezed my eyes shut and felt the serene comfort of him. This was what I'd missed.

"All right," Chris said. "Now let's figure out what you can do about it."

We talked for an hour. And despite how badly I felt about Alexa, I felt wonderful with Chris. This was what a husband and wife should be like. This was what I'd assumed we would be like when we were married. Why there had been so precious little of this, I couldn't say, but I loved the closeness now. I loved him.

We decided I would speak to Roslyn the next day. I would admit I'd made a mistake and try to get Alexa her job back. By the time Chris led me to bed, I was exhausted, but I was calm with my decision. I murmured thanks and fell asleep.

"Absolutely not," Roslyn said.

My calm from last night evaporated as if the air had been sucked from the room.

We were sitting in Roslyn's office, a cool space decorated with black and white prints of chilly winter landscapes.

"Why?" I said, trying to stop my legs from jiggling up and down. "Why can't we rehire her, if I admit I made a mistake?"

Roslyn shook her head and gazed at me, clearly disappointed. "Remember when you brought up the topic of letting Alexa go, and I told you it had to be your responsibility?"

I nodded and chewed anxiously on the inside of my lip.

"Well, that remains true. Once you're in management, you have to make some tough decisions, and you have to stick by them."

"Of course. I know that, and I agree, but I think just this once—"

"Can't do it, Billy."

"But why?" My anxiety was replaced by desperation. If I

couldn't somehow reverse what I'd done, Alexa's family would suffer. I wouldn't be able to shake the thought of that bleak apartment from my mind.

"When you let Alexa go, did you read the HR manual?" Roslyn asked.

I nodded, although I'd really only skimmed it, too set on sacking Alexa ASAP.

"So then you'll probably recall," Roslyn said, leaning forward on her desk, "that once someone is terminated, they cannot be rehired. Laid off, yes, we might be able to bring them back, but not if they were terminated for cause."

I sagged in the chair. I had rushed forward to something I wanted—getting Alexa out of my little world—without knowing or paying attention to the consequences. "There's nothing I can do?"

She shook her head. Then her face brightened. "But on a better topic, how's the budget going for Odette's book?"

I held back a sigh. Budgets, budgets, budgets. The new staple of my work life. How I hated them. "Just fine," I said.

"Great!" Rosalyn was chipper now that we'd dealt with the unpleasantries. "Well, see if you can get the numbers up. We've got to make some money off of her. And don't forget we've got an officers' meeting this afternoon."

That made me sit a little taller. I wasn't sure what went on in such meetings, yet they sounded official, exciting. Evan had told me otherwise, but I always believed he'd made them sound painful because he knew how badly I wanted to attend. And now I would. My first officers' meeting.

"I'll be there," I said.

Having your toenails pulled out with tweezers.
Listening to a Ted Nugent song for eternity.

Bleeding from the eyes.
Being run over by a lawn mower.
Watching a four-day Three Stooges marathon.

I sat in the boardroom making a list of things that might be more painful than the meeting itself.

Evan hadn't been patronizing me or trying to make me feel better when he'd said officers' meetings were boring. In fact, the word "boring" itself was a rip-roaring riotous party compared to what this meeting really was—monotonous and brainless.

We were on the topic of whether to have carbonated mineral water put in the pop machine. Lester, a VP from accounting, pointed out in a speech as long as a state of the union address, that the pop machine was really just for soda and we'd already compromised that sacred concept by adding regular water. Another man, clearly Lester's nemesis, argued that Lester was promoting a prejudiced attitude toward water, and that surely water of all kinds should be allowed the same rights as soda and permitted to mingle in the same areas.

"And you're missing a big point," the nemesis said. "We make money on that machine. The sparkling water will sell as fast as hotcakes."

Lester huffed and puffed about the importance of tradition and doing things the way they've always been done. I scribbled on my pad, *Sell as fast as hotcakes.* What did that mean anyway? What were hotcakes, and did they really sell so quickly? Maybe we should put those in the machine.

Lost in tedium, I began to write other sayings that didn't make sense.

Colder than a witch's tit. A witch was a mammal, wasn't she?

And therefore, why would her breast be colder than anyone else's?

Snug as a bug in a rug. Never understood this. Is the bug supposed to be rolled up in a rug, or just happy to be lolling in carpet fibers?

Clean as a whistle. Whistles were coated with saliva with every use, and therefore wouldn't exactly qualify as clean.

I felt someone's eyes on me and looked over to see Evan staring at my legs. I'd worn a light blue, pleated skirt that was rather schoolgirl and saucy. Apparently, Evan agreed. He raised his eyebrows and gave me a salacious smile. Feeling bored and bold, I crossed my legs, and the skirt rode a little higher. Evan's mouth fell slightly open, his gaze never leaving me. That gaze carried with it a certain power, wholly different from the power I'd felt when I fired Alexa. This power was sexual, ragged—the intensity thrilled me, yet scared me too. *This* power was great enough to carry me away with it, right when my marriage had gotten back to the place I wanted.

"Excuse me for a moment," I said, standing up.

Everyone in the boardroom looked at me with surprise. I thought I saw Evan grinning.

"Ladies' room," I said.

More stunned looks. Evidently, no one in the history of Harper Frankwell had ever left an officers' meeting to use the restroom. I considered sinking back into my seat fast, but between the boredom and Evan's eyes, I had to escape.

"Ladies' room," I said again, before I scooted toward the door.

By the time the meeting ended *two goddamned hours later,* no one seemed to remember my departure from the room or the way I'd snuck back in. I barely had time to do any work before I had to leave to meet my mom, but with my excitement to see her I couldn't have cared less. I headed for the parking lot.

As I steered my car onto the highway, my cell phone bleated from inside my purse. I reached over to the passenger seat and answered it.

"How's traffic?" Chris said.

"Same as five minutes ago. What's with you?" I had talked to Chris three times at work today, and once since I'd pulled out of the lot.

"I just wish I could go with you."

I laughed. "Since when?" Chris had never had such a keen interest in seeing my mom.

"I want to be with you." There was a plaintive note in his voice.

"Chris, you were with me last night and the night before that, and this morning."

"I want to be with you all the time."

Internally, I repeated, *since when?* Why, exactly, had Chris come back to me so quickly, when for years he'd distanced himself? I hadn't wanted to ponder that question—I just wanted to be happy with the new closeness we'd found— but Chris's near desperation baffled me. Even in our happiest days, we'd never been the couple who lived hand-in-hand.

"I'll see you when I get home," I said.

"Baby doll!" My mother swept into the bar at Milrose Brewery and pulled me into a hug.

I squeezed her tight, inhaling a new light, floral perfume. Over her shoulder, I could see other patrons at the bar checking her out. And for good reason. Her black hair was pulled elegantly into a chignon, and she had on huge dark sunglasses and a tangerine wrap around her shoulders that made her look more Parisian-urban than Barrington-suburban.

"Are we eating?" She pulled away and glanced around, as if the maitre d' might materialize and whisk her to a corner table.

"I'll tell them we're ready."

A few minutes later, my mother and I were tucked away in the loft section of the barnlike restaurant. "Mmm," my mother said, perusing the menu. "What to get, what to get."

"Tell me about Italy," I said.

"Oh, it was divine. You've been telling me for years that I should go, that I shouldn't be afraid to do things on my own, and you were right! I made so many friends." From her bag, which looked suspiciously Prada-esque, she whipped a small, red leather album. "Here's Claudia." She pointed to a photo of a stylish woman around fifty with ash-blond hair swept off her face. "Here's her husband, Thomas. What a dear."

For the next twenty minutes, I heard about Claudia and Thomas, and their Milanese friends, Paola and Stefano, and every fashion show and party they'd attended the last two weeks. I was delighted for my mom. To see her so vivacious again, so lustful for her life, was heartwarming. But my own heart needed warming of the maternal kind. I wanted her to say, *now tell me about you, baby doll.*

When our entrées were delivered—rigatoni and chicken for me, halibut for my mother—I jumped in. "I got the vice presidency," I said, blurting it out.

"What?" My mother clapped her hands. "Fantastic!" She waved the waiter over and ordered champagne, while I preened under her attention.

But I was barely into my story, when my mother interrupted. "You'll be needing some different clothes now that you've been promoted, am I right?" she asked.

"Oh, not really, I—"

"Don't be silly. You have to dress the part. And I've got just the thing." Out of her bag came another album, this one filled with designer sketches. "Look here, darling." She pointed to a drawing of a woman in a yellow suit with black lapels and wide shoulders.

"I think that's a little much, Mom."

"Nonsense. I'll get it for you. You deserve it! And there are others."

Soon we had pushed our dinners away and were poring over sketches that now lined the table. I didn't have the strength to fight her enthusiasm, and somehow, I agreed to have three suits made for me by an Italian designer called Pravadelli. After an hour of this, my mother abruptly claimed jet lag and said she needed to get home. "I'm playing bridge tomorrow with Marjorie and Carol," she said offhandedly.

"*Aunt* Marjorie and *Aunt* Carol?" My mother, like me, had two sisters, but they both lived on the North Shore, and they weren't close, due in large part to the fact that the sisters had disapproved of my father so many years ago. I'd often told her that she should make up with them and get back in each other's lives.

"Yes, you were right about that, too. No need to hold grudges."

"That's great, Mom." My mother needed her sisters, her new friends, but I needed her too. And yet for some reason, I felt her slipping away.

When I got home, I slid my key into the lock, anticipating the cool, inky darkness of the condo. I would put on my red checked pajamas that had been washed to a soft sheen, I would make myself a cup of tea and I would read for a few quiet minutes in the big chair, under a soft pool of light. Later, I would slip into the bed, already warmed by Chris's sleeping body. I nearly sighed with anticipation.

But our place was bathed in light, and there was Chris, wearing an apron over sweatpants and a T-shirt.

"Hi, sweetie," he said. He crossed the kitchen, wiping his hands on a towel, and kissed me.

"What are you doing up?"

"Making you crème brûlée."

"Now?"

"Sure, what's wrong with now?"

"It's Tuesday night, and it's practically midnight."

"Only the best for my wife. It'll be done in five minutes." He spooned a fluffy concoction into small white dishes. "So tell me about your mom. I want to hear everything."

"She's good. She's great actually."

"And how about you? I know you've missed her. Was it nice to see her?"

"Yeah, sure," I said. I felt weary from these questions, all of them designed to let us talk for hours, when for the last few years we'd barely spoken for minutes at a time.

Chris switched on a mini blowtorch and went at the top of the desserts, turning them a golden brown. "Chris," I said, over the loud, humming noise of the torch. "Thank you. This so sweet, but I can't eat crème brûlée now."

"What's that?" He kept at his work.

"Honey, I just had pasta with my mom. I really can't eat anything else."

"Voilà!" Chris said in a goofy way. He handed me a dish of crème brûlée piled high with red raspberries.

"Did you hear me?" I pined for my fantasy of the cool,

silent apartment and me alone in it. It seemed I rarely had a second to myself anymore.

"What?" He picked up a dish for himself and dug into it with a spoon. "Mmm, it's perfect. You'll love it."

"Chris, thank you. I appreciate it, but I simply can't eat it. I'm full, and I want to go to bed."

"Well, in that case," he said, raising an eyebrow. "I'll take you there."

"No, Chris, not tonight." I couldn't believe the words coming from my mouth, but we'd had so much sex over the last week that I really wanted a quiet evening.

"C'mon, have a few bites." He handed me a spoon. "I made it for you," he said with his mouth half full.

"I know, baby. I really do appreciate it, but I just can't."

"Sure you can."

"No, I can't!" My voice shot up a few decibels, surprising both of us.

Chris stared at me with the look of a forlorn child.

"I'm sorry," I said.

"I just want to make you happy," he said softly.

"You do."

Chris shook his head.

"You *do*," I repeated.

God, what was happening here? I'd longed for some attention from my husband, but I'd gotten constant passion and attentiveness. It was too much. A real marriage had to exist somewhere in the middle, didn't it? But how could I explain this now to Chris, whose eyes were filled with pain?

I reached out and squeezed his hand, then I lifted the spoon and broke the hard shell of brûlée.

chapter nine

Around noon on Wednesday, I called Alexa from my cell phone. I stood outside my office building on Michigan Avenue, surrounded by bored smokers and workers hustling to run errands during lunch.

"*Hola,*" a woman's voice answered.

"Is Alexa there?" I squeezed the phone tight. I half hoped she wasn't around, since I had no idea what to say or even why I was calling, except that I couldn't shake my guilt.

"*Un momento.*"

Some scuffling sounds, some Spanish being spoken, and then the phone being picked up. "Alexa Villa."

I squeezed the phone tighter. The optimistic, professional tone of Alexa's voice made me feel worse. She'd obviously been hoping this was a work call, maybe someone responding to one of her résumés. She pronounced her last name like "vee-ya," I noticed; while at Harper Frankwell, everyone had said "villa" like a villa in France.

"Alexa, it's Billy."

Silence.

"Look, I'm sorry to bother you, it's just…" *It's just what?*

"What do you want, Billy?" Her voice had lost the cheery professionalism.

"Could we meet? Maybe for coffee?"

"Why?"

"I don't know. Because I want to apologize, I guess."

"You already did that."

"Please."

More silence. Finally, she spoke again. "I can meet you in forty-five minutes."

"Oh." I was surprised she'd accepted, surprised she'd suggested today.

She snorted. "Don't worry about it. You have to *work*, right?"

"No, it's okay. That's great. Where?"

"Do you know the Bongo Room?"

"Yeah, but—" I was about to point out that the Bongo Room was all the way over on Milwaukee Avenue. I might as well forget work for the afternoon. But then I remembered the legions of people living in Alexa's apartment, counting on her. "That's fine."

Forty-five minutes later, I was seated in a booth in the restaurant, a funky place with walls painted purple, orange and green. Alexa arrived, wearing dark jeans, a crisp white blouse and a silver necklace with a pendant shaped like a leaf. Her dark hair tumbled around her shoulders. She looked human, pretty. So different from her office look.

"Hey," she said, slipping into the seat across from me. Her tone was light, but her expression was hard.

"Hi."

Now what to do? I looked at the menu.

"Have you eaten here?" she asked.

I shook my head. "Always wanted to."

"The French toast is delicious."

The waitress stepped up to our table, and I ordered the French toast, even though I preferred pancakes, and a cup of decaf coffee.

"I'll have the same," Alexa said, "but make mine regular."

When the waitress was gone, we stared at each other. "I wanted to apologize," I said.

She shook her head. "You did that when you came to my house."

"Just hear me out." I sipped my water, wishing the coffee would come, something else I could do with my hands. "I do believe you had some—" how to put this lightly? "—*things* you needed to work on in the office."

Her expression was blank.

"And you and I never got on very well," I continued. "However, I shouldn't have fired you. I admit that. And I wanted to say I'm sorry. I tried to get you your job back, but—"

"The company has a policy that it doesn't rehire people terminated for cause." She said this swiftly and without expression.

"That's right." Which made me feel even worse. The girl could quote company policy chapter and verse. "So, I guess I don't know what else to do, except to once again say I'm sorry."

She blinked a few times, then her eyes shot to the table. "Well, I'll admit, I didn't make it easy for you. I can be such a bitch, especially when I'm envious of someone."

"Why would you be envious?"

She shrugged. "You seem so smart and together, and I knew you had a shot at being a VP, even though I tried to piss you off and make you think you didn't."

"Wow. I didn't know that."

The coffee came then. I eagerly pulled the cup to me and began doctoring it with drops of cream poured with scientific precision, and a packet of Equal, which I took elaborate pains to shake and snap before pouring every bit into my mug. Alexa sipped hers black.

"I have a favor to ask," she said.

"What's that?"

"Help me get another job."

Alexa reached into her bag and pulled out a file. Inside, she had lists and graphs and charts, all apparently cross-referencing the PR firms in town, along with their clients and staffing needs. "I've done some research."

"I see that."

We talked for the next hour, picking apart the French toast, which was, incidentally, topped with an utterly sinful dollop of butter mixed with crushed Heath bars. We discussed the other firms in the city, gossiped about the people Alexa might contact and what we'd heard about them. This was the first time I'd had a real conversation with the girl, and I found that she was smart and strangely funny in a deadpan way.

"I've considered suicide," she said at one point, causing me to cough up a chunk of Heath bar butter. "But," she continued without glancing at me, "I've decided that the only way I'd want to go is death by overdose of Mint Milanos, and have you ever noticed how expensive those cookies are?"

My coughing turned to laughter. But I felt worse and worse, because as we brought the conversation back to other PR firms, I realized that I'd looked into all those firms myself.

"I have to tell you," I said at last, "I don't know how many firms are hiring."

Alexa pushed her plate away. "I know. But I have to try."

"Of course."

"You know what I'd really like to do?" Her face brightened a little. "Open my own firm. One that caters to Hispanic businesses. There isn't anyone like that in Chicago."

"That would be amazing!"

She shook her head. "But that takes money. And I don't have it."

My guilt seeped further into my bones. "Maybe someday?" I said weakly.

She sat up taller. Her earlier hardened expression had returned. "Look, thanks for talking. If you hear anything or talk to anyone…"

"I'll let you know," I finished for her.

She took out her wallet and withdrew a twenty.

"I got it," I said.

"No." All traces of the friendliness I'd seen during our talk vanished. "I don't take handouts."

"Okay." I fumbled around for my own wallet.

She dropped the twenty on the table. "See you," she said. She turned and left.

I hailed a cab and gave the office address, filled once again with guilt about Alexa, but also feeling a low-grade anxiety that seemed to permeate everything these days. I called Tess, but she was on her way to a Mommy & Me yoga class and couldn't talk. I tried my own mom, but I got the *Ta-ta!* message again. I'd talked with her this morning, but our chat had been overwhelmed by her social calendar—tennis with friends in Barrington, shopping with her sisters, dinners with neighbors. I called Chris at work. He was in a deposition, I was told by his secretary, but she was to interrupt if I called.

"Oh, no, don't do that," I said, but it was too late.

A minute later, Chris was on the phone. "Hi there," he said, "I'm so glad to hear your voice."

"You, too, but you didn't have to come out of your dep."

"Shit, we've been in there for four hours already. We needed a break. How's your day going?"

"Well, I just had lunch with Alexa."

"How in hell did that happen?"

I paid the cabbie and slid onto the street. "I called her."

"Why?"

"I don't know. I'm still feeling guilty."

"Billy, you've got to get over that. You had every right to fire her."

I felt a rush of gratitude for Chris's blind support of everything Billy, but I knew he wasn't correct on this one. And somewhere deep inside, I felt irked at that support. I wondered if I confessed to a fake murder if he would support me so blindly. I had a sneaking suspicion he would.

"I had the right to fire her, given my new position," I said, "but I still shouldn't have done it. I got drunk with power. It wasn't the proper decision."

"Of course it was."

I sighed.

"Well, let me make you dinner," Chris said. "That will make you feel better. And then I'll give you a bubble bath, and we'll talk it all through."

I smiled a sad smile as I stood on Michigan Avenue in front of my office building. How I loved my husband. But I wanted Chris to be honest with me, the way Tess was. I wanted him to smack me upside the head (metaphorically, of course) when I fucked up. Instead, he seemed to talk and talk and talk without ever acknowledging that I made a misstep somewhere. It was as if someone had slipped Chris a pill that made him unconditionally supportive—something

I'd always wanted *in theory*. In reality, I wanted less intensity and more authenticity.

"I might have to do something for work," I answered. After taking two hours out of my day to eat at the Bongo Room, I definitely had work awaiting.

"You're sure? I'm supposed to be here late on this merger, but I can get out early for you."

"No, no. You do your thing. I'll see you later."

At seven-thirty, I roamed the halls of Harper Frankwell in search of coffee and found Evan in the kitchen, pouring his own.

He smiled when he saw me. He held up the pot.

I nodded. It was blissfully quiet in the office right then, with only the hum of nearby computers.

Evan poured coffee into a mug and handed it to me. Our fingers touched briefly. My belly clenched. We stood silently in the kitchen, drinking our coffee. Neither of us had spoken, and it was so nice to simply coexist at that moment, free of the constant talking and analyzing that had characterized my relationship with Chris lately. Of course, the talking and analysis and sex had been exactly what I wanted, but getting it overnight and without explanation had the effect of shopping for your own birthday present.

At last, Evan spoke. "This coffee sucks. I need a beer."

"Heading to Wrightwood Tap?"

"Nah. I've got a party. Want to come?" He dumped his coffee in the sink.

"A party on a Wednesday night?"

"It's somebody's birthday. And this is an interesting crew. They don't care if it's Sunday morning."

"Where is it?"

"Old Town. Wells Street."

Close to my condo. "I don't know. I should probably keep working." The prospect made me want to cry with boredom.

Evan took a step closer. "Come with me."

Tess's warning flew through my head. *Be real careful.* But I could handle myself at a party. There would be other people around, and I could escape and walk home whenever I wanted.

"I'll get my purse," I said.

The apartment on Wells Street was filled with about twenty people, most of them dressed in black, most of them young and impossibly hip, the type of people who slept until three in the afternoon and hit the clubs after a very late, very light dinner. A number of people had martinis in hand. There was the unmistakable scent of pot in the air.

"Billy, this is my friend, Carly." Evan introduced me to a small woman wearing a black, spaghetti-strap dress. She had straight blond hair, parted in the middle to show the smooth skin of her face and light blue eyes ringed with dark liner.

We shook hands. "How do you two know each other?" I asked.

"Evan and I used to fuck," Carly said.

"Oh." I felt a little zing of shock and then envy toward this tiny blond thing. I couldn't help imagining the two of them together. They must have looked amazing, with their blond hair, their smooth skin close together. I flushed at the thought.

Evan and Carly cracked up at my reaction.

"Sorry to be crude," Carly said, "but let me explain. When we were together, Evan kept asking me if I'd ever been with a woman."

I glanced at Evan, who shrugged. "Two women together— that's hot," he said. "I just wanted to hear about it."

"But it backfired on him," Carly said. "He got me to thinking, and then the thinking got me to doing."

"And the rest is history," said a tall woman, entering our circle. She laid a soft arm around Carly's shoulders. She had black ringletted hair and a voluptuous body.

Carly, Evan and the woman laughed.

"So you, two?" I pointed a finger between Carly and the woman.

"Yep," the woman said. "It's been four years." She leaned down and kissed Carly on the forehead.

"Wow, that's great." I said. My spirits buoyed with the thought that Carly was off the market.

"One of these two should have introduced me," the tall woman said. "I'm Sharon." We shook hands. "And it looks like you need a drink."

"Please," I said.

Soon, Evan and I were in the kitchen holding mandarin martinis. The drink went down my throat in a smooth, tangy rush. The rest of the guests seemed light years ahead of us in terms of intoxication, and I sipped my drink quickly in an effort to catch up. A funky song with a strong bass and violins in the background surged from the overhead speakers. In the room next to the kitchen, people were dancing.

"These things are too sweet," Evan said, staring at his martini with disdain. "I need a beer."

"I'll keep yours as backup." I took the martini from his hand.

Evan grinned.

"What?"

"Nothing." He reached around me to the sink, which was full of ice and beer. His shoulder brushed mine. I set Evan's drink down and took another sip of my martini.

When he'd grabbed his beer, he was still smiling.

"What are you grinning at?" I asked.

"You."

"Explain, please."

"You were jealous when Carly said we used to sleep together."

"She said you used to fuck."

"Yes, we did. And that made you a little crazy, didn't it?"

"Don't kid yourself."

Someone opened the refrigerator door behind Evan, jostling him toward me. He put his face close to mine, his mouth near my ear. "You imagined it, didn't you?"

I froze. I could barely breathe, much less respond.

"You thought of Carly and me together, and it made you hot."

A coarse breath broke into my chest, causing it to rise and fall rapidly. I couldn't have hid my reaction from Evan if I'd tried.

"And then," he said, moving even closer. "And then you imagined *us,* didn't you?"

The scent of marijuana became stronger in the air. I wondered if there was any truth to the secondhand smoke business because I felt almost stoned. The temperature in the kitchen seemed to have shot up ten degrees. I could feel the heat of Evan's body. I could hear my own sharp intakes of breath. But I still couldn't talk. Instead, I gulped the martini, imagining the cool liquid cleansing my insides. At the same time, I couldn't stop imagining Evan and myself, our mouths together, our bodies entangled.

I coughed to scare away the image, and reached around Evan for the backup martini. When I looked up at him, his eyes were locked on my face, his lips slightly parted. "You've thought about it, haven't you?" he asked.

I nodded.

"You know just what it would be like, don't you?"

Another nod.

Someone cranked up the music. Everyone in the kitchen turned to look into the adjacent room, where Carly and Sharon were now dancing, the others standing back to watch. The two women wound around each other with their moves, almost stalking. These were people who clearly knew each other's bodies well. Every so often, one of them reached out to stroke the other's arm or hair. Evan moved closer to me so that we were side by side, his arm around my back. I felt the pulse in my back, right where his hand was; I felt it in my head, in my stomach. Everyone in the room was riveted to the two women.

Carly and Sharon moved closer to each other, until their bodies pressed together, still moving. Carly's cheek rested momentarily on Sharon's breast. Sharon threw her head back, hips swaying, and touched Carly's head. Carly's hands went to Sharon's undulating hips. The two of them moved like one body. And then Sharon was looking down, Carly up, and still swaying, the two of them began to kiss—open mouths, pink tongues.

My own mouth was a little open now, my body hot.

I felt Evan's hand on my elbow. "Come with me," he said, his voice low and rough.

I let him lead me out of the kitchen. We skirted the living room, where Carly and Sharon were still embracing. We walked down a hallway. I didn't ask him where we were going. I didn't want to know. I didn't want to talk. Evan opened the door at the end of the hallway. It was a small bedroom with a tiny lamp next to a double bed.

"Is this their bedroom?" I said, glancing at the pile of coats on the bed.

Evan shook his head. "Guest room."

He crossed the room and switched off the lamp light. The room went black.

"Ev?" I said. I reached out, and he was there, his arms wrapping around me, his mouth coming down hard on mine. We kissed, fast and greedy, as if this had been waiting for us forever. He pushed me against the wall and pressed his body against mine. I grabbed his hair as we kissed, pulling it, embracing him tight. His hands were all over my body, touching me through my clothes. I did the same, grabbing—*finally*—that hard chest through the soft cloth of his shirt, pushing my pelvis into his thighs. And in my head, I was imagining what it would be like to shed the clothes from my body and to have him push hard inside me.

"Oh, yeah," Evan grunted. "Yeah."

His words made me hotter. I bit his neck. He groaned, and I was grateful for the music banging outside.

His hands felt for the hem of my sweater, and I thought, *here we go.*

He pulled the sweater up, his fingers on my bra. I felt a hard tug as he pulled that up as well, so that my sweater and bra were in a ring around my neck. His hands were on my breasts now, Evan's warm, large hands.

I froze. Those hands were foreign. They weren't Chris's long, smooth fingers. No one else had touched my bare skin in so long that I couldn't ignore how shocking the sensation was. Why I hadn't noticed the difference between Evan and Chris during our kiss, I couldn't say, but now it was palpable.

"Evan," I said, pushing him away slightly.

His hands dropped, roaming my hips, but I couldn't shake the sense of surprise, of something wrong.

"Stop," I said. "Please."

The air felt cool as he stepped back. "What is it?"

"I can't."

"What's wrong?"

I laughed, a desperate shaking laugh. "I'm married!" My voice sounded hysterical. Near tears. "And I love my husband. I really do."

Somehow kissing Evan, and the dismay I suddenly felt at my betrayal, had made Chris and me seem as clear as new glass, where the image had been foggy before. Somewhere in our history, as well as in the recent weeks, I'd had passion with Chris, I'd had affection, I'd had caring. I'd had the whole deal. It wasn't lost, as I'd feared over the last few years. The intimacy just needed to be worked at and maintained and balanced. We needed to put together the passion and conversation of recent times, with the independence of old. We still had the pieces and the very real love for each other. This thing with Evan, on the other hand, was just a shard of something, a splinter of sexual longing.

"Okay," Evan said. "Hold on."

I heard him moving through the room, swearing as he bumped into something. Then the small lamp went on. Evan was sitting on the edge of the bed, panting. His shirt was askew, his hair standing at odd angles.

"I'm sorry," I said. I tugged my sweater and bra into place and crossed my arms. I leaned against the closed door.

He shook his head, straightened his shirt. "No, it was my fault."

"It was both of us."

"Right." He looked at me, a questioning look that said, *What do we do now?*

"I've got to go." I opened the door, and left Evan sitting on the bed.

★ ★ ★

"Where have you been?" I heard Chris call from the living room as I opened the door.

It was only nine o'clock when I got home, but I felt as if it were the middle of the night. The martinis, the fevered kissing and the shame had made me exhausted.

I leaned my head against the doorjamb. "A party," I said softly.

I stepped inside and closed the door. Chris sat on the big chair, smiling, as if I were the only person he'd want to see at that moment. I fought not to cry.

"A party on a Wednesday?" he said.

"I know. Weird, huh?" But it was me who sounded weird, my voice small, hollow, as if it came from a tin can.

"Let me guess. Evan's friends?"

At the word "Evan," the remorse flattened me. I could barely stand.

"You all right, Treetop?" Chris came to me, his arms encircling my body.

But I couldn't stand his touch, not when Evan's arms had been there only fifteen minutes before. "Fine, fine." I pulled away.

"Did you eat dinner?"

"No."

"Great, I'll make you some pasta with truffle oil. It's a new recipe I'm trying out."

"Chris, don't." I couldn't bear the thought of his kindness. "I'm going to take a shower."

"Well, I'll join you." He ruffled my hair, leaning his tall body down to kiss my neck.

I pulled away again. "I…I can't."

"You can't what?" Chris's face was confused.

I can't live with myself.

But instead, I said, "I'm just so tired."

"Okay, sweetie, I'll start the water for you."

"No, don't." The thought of him doing anything was too painful, making the shame unbearable.

Chris's face fell at my harsh words.

I was fucking up everything, hurting everyone. My head swam with flashbacks of what had happened tonight with Evan. Not one cohesive thought could take hold. "I'm just going to go to bed," I said. I went into the bedroom. I stood for minutes, glaring at the frog until I finally turned off the light.

chapter ten

Infidelity is not a warm and fuzzy concept. It's not a word you'd find embroidered on a pillow or placed in a calico frame. And yet, infidelity has so strong a pull for so many people. I'd never considered myself part of that unfaithful population, or even on the outside looking in. In fact, the only real person that I knew who *might* have had an affair was my father.

He was gone from our house one day, just gone, like a bird that had flown south for the winter. My mother was grief-stricken. She cried. She stared out windows, as if waiting, praying, for his gold Cadillac Eldorado to pull down the drive. And yet at other times, she was matter-of-fact about it, even stoic. She sold our white house with the two-story columns, and she moved us across town to the apartment by the old hospital.

Often I traipsed down the back apartment stairs, which smelled like a strange, sweet smoke from the Indian couple who lived on the first floor, and went into the cement yard. An old picnic table, gray from the weather, was chained to the side of the building, and if I stood on it, I could see the cupola on our old house—a tiny, white-painted room made all of windows, peeking over the town.

One day, my sister Hadley came outside while I was there. She wore yellow pants and a white T-shirt with a dark smear near the shoulder. There was a scratch on her face, probably from getting in another fight at school. The fact that she and Dustin had these brawls with classmates made them seem like different beings. Not normal girls or sisters, certainly nothing like me. "What are you doing?" she said.

"Just looking."

In one fluid leap, Hadley was on the table next to me. We stared at the cupola in silence.

Finally, Hadley said, "He's probably got a girlfriend."

"Who has?"

She scoffed. "Dad. That's why men leave. To get other girls."

"Oh." This was new information. My mother had always said that he had business to take care of, that he would be back eventually. I'd stopped believing that he would return, but for some reason I'd never questioned the statement that he'd left because of business.

I never learned what the real story was, which only made my anxiety, disappointment and obsession about my father grow. Infidelity was always a possibility, though, one I abhorred on behalf of my mother and her tearstained face.

Now, I was busy hating myself, too, for what I'd nearly done the other night with Evan. What I'd wanted very much to do.

To tell or not to tell? *That* is the goddamned question.

Confessing to Chris was the right thing to do, wasn't it? Certainly hardcore honesty was the way to go. Or was I only trying to assuage my guilt by considering such a thing? Wasn't I hoping Chris would absolve me from the shame? And if so, wouldn't I be a better person to simply live with that shame instead of hurting Chris when really nothing had happened? But something *had* happened, even if it wasn't full-on sex. Which brought me around to square one.

I called Tess, and we met at a coffee shop on Clark Street. We took our foaming lattes outside to a black metal table. She was beaming now about her pregnancy—it had settled around her.

"Maybe someday you and Chris will join us in Baby Land," she said, smiling serenely, patting her belly.

"Maybe." I knew in that moment I couldn't tell her. Her husband, Tim, worked with Chris. She and Tim had introduced us. If they knew, it could affect all of our friendships. I drank my latte and kept quiet.

When I left Tess, I tried my mom. But when we met at Milrose again—me brimming with my secret, with my need for some seasoned, even harsh, maternal advice—she had brought two women from her neighborhood.

"Ellen and Mary," she said, "this is my daughter Billy."

I smiled. I shook hands. I shelved the thought that my mother and I would ever again have a heart-to-heart.

The next day I called Dustin in San Francisco. I wasn't sure if I could confide in her, since we so rarely did that kind of thing, but I was willing to try. The scene with Evan was eating at my insides, clawing its way to the surface.

"Hi, Billy!" Dustin said, sounding pleased to hear from me. I'd caught her at home for once.

"How's Robert?" I said, asking after her husband.

"He's on a golf trip." She laughed wryly. "Remember how dad used to golf all the time?"

I blinked at the mention of our father. "No." I had no recollection of my father ever holding a putter or even talking about golf. And that realization made me sad. He was gone from me in so many ways. Physically, of course, for over twenty years, but since that morning I woke up with the frog on my nightstand and with everything changed, he'd been gone from my heart, too. I really didn't miss him anymore. I didn't wonder why he'd left. But somehow I *missed* the missing of him. I was starting to realize that my old obsessing, my never-getting-over-him had been the way I held on to him. He was really and truly gone now.

"Oh, well," Dustin said, onto a different topic. "What's going on with you? I hear you're a big VP now."

"Yes, it's true. I got promoted."

"My little sister! A vice president! I'm so proud."

"Thanks, Dustin." But the congratulations was bittersweet; hearing the words now reminded me that she hadn't even called or e-mailed to congratulate me on my promotion when it first happened. Not that I needed her approval, but the lack of it reminded me how distant we were. So I knew I couldn't tell her about Evan. After a few minutes of mindless conversation, we were off the phone.

Which brought me back to my dad. He might have been the one family member I could have talked to about this. If what Hadley had told me all those years ago was true, he might have understood. Father and daughter, united in guilt.

"What's it been like?" Alexa said.

"What do you mean?"

"Being vice president. What's it like?"

We were sitting outside near State and Rush having lunch on a sunny, Friday afternoon. Alexa had called me this time, and after a long, painful week (both emotionally and professionally) I'd quickly cleared my schedule of budgets and board meetings and assistant hand-holding to meet her. I hadn't been sure *why* she wanted to meet, a mystery that became even more curious as we ate and chatted. Just chatted. About her brothers and sisters and the silly things they did, about where we went to college and how we got into PR. It was a pleasant experience—especially given the bright, seventy-degree day, the crowds strolling the street and my desperate need for a girlfriend. This afternoon was small relief from my agitated mind. But at the same time, I kept waiting for the Mexican curses to fall, for a quick turn of Alexa's suddenly engaging personality.

But now this question about my new position. This was why she'd called, I supposed, and although Alexa was the last person I wanted to have this discussion with, I thought I owed it to her.

"It's all right," I answered.

"Just all right?" She shook her hair away from her face, and I noticed two guys at the next table staring openly. When she wasn't putting on her tough-PR-girl image, she was gorgeous.

"The role is not exactly what I thought it would be."

"What did you think it would be?" Alexa leaned forward.

I shifted around in my chair. I didn't want to sound ungrateful about the vice presidency, but I really did want to talk to someone, especially someone in the PR world.

"Being a VP is a bit dull," I said.

Her eyes narrowed to slits. "You're just saying that to make me feel better."

"No, I'm not. I thought it would be more exciting and glamorous, but I miss my old job a hell of a lot."

"Why?"

"I miss the creativity. My new job is all administrative, all the time. It's looking at the P&L sheets and going to officers' meetings and arguing about the damn pop machine and making personnel decisions."

I stopped short, realizing I was sitting on State Street with one of those personnel decisions.

But Alexa blew right by it. "That's what's exciting about it!" she said. And indeed, she looked excited just by the topic. "You're getting to focus the direction of the firm. You're making real decisions about which of the firm's resources to put where. That's power." I dropped my head a little. Here in front of me was someone clearly cut out to be a VP at Harper Frankwell, someone who would have relished it as much as she succeeded in it.

"I suppose you're right," I said in a weak voice.

"It's absolutely true. That power is something to be respected. Most of the people I grew up with will never know that kind of power."

Her talk embarrassed me. My new power had led me like a stumbling drunk bent on breaking something. What I'd broken was Alexa's career. "Any luck with the job search?"

She shook her head.

"I'm sorry."

"You've got to stop saying that. Someday I might thank you for firing me."

"God, I'd really like that." We both chuckled. "But why do you say that?"

She shrugged. "Not working every day is making me think. And what I think is that I really want to open my own PR firm like I mentioned before, one that will work primarily with Hispanic people and businesses."

"That's wonderful."

"Well…" She shook her head discouragingly. "It's great that I know what I want to do, but I really don't know where to start."

We sat quietly for a moment. The guys at the next table left, smiling at us. Alexa didn't even notice. The crowds on State were getting larger as the afternoon grew longer and the sun heavier and more golden.

"So, are you dating someone?" I'm not sure why I asked her that question. I wanted to get off the topic of being a VP, and I guess I was hoping she did have a boyfriend, someone to cushion life's blows.

"No."

"Oh."

"You're married, right Billy?"

"I am."

"And do you love him?"

Jesus, what a question. "I do. I love him very much." I looked at my hands in my lap. I let the guilt swim through me. "We've had our problems. He was very distant for a long time, and I sort of let it stay that way." I noticed, in the back of my brain, that I was talking about very intimate things with Alexa, of all people. "And then we had the opposite problem. We got too close. He was around all the time, and I couldn't seem to get enough space from him. And I made some mistakes."

"Sounds tricky."

"It is."

Alexa smiled a little. "You know who I always had a thing for?"

"Who?"

"Evan O'Reilly."

At his name, my body tingled, then the acid churned in my stomach. Still, I could feel his hands on my face, the back of my neck, my breasts.

"Really?" I said, trying for nonchalance. I couldn't imagine the two of them together. Evan went for thin, waspy girls much younger than him, and Alexa…well, Evan just didn't seem her type. But then I suppose a hot blond guy is most women's type.

"I think he's very smart," Alexa said. "I like the way he thinks about things. Like when he's in those pitch meetings?"

"You mean when he's always calling Roslyn 'Roz'?"

"Oh, I do hate that," Alexa said, laughing. "But no, I like how he listens to people. He sits back and watches the conversation and takes it all in. When he opens his mouth, you respect what he says because it's thoughtful. Have you ever noticed that?"

"I suppose." I was usually too busy noticing Evan's pecs beneath his French blue shirts.

"And he's nice to everyone," Alexa continued. "In a genuine way, I mean." She looked embarrassed. "I don't know what I'm going on about."

I sure did.

When I got home that night, I skipped my usual protocol. I didn't check the phone messages or the mail. I didn't flip through the TV channels. Instead, I went straight to my bedroom. I glared at the frog, then I stripped off my clothes, leaving them in a pile by my side of the bed, and I slipped under the covers.

It was only 6:00, and the sleep I craved didn't come. I was depressed enough to want to snooze the next four months away, but my body wouldn't allow it. I lay in our bedroom, light seeping boldly through the blinds. I thought of all those people heading out for a spring Friday evening—maybe off to Wrigley Field for a night game, maybe dinner outside at Jack's Bar on Southport—and yet here I was, in bed. Alone. This was how I wanted it, but I wanted to be unconscious. Unable to feel the questions, the shame, the wonder of whether I could ever truly be happy when I wasn't happy now, even after I'd gotten everything I'd thought I wanted.

I threw off the covers and sat up. Chris was still at work. Probably would be for a long while, since I'd told him I was working late in order to avoid seeing him. I'd been doing this for the last few days. I couldn't bear his sweet face, his unconditional love.

If I could just tell someone about Evan. Hell, about *all* of it—getting what I wanted overnight, how none of it had been like I'd imagined—maybe I could set it right. But I'd exhausted my list of potential advisors, both friends and family. I needed someone who could be objective, who could listen and tell me honestly what in the hell to do.

Blinda. That was the person who came to me then, because this need for an objective viewer of my life was what had brought me to her in the first place. And hadn't she started all this with her mantra of *look inside, Billy,* and her gift of the frog?

I glanced at the frog on my nightstand as I dialed her number. Surely she was back from Africa by now. The phone rang five times—a hollow, distant sound—then a click. She *was* there! But then the whir of an answering machine and Blinda's musical voice, "I'm out of the office for a while, but please leave me a message. Peace."

I felt an irrational desire to say, *Yeah, peace to your mother,* and hang up, but I composed myself and asked her to call me as soon as she got in.

Days went by without word from her. I avoided Chris. I said I had to work, then sat in my empty office over the weekend, listening to the steady whir of the air-conditioning, finally throwing myself wholeheartedly into work, hoping it would chase away everything else. But my mind kept coming back to Blinda and the conversation we'd had when she said she was leaving for Africa. All I could recall was that she would be out of town *for a while*. What did that mean, exactly? Weeks, months, years?

Frustrated, I dug up the few names of other therapists who'd been recommended when I started entertaining the idea of therapy. One was on East Ohio Street, not too far from the office. On Monday, I called the number, spoke to a receptionist and made an appointment for five o'clock that same day. I hung up and felt myself breathe fully with relief. I simply needed to talk to a professional. That was all. Soon I would have this whole mess figured out.

Her name was Dr. Hyacinth Montgomery, "but everyone calls me Dr. Hy," she said with a smooth smile. She looked like a presidential candidate—a perfect figure in an impeccable black suit, subtle makeup and a stylish brunette bob.

Her office was wood paneled and lined with books like an English library. A vase of white tea roses sat on the coffee table next to the patient couch. The effect was elegant, but I missed the cracked Asian pot and the wooly red and orange sofa in Blinda's place.

"Please, sit," she said. "Now tell me what brings you here."

I explained that I already had a therapist, someone I'd been seeing for a few months, but that she was out of town and I needed to talk to someone.

"Fine," she said. "That's just fine. What seems to be on your mind?"

"Well, uh…" The words dried up in my mouth. How to explain this? Best to just get it out, I decided. "I was seeing my therapist because I was unhappy with some aspects of my life."

"Mmm, good," Dr. Hy said.

"So, there were these aspects I wanted to be different," I continued. "They really weren't anything earth-shattering. I wanted my husband to pay more attention to me, I wanted to be promoted at work, I wanted my mother to stop living her life through mine, I wanted to get over my father, who took off when I was young, and I had this somewhat irrational hope that this guy at work would have a crush on me."

Dr. Hy laughed, a soft tinkle of a laugh. "I think those are all valid wishes."

Confident now, I charged on. "I told my therapist all of this, and she asked me if I'd done enough to make these thing happen. Then she told me to look inside for my happiness."

Dr. Hy nodded, a small smile of agreement.

"But she also gave me this frog," I said. "I should have brought it to show you, but the point is, she gave me this frog and told me that in the Chinese culture the frog was believed to bring good fortune. I didn't think much of it, and I put the frog on my nightstand. When I woke up the next morning, everything had changed." I held my breath, waiting for her reaction.

There was a crease between Dr. Hy's eyebrows now. "How do you mean?"

Too late to turn back, I thought. I'm paying her. I might as well blurt it out. "I got everything I wanted overnight," I said. "I know this sounds crazy, but it's absolutely true. The very next day, my husband was great, the guy at work had a crush on me, my mom was in Milan, my dad was just gone from my head and I was a vice president."

The crease deepened. "Overnight, this happened? Do you mean 'overnight' as a figure of speech?"

"No, no," I said. "Literally, the day after I saw her, after I got this frog, my whole life changed."

"Maybe it just felt like that."

"No, it did. I know how odd this sounds, but please, trust me."

Dr. Hy leaned forward. "Just to make sure I understand you, you're saying that your therapist gave you a frog, an icon of some sort, and the next day your life was very different. You'd gotten everything you wished for."

"Exactly."

"Were you on any medications at the time?"

"No."

"Do you use drugs or alcohol extensively?"

"Well, I've been known to have one too many glasses of wine on occasion, but no."

"And Billy, do you really believe that your life was entirely different in one day?"

"It absolutely was. I woke up that morning with the frog on my nightstand, and it had all changed, just like that." I snapped my fingers for effect. "Please. Can you help me straighten this out? I'm not sure where else to turn."

"Are you taking any medications now?"

"Just vitamins and stuff. Why?"

"Have you ever been prescribed antipsychotic drugs?"

"What? No! I mean, I guess I can't blame you for asking, but I am not psychotic."

"Of course not, and I wasn't suggesting that. It's simply that on these drugs many people feel more…" She paused, as if looking for a word in her mind. "Stable."

"I'm perfectly stable." I paused. "Well, I'm pretty stable anyway. I just don't want my life to be like this anymore. I want to have some say in it. I *thought* I wanted to get everything overnight—I mean who doesn't?—but it hasn't been as great as I'd hoped. And I feel like everything is preordained somehow. Like I didn't have a hand in it. I think it

has something to do with the frog or Blinda, but I can't figure it out."

"And where is this Belinda now?"

"It's Blinda, not Be-linda." I wasn't sure why this mattered,
but I felt the distinction needed to be made.

"Okay, sure. And where is *Blinda* now?" The way she
drew out Blinda's name made it sound as if she thought I
had an imaginary therapist, the way children have imaginary
friends.

"Africa. She used to be in the Peace Corps."

"How long has she been in Africa?"

"It seems like a long time, but it's really been a few weeks."

"I see." She smoothed her already sleek bob with her
hand. "Billy, I should also mention something—and this is
just for you to tuck away in case you need it later—but there
are a number of top-of-the-line inpatient facilities in the city
for people who just need a break from everyday stress."

"Inpatient?" I began coughing. "You want to hospital-
ize me?"

"I'm just naming some options."

I stood from the couch. "Thank you for your time, but a
better option is for me to just get out of here."

chapter eleven

The next day, I sat at my desk stewing, the door closed. How could Blinda give me the frog and then take off? It was like giving someone a ballistic missile without the owner's manual.

I clicked on the Internet and spent an entirely useless fifty minutes searching Google for *jade green frog* and *wish fulfillment* and *Chinese prophecy*. I got a whole lot of nada.

Lizbeth buzzed me. "Evan is looking for you."

I drew in a fast breath. Evan had been looking for me for nearly a week now, and I'd managed to avoid him by getting in early, leaving late and keeping my door closed. Yet I could feel him; I remembered those kisses. The memories made me hate myself.

"Tell him I'll call him," I said.

I hit the off button and sat back in my butter-yellow chair. (At least I loved my chair.) How odd that I should be putting off the great Evan, the Everlasting Crush. Yet the thought brought me no triumph, only a reverie that led me back to Blinda and the frog.

Suddenly, I struck on a thought. I sat up in my chair, my feet pushed to the ground, as if I might leap and run.

If indeed the damned frog had given me what I wished for—and it certainly seemed that way—then couldn't I just get rid of the frog and get rid of everything that had happened? I'm not sure where I got this idea, but it seemed intuitively correct—lose the frog and lose the wish fulfillment, too. Then I could start over, wherever that start-over point was, and make it all okay.

I needed to go back to that place where I didn't get what I wanted simply because I'd wished it to a therapist and a frog. I needed free will in my life again. I needed everyone else to have free will, too. I didn't want Chris to love me (or Evan to lust after me) only because I'd wished it so. I didn't want the promotion because I'd pined for it; I wanted to deserve it. And my mom? Well, I did like my mother having her own life, but again, wasn't that simply because I'd hoped it into existence, the way I'd hoped for the dispelling of my father from my mind? The frog had brought what I'd wanted, at least as I'd thought I'd wanted it, but without the ability of others to choose for themselves.

And of course, the things I'd wanted weren't faultless. They each brought their own problems that were, in many ways, much trickier than the problems I'd had before. If I could just rewind and do it all the old-fashioned way—take action, make choices, let everyone else do the same—I would look more closely to see what I *really* wanted. And I'd handle achievement better when it came my way.

The conclusion was clear. I stood now, fighting back the urge to raise a determined fist in the empty confines of my office.

I had to destroy the frog. I had to kill it. Period.

★ ★ ★

I went straight home and marched to my bedroom. I moved aside the alarm clock and the novels on my nightstand and stood staring at the frog as if it were a four-hundred-pound gorilla, rather than a scrap of faux jade.

"Time for you to go," I said out loud. I was inexplicably nervous.

I reached out hesitantly, as if it might bite me. I snatched the thing in one quick movement, closing my fist around it. I held it tight and carried it to the kitchen, where I dropped it in our kitchen garbage can. That hardly seemed final enough, so I fastened the bag with a twist-tie and took it outside.

The Dumpster behind the condo was large, gray and battered. I lifted the heavy metal top and dropped the bag inside. When I let the top go, it slammed closed like a prison door. A perfect resting place. I almost felt as if I should bow my head, maybe mumble a few words as if at a burial, but right then one of the other condo members, a man in his mid-sixties, came by with his own garbage bag.

"Hello!" he said jovially. "Nasty weather, huh?"

I glanced around. I had been so concerned with the frog that I'd hardly noticed the weather. Sure enough, the skies were foggy and ominous, the air a chilly fifty degrees. "Nasty, yeah," I said.

I went to turn away, but then the man raised his arm to lift the Dumpster lid. I felt an irrational fear as he did so. "Oh, don't…" I said, moving toward him.

The man froze, the top already a few inches up now. "What's that?" he said, looking at me strangely. He kept hoisting the lid, and I felt the breath catch in my lungs. What I was afraid of, I didn't know. Nothing happened. He threw his bag on top of the others and let the lid fall with a satisfying clang.

"I was just saying have a great day," I said.

"You, too."

I trotted back to my condo. I looked around trying to feel the shift that must be happening now that I'd gotten rid of the frog.

The next morning, I was awoken by a nudge. When I blinked my eyes open, Chris was standing over me with a tray. "I made you breakfast," he said. "And you're going in late today, because I have plans for us." He gave me a lascivious wink.

I coughed. "Oh, honey. That's so nice, but I can't be late, and I've told you I really, really don't like breakfast."

"Sure you do." He nudged me some more with his knee. "Scoot."

I moved over and sat up. I sensed something, as if someone were in the room with us.

With trepidation, I turned my head ever so slowly toward the nightstand. And my eyes came to rest on something little. Something green.

"Chris!" I said, scrambling into a kneeling position. "Did you take that out of the garbage?"

"Whoa!" Chris said, holding tight to the tray to stop the food from sliding. "Don't be rude. I made these eggs myself."

"Not the eggs," I huffed. "That!" I pointed at the nightstand.

"That frog has been there for weeks," Chris said.

"But I threw it away yesterday."

"Why?" His face creased in a confused frown.

"It doesn't matter why. Did you dig it out of the Dumpster?"

"No." He laughed.

"Well, then how did it get here?"

He shrugged. "Maybe you meant to throw it away, but you forgot."

"I did *not* forget. I threw it away after work. How did it get out?"

Chris laughed again. "My wife has gone crazy."

That day, I left my office early and hurried to the elevator with purpose. The doors opened, and there stood Evan. Instead of exiting, he waved an arm as if inviting me into a party. Another one.

"Aren't you getting out?" I said.

"Not now." He grinned.

"Well…" I stood there, unsure, not trusting myself. The doors began to slide shut. Evan stuck his arm out to stop them, then grabbed my hand and pulled me inside.

"How are you?" he said. Normal words, casual words, but his voice was low and deep, and his hand still held mine.

I pulled it away. "Fine, thank you. You?"

"What's with the formalities?"

I couldn't think of an answer.

"Are you leaving for the day?" he asked.

I nodded.

"I'll go with you."

"No, Ev. You can't. I can't."

Ignoring me, he moved closer. "We'll pick up from where we left off last week." He put one arm on the wall behind me. My mouth went dry. I licked my lips, which Evan seemed to interpret as a come-on. His eyes closed and his mouth parted. He leaned toward me.

"Goddamned frog!" I said.

His eyes shot open. "What?"

"Sorry. Nothing." I wriggled out from under his arm, just as the elevator reached the lobby. "Got to go." I darted through the lobby and onto Michigan Avenue before he could stop me.

When I reached my condo, I asked the cab driver to wait.

With the sense of purpose back in my step, I went straight to the bedroom and grabbed the frog. I was no longer scared of it; I was sick of it.

"Can you take me to North Avenue Beach?" I asked the cab driver.

"Whatever you want."

I jumped out when the cab pulled behind the beachside restaurant, and I walked to the wide sidewalk edging the lake. The weather was beautiful again, and joggers, bicyclists and in-line skaters jockeyed for space. A few eager souls were lying in bathing suits on the smooth sand. The lake was teal-blue and calm. I joined the crowds on the sidewalk and headed for the cement pier that would take me directly over the lake. I walked to the very end. A lone fisherman sat there, his chin tucked into his chest, dozing.

I slid my hand in my pocket and took out the frog. Without looking at it, I ran my hand over the little bumps on its back, the rounded haunches. I was slightly more mellow now that I was surrounded by Lake Michigan. The frog wasn't a bad thing, I thought, just something that needed to go. Its time with me was over.

I stared down at the lake, too deep to see the bottom. I turned and looked across the expanse of it. Indiana and Michigan were somewhere over there, but this lake was large enough to hide them. Was it big enough to hide a little frog and keep it hidden?

With one movement, I drew my shoulder back, imagining myself as a baseball pitcher, and with a whip of my arm, I launched the frog. It sailed about thirty feet, making a beautiful streak of green across the pale blue sky, before it landed with a smooth *plunk,* barely causing a ripple.

"You little fucker."

"Hmm?" Chris said, and rolled over.

I stood up from the bed and crossed my arms, looking at the nightstand. It was back. The damned thing was *back*. "How did you get out of the lake?"

"What?" Chris said.

I grabbed the frog, along with the cordless phone, and took them into the bathroom. I set the frog on the counter, facing it away, but the reflection of its eyes still stared at me from the mirror. I dialed Blinda's number. I knew it by heart from all the times I'd tried it. Again, that same damned message with that same musical voice of hers—*I'm out of the office for a while.*

"Goddamn it!" I yelled.

"You okay?" I heard Chris say from behind the door.

"Fine," I called back, but I then muttered again, "you little fucker."

I swiveled the frog around and studied it, as if it would give me the answer on how to properly execute it. Its slash of a mouth looked wider, its tiny face more pleased. I would have to try harder. I *would* kill this thing.

I took the frog to Lincoln Park Zoo. When no one was looking, I lobbed it into the corral with the elephants, smiling at the thought of those massive gray feet squashing the crap out of that little green amphibian.

The next morning, it was back on my nightstand.

I took it on the El platform, and threw it under the tracks before the train passed.

The next morning, it was back on my nightstand.

The day after my El trip, I left the office at lunch and went straight to the Art Institute, patting the lion at the top. I'd been to the Institute when the bizarreness started a few weeks ago, and although the ancient loveliness of the paintings and artifacts hadn't helped erase my worries then, it was worth trying again. A jittery dread had taken over my body, a feeling of moving on a predetermined highway from which there was no exit.

It was a Friday, so the museum was fairly crowded. Instead of heading for the busier rooms, I slipped in the Chinese/Japanese hall, which I usually overlooked. But today I felt pulled inside, as if something was waiting for me. And it was. At the back of the room, next to a thin jade vase was a tiny, wide-mouthed frog the size of a nickel, also made of jade. It looked precisely like *my* frog—there was the lily pad beneath the frog's rounded legs; his mouth was a long slash that ran under the eyes. I peered closer, my arms behind my back. Near the frog's case was a white printed card that read *Shang Dynasty 1700 B.C.—1050 B.C. Originally part of a pair, the frog-on-lily icons were initially said to have brought great fortune to the dynasty. After disaster befell many family members, it was believed the frogs had brought about ruin.*

I stepped back from the card as if shocked with a cattle prod. *Ruin,* I thought. A powerful word that seemed to signify volcanoes and locusts and mayhem. Was that what would become of me if I held on to the frog? Ruin? And was it possible that my frog was somehow the other side of the pair?

I swiveled around and marched through the halls until I found the administrative offices for the Institute.

"May I see the curator?" I said to the receptionist, a woman about my age.

"Do you have an appointment?"

"No, but it's important. I have something to donate."

"Are you from an organization?"

"No, I'm…a private collector." I liked it as soon as I said it. *A private collector.* It made me sound worldly and learned, like someone who'd just hopped off a private plane from a dig in Egypt. I was glad I was wearing a suit.

"Your name?"

"Billy Rendall."

"Will you wait a moment?" She gestured to two chairs upholstered in tan brocade.

"Certainly." I didn't usually say "certainly," but it seemed a word that a private collector would certainly use.

A few minutes later, the receptionist was back with a small, balding man, wearing round copper glasses and an ill-fitting pinstripe suit. "Ms. Rendall," he said, shaking my hand. "I'm Charles Topper, an assistant curator here. Will you follow me?"

In his office, which, strangely, lacked art or decoration, Charles Topper got right to business. "What can I do for you?" he said, when he'd taken his chair behind his desk.

I squirmed to sit higher in the leather chair. Now that I was here, how to say this? "I believe I have something to donate to the Institute. I believe it dates back to the Shang dynasty."

Mr. Topper's eyes grew large. "Is that right? Well, that's fantastic. May I ask how you acquired this piece?"

"It was a gift."

"And can you describe it for me?"

"It looks like a piece you already have. The frog on the lily pad?"

His eyes grew narrow now and his mouth pursed. "You're speaking of the Shang dynasty frog, which was part of a pair."

"Yes, that's right. I can't be sure that I have the exact one, but it closely resembles it. And I have no use for it anymore." I said this last part breezily, as if I was accustomed to donating artifacts to museums around the world. "I'd like to give it to the Institute. If the piece is of interest to you, it's yours. And if not, you can get rid of it." I hoped that there was a massive incinerator employed for such a purpose.

"Ms. Rendall," Mr. Topper said, taking off his glasses and pressing his thumb into the center of his forehead. "I should tell you that there is quite a legend surrounding that pair of frogs, or at least one of them. Something like the Hope Diamond."

"You mean where everyone who had the diamond was killed or cursed?" I felt a sweat break over my body.

"Well, yes, that's the lore associated with the diamond, but in this case, with the Shang frogs, it's something more mystical. You see, the Art Institute has had the one frog for over a hundred years. But you're not the first person who's tried to give us the other half of the pair. The fact is, ah… How should I express this?" He put his glasses back on. "We can't seem to hold on to the other frog once it's been given to us."

"What do you mean?"

"It's rather embarrassing, but it just disappears. The Institute reported it as a theft the first few times. Now…well, we're not sure what to do anymore."

"But you'd be interested in looking at my frog, wouldn't you? I mean, it might be a different frog. Or maybe you can hold on to it this time." I held back from saying, *Please. Please take this thing off my hands.*

He scratched his head. "There's a whole protocol that has to be followed with such a donation. You'd first have to fill out the paperwork—"

"You know what?" I said, interrupting him. "Let me just pop home and get the frog to show you. If it seems like you might be interested we can take it from there, okay?"

Before he could answer, I was out the door. I hailed a cab home and told the cab driver to wait. Inside my condo, I snatched the frog, holding it tight in my fist. I ran back to the cab and asked him to take me back to the Institute.

"Hmm," Mr. Topper said, when I'd placed it on his desk. "You should know I'm not a spotter."

"A spotter?"

"Someone who can authenticate these things. But this certainly looks like the other one." He shook his head. "Remarkable."

"So, you'll take it?"

"We'll try." He smiled. "I'll get the paperwork."

The next morning, it was back on my nightstand.

I became desperate. If this was some kind of cosmic test, I was determined to pass. If I could simply destroy the frog for good, I was certain I'd be back to square one, back where I'd started that night I'd seen Blinda weeks before. I could erase everything that had happened and begin again. This time I would do it right. I would try to take Blinda's advice and look inside for my happiness, but I would also work to get those things I wanted. I would actually address them. Someone once said that life was not a spectator sport. Unfortunately I'd been sitting on the sidelines lately—way, way back in the bleachers.

Soon, I could think of little else but obliterating the frog. I began watching TV for particularly heinous serial killer stories, hoping for some tips. I took to carrying the frog around with me during the day, looking for that perfect, destructive opportunity.

On Sunday afternoon, I rode the train to Armitage Avenue and walked the street, heading for Lori's, my favorite shoe store, thinking that since I couldn't see my therapist, maybe a little shoe therapy would help. Right before I reached the store, I passed a church. One of the doors was open, letting in the cool May air, and I could see a memorial service inside. There was an open casket at the front, mourners lined up to pay their respects.

I had a thought.

But then a war in my head. *Don't do it. Don't even think about it,* the sane side said. *This might work,* my crazy side retorted. *This might actually do it.*

Without thinking about it more, I joined the line shuffling to the casket in the front. There were approximately sixty people in the church, most of them murmuring quietly to their neighbor while organ music played in the back. As I reached the casket, I saw a man inside. Either the mortician was not particularly gifted, or this man had been very, very old. His face was as white as the little tufts of hair on his bald head, but there was a serene smile on his face. I panicked. This wasn't some game. This was a funeral for a very real person, an obviously much better person than me. Guilt twisted my insides. I was a terrible person to intrude.

I shuffled to the left—I had to get out—but then I felt soft pressure on my arm. The priest.

He nodded at me. "It's okay. We all get scared sometimes. Just pay your respects."

"No. I… I don't… I can't. I didn't even—"

He nodded again. "It's okay." His hand propelled me toward the casket.

"No, I…" But I saw a few people glancing at me, worried expressions on their faces. This was horrible, disrespectful. But protesting further would only create more of a stir.

I took the few steps to the casket and touched the rim with one hand. For some reason, tears sprang to my eyes. "I'm sorry," I whispered to the man. He looked like someone's kind grandpa, the type I'd always wanted to have.

The frog was still in my left hand. I had a thought—*What could it hurt?* More wars in my head. More wavering. I heard the people behind me shuffling their feet impatiently. The organist began another song.

Finally, without thinking about it anymore, I brought my left hand to the casket and dropped the frog inside. It slid down the side of the casket, invisible in the folds of ivory satin.

The next morning, it was back on my nightstand.

Spring in Chicago can mean fifteen inches of snow or an eighty-degree scorcher. But one Monday, with the end of May quickly approaching, the city hit on the most perfect of spring weather—a balmy breeze, and puffy white clouds dotting a powder blue sky. I'd spent the weekend trying with more and more ferocity to kill the frog, but it was apparently the *Terminator* of icons, because it would not die. Luckily, Chris had stayed with his parents on Saturday night after a family birthday party, one I'd managed to avoid. I had been nothing but cranky and miserable, and yet when he was around, Chris kept offering food and conversation and love. I wanted that love. More than *anything*. But it was hard to accept it when I felt that I'd wished it into action, rather than Chris having desired it on his own.

Now, on Monday, I walked back from lunch with two of my clients. I'd told them that I had an appointment on Franklin Street, so I could accompany them to their office. Really, I had no such appointment, and I'd gone totally out of my way, since my office was blocks away, but this was something my first boss had taught me to do; spend as much time with the client as possible, time other people don't. I'd gotten in the habit, and now it was my routine. But I also loved the client contact, which I got so little of these days, and then there was also the small fact that by avoiding the office, I was avoiding Evan and his unconditional lust.

As we walked, I smiled and laughed at the appropriate times. I gossiped a little about a crisis I'd heard about at another PR firm. I was putting on a good show. Really, I was thinking about the goddamned, fucking frog. It was in my black suede saddle bag, tucked inside the zippered pocket. I could feel it there, pulsing, sending out waves, telling me that I had no control over my life, that there was no free will, that it was all preordained, at least for me. I would always be able to have whatever I wanted, and I would never be happy with it.

Right then, we passed the Sears Tower. "Geez," said Teresa, one of the clients. "I haven't been up there in a while." She glanced up, holding her long brown hair back from her face as the wind picked up and barreled down the street.

We all craned our necks, staring up at the black mirrored building that towered over us like a mountain. A piece of white cloth, possibly an old T-shirt, sailed into our field of view and landed near our feet.

"Where did that come from?" I said.

"It's like someone dropped it," Teresa said. We all looked up again.

"Can you imagine falling from there?" said the other client. "Nothing could survive that."

I stood, still looking up. Teresa and John began walking again, then halted a few feet ahead. "Coming, Billy?" John said.

I managed to drag my gaze away. "I'm going to...um, I'm going to run a few errands, so I'll leave you here."

I shook their hands, and managed to make suitable farewell comments, yet the whole time, the frog was calling louder. *Time for you to go,* I thought. *For good.*

I waited a second, watching their backs as they walked away. Then I walked to the door that said, "Sears Tower Observation Deck."

Hours later, I climbed down one hundred and ten floors from the top of the Sears Tower, still shaking violently from the force of the wind and the thought that the frog might really be gone now. When I got outside, a dusky twilight had settled into the Loop. Most people were already on their way home, but a few stragglers walked the streets, a couple of lone cabs circled with roof lights blazing.

I hailed one of them and whispered my address. The experience on the roof had taken the power from my body. I was exhausted.

When I got home, I was relieved to see that Chris wasn't there. I stripped away my clothes. I turned off all the lights and crawled in bed, pulling the covers over my head.

When I woke up early, the first rays of sun were pushing through the curtains I'd forgotten to close. I looked first at Chris, asleep with his dark lashes lying against his pale cheeks. I took a breath and rolled over.

And there was the frog.

I began to cry softly. I couldn't get rid of it. Nothing would ever change.

chapter twelve

"Your mother was a voodoo priestess, right?" I asked Odette. She glanced up from the proposal I'd given her, her almond-shaped eyes amused. "What kind of transition is that? I thought we were talking about my press release."

I laughed. "Sorry."

We were in the basement office of her restaurant, having one of our routine evening meetings. Well, they used to be routine until I became a VP. Now I'd had to make excuses to attend this meeting, instead of the account rep. When I'd waitressed in college, the main office there was a pitiful place with rotting walls and mice droppings. Odette's office, in sharp contrast, was a vibrant space with brightly colored wall hangings, a wood desk painted yellow and a comfy blue visitor's chair.

"It's all right, Billy," Odette said, in her slow southern voice. "You've been distracted all night. Tell me why you're asking about my mother." Odette was a heavyset, black woman with long braided hair. Sitting back, she drew her braids over her shoulder, the beads on the end clicking sooth-ingly.

"You told me your mother was a voodoo priestess, isn't that what you said?"

"I can't possibly imagine why you're asking me this, but yes, my mother is well known around New Orleans. Not that most people believe in that stuff, especially not up North."

"I believe in it."

"Since when?" Odette adjusted the collar of her chef's whites and smiled patiently, as if she didn't quite believe me.

"Since…well, since the last month. Since something hap-pened to me."

"What do you mean?"

"I changed overnight. My whole life did. And I think it was because of this therapist I went to. Or maybe because of this frog she gave me." I stopped. How to put this into words? I didn't want her to think I was crazy, like Dr. Hy did.

"You want to explain what you're talking about?" Odette sounded concerned, but interested.

"Well…" I drifted off.

"Billy, I can handle anything. Hit me."

And so I plowed on. I told her the whole story of Blinda and the frog and how I'd gotten everything I wished for overnight. I explained how all those things I wanted had brought about their own set of issues, which I hadn't han-dled very well.

Odette nodded continuously. She muttered, "Uh-huh," and "Okay," and I kept talking. I told her about firing Alexa and how I wanted desperately for things to work with Chris but how he was killing me with food and conversation and constant sex. I told her how I missed my mom, how I even missed the obsessing and wondering I used to do about my absentee father. I told her about Evan flirting with me but left out the part about actually kissing him. It was the one part of my story I hadn't been able to tell anyone so far. I was too ashamed.

"So I want to erase it," I said, getting to the end of my story. "I don't want people to love me or desire me because of some wish I made. I want to just go back to the day this all began so I can get my life right."

"You want to get your life right?" Odette repeated.

"Yes, exactly," I said, my voice getting a little louder, faster. "I'm realizing that I had been pretty passive about things. I knew Chris and I had problems, but I didn't do much to remedy that. I wanted the vice presidency, but I didn't do everything I could to make that happen. But I have a hunch that if I get rid of this frog, and all that went on this last month, I can start again and do it properly, you see? I thought I wanted my life to be easy—or at least easier—but what I realized was that I want to be responsible for what I achieve."

"So it's the journey that counts, not the destination. And all that New Age crap?"

I laughed. "Yes."

"Okay, well you still haven't told me what you want from my mother." Odette shifted her weight, crossing her arms.

"Do you believe what I'm saying?"

Odette smiled kindly. "Of course. I've seen much stranger things than this."

"Like what?" I asked, incredulous.

She shook her head. "Tell me why you asked about my mother."

"I don't know. I thought maybe she could help reverse this…this spell or whatever it is."

"So that you can go back to the beginning and start over?"

"Do you think she can help me?"

Odette shook her head. "Sweetie, you don't need voodoo."

"But I do!" My voice was getting even louder. "I'm desperate. I need to do *something.*"

"So do it," Odette said. "You don't need voodoo for that."

"I do if I want to go back to how things were."

"No, no, Billy, don't you get it?"

"What? What's to get? I have to reverse all this. I think my best shot is just to get rid of the frog and get rid of what happened and then I can do something—"

"Billy," Odette said, standing. She moved around the desk and put a hand on my shoulder. "Listen to me. You don't need to go back. You just need to begin today. Start doing something. *Now.*"

I walked through Odette's crowded restaurant in a daze. A long-haired guy sitting at the bar waved to me. I squinted and realized it was someone I'd known at Northwestern. Normally, I would have sat down and spent the next hour catching up. But now, I barely managed to raise my arm in a wave, before I kept moving, in a trance, through the restaurant and out into the mild night air.

The restaurant was on West Chicago, over two miles from my condo, but I didn't want a cab whisking me home yet. I put one leaden foot in front of another and walked east, thinking that Odette was right. Exactly, one hundred percent right. She hadn't said much, but her words about taking action now had made such sense. I'd thought that by getting rid of the frog, I had a chance to go back to the way things had been before. But I hadn't stopped to think what that would mean. Chris would return to his usual incommunicative ways, Evan would still pat me on the back like a football player, I'd still be slaving in my cubicle (but happily creating), Alexa would still have her job (and still be annoying the hell out of me), my mom would still be miserably locking herself in her house in Barrington, and I'd still be pining for my father. No, I didn't want that old life back. But I did want to take control of my life.

Before all this happened, I'd had all sorts of control, only I didn't know it or I didn't use it. I could have talked to Chris more about the obvious rip through our marriage, and I could have insisted that we get therapy, together. I could have told my mom she needed to back off a little; I could have encouraged her more to take a tennis class or join a book club. And at work, I could have done more than bitch about not being promoted.

I could have done all sorts of things—I saw that now—but I hadn't. And then the frog had given me what I wanted. Only getting what you want isn't perfect. It doesn't mean automatic happiness. Those things I'd desired had brought along their own host of concerns and troubles. Plus, they weren't as satisfying when I'd had nothing to do with attaining them.

Now it was time to start fresh. Yet *where* to start?

I thought about calling my mom from my cell phone, to bring her back into a world where we shared our lives, even though we lived apart. I glanced at my watch as I passed under the El tracks at Franklin. Already 10:00. She would either be asleep or out socializing with her new, fabulous friends.

Evan. I definitely needed to set things right there. We worked together. I couldn't put that off forever. And speaking of work, I needed to start over there, as well.

When I reached Dearborn, I took a left and walked the softly lit street, past old brick townhouses, the small green plot that was Bughouse Square, and the stately, stone Newberry Library. I was almost home. Which brought me to the most important thing I had to do. The most important thing in my world. Chris.

★ ★ ★

"Hey, is that my girl?" Chris said as I walked in the condo. He was on the computer in jeans and a black T-shirt.

"It's me," I said, weakly.

He stood and enveloped me in a hug, one I didn't deserve. I held him tight, wondering if this might be the last embrace for a while. If I told him about Evan, he would pull away, rightly so, but I still wasn't sure if I *should* tell him. We had to get to the base of our original problems—Chris being all attentive and loving for the past few weeks couldn't erase that. Yet I wanted to tell him about Evan. I wanted to get that horrible secret out in the open. But wouldn't it just hurt him? And wasn't that unnecessary if I knew I'd never do it again? Or was I kidding myself and making excuses?

"How was Odette?" Chris said, releasing me. "I was going to make you dinner, but I figured she'd feed you."

"She did. She's fine." My was voice flat.

Chris peered at me. "Something wrong?"

"Can we go in the living room?"

Chris led me there, and I pulled him onto the couch.

"Oh, I see," Chris said, with a little growl.

"No, Chris, it's not that."

"Well, let's make it that." He began to kiss my neck.

"Chris, please." I pulled away.

"Okay, hon." He stroked my arm.

There was a second of silence, and I seized it. "Why did you get so distant after the wedding?"

"What?" Chris looked perplexed.

"It might have even been during the planning of the wedding. You became very distant, and really it's stuck around the whole time we've been married. We haven't been happy. Not since we were dating."

Chris blinked rapidly. "Haven't we been happy the last couple of weeks?"

"Yes, of course, but that's—"

"That's what?" He looked hurt, his eyebrows drawn together.

Did I say, *that was only because of the frog?* No. It didn't matter what had caused the change in Chris, because I was putting things right, starting now.

"Chris, I know things have been…better recently, but that doesn't change how we were practically strangers for years. We've got to figure out why that happened."

He shrugged. "What does it matter? Why do we need to revisit that time if we're fine now?"

"Because how do we know we won't slide back into that pattern?"

"We won't."

"You can't say that. You don't know. And I *do* want to know about the past. I want to figure out why we drifted apart. We can't just pretend everything was fine."

"I'm not pretending, I just don't think we need to rehash old news."

"But it's not rehashing, if we've never talked about it!"

I'd raised my voice, but Chris barely blinked. "Just leave it, Billy," he said, his voice low and sweet. "I love you."

"I love you, too, but—"

"It's fine. We're fine."

"We're not."

"Of course we are, sweetie." He scooted toward me on the couch, his arms out as if to hug me again. He was never going to stop being so kind, so loving, so intent to let the past lie, and with the secret in my chest too large to bear, I could never go forward as Odette had said. Maybe it was selfish, maybe it was the right thing to do. All I knew was that

I couldn't keep such a thing from my husband and just move forward.

"Chris, stop," I said. "I have to tell you something." I grabbed both of his hands in mine. As I looked down at them, one tear fell and splashed on his skin. "I am so, *so* sorry, but…" I trailed off for a second, wondering how to explain. *Just say it,* I decided, *just get it out.* "Chris, I was with someone else."

We were frozen there, like two actors at the end of a play before the curtain fell—Chris's body in midlean, his hands still in mine. His mouth was open, his eyes unblinking. The only sound in the room was the *womp, womp, womp* of the pulse in my ears.

He stood, looking down at me the way someone looks at a bug who has crawled into their house. "Get out."

"What? You can't—"

"I can't what? I can't kick you out for sleeping with someone else?"

"Whoa, Chris." I stood and grabbed his arm. "I kissed him. That was it. I should have said that right away, I'm sorry. I did not sleep with anyone else."

He yanked his arm back, but didn't move away. His face was confused. He looked like a little boy, suddenly hurt by the world.

"Oh, God, don't look like that," I said. "Please. I had to tell you. I couldn't go on not telling you, but it was just a kiss."

"Who?" Chris backed away from me. He leaned heavily against the wall as if that were the only thing keeping him from sliding to the floor in a heap.

I stayed where I was, mortified by the question. "What do you mean?"

"Don't, Billy. You *know* what I mean. Who was it?"

In all my thoughts about confessing what I'd done, I had somehow never considered having to tell him it was Evan. Evan, who Chris truly liked. Evan, whom I suspected was sometimes envied by Chris for his freewheeling lifestyle and bevy of women. How to tell him I'd joined the damned bevy?

"It doesn't matter," I said, hearing the cliché words, which I must have picked up from watching *Days of Our Lives.*

"Give me a fucking break," Chris said, spitting out his words. He rarely swore.

I took a breath. I let it out. I stepped cautiously closer to my husband. "Evan."

Chris laughed—a raw, choking kind of laugh. "I don't believe you! I know this guy. You couldn't pick someone I didn't know? You couldn't at least give me the fucking courtesy?"

"Chris, I'm so sorry."

"Jesus, I *knew* you had a thing for him."

"I don't have a thing for him."

Chris gave me an incredulous look that made me want to shrink into the earth. My guilt reached monstrous proportions. Because he was right. I'd had "a thing" for Evan for years. Not only that, but I'd wanted Evan to do something about it. I wanted to play with fire, sure in the knowledge that I'd always be able to blow out the flame. I'd been wrong. I wasn't strong enough. Or maybe I simply hadn't been protective enough of my marriage.

"I don't have a thing for him," I said. "Not anymore." I took a step closer, but Chris shooed me away with a harsh, fast motion of his arm.

"Don't," he said with finality. He looked around as if seeing our living room for the first time. "You know…you know what? I could have cheated on you or kissed someone else a million times."

I wasn't sure if this was supposed to make me feel better or worse. "Okay."

"When you were planning the wedding, and you cared more about the goddamned place settings than you did about us—you don't think I could have done something then? Or after, when you were more concerned about your job than me?"

"Of course you could have. I'm sure. But wait. What do you mean, I didn't care about us? And when have I ever been more concerned with my job?" Despite the guilt, the fear, the sheer horribleness of the situation, I saw a glimmer of hope. *This* was why I had told him—so that we could finally face what had been wrong with us. We couldn't move on, we couldn't be truly happy, if we couldn't do that.

"Forget it," Chris said, his head sagging in his hands. "Forget it." His last words were muffled, and somehow that muted volume had let the dust in the room settle. I saw then that there was no quick fix. I had done something that had taken maybe forty seconds, but would take so much longer to repair the damage. That is, if the damage, combined with what had already been lying in wait, could be repaired at all.

Chris raised his head. "Billy, I'm not trying to punish you or anything, but could you please leave?"

"I'm not leaving! I'm not leaving you." What was happening? I was supposed to start over, start clean. "We have to talk about things," I said, plaintively. "I want to explain about Evan. It was—"

"Don't!" Chris said. His voice was harsh and ragged. "Don't make me listen to it! I won't."

"Seriously, it was just kissing. It wasn't anything—"

"Jesus, Billy, don't you get it? It's not just what you did, it's the fact that you did it at all. I never, ever thought you'd do something like this." He gave me a look that made me see him as if he were eight years old and someone had picked him last for softball. "How can I trust you not to do it again or not to do something worse? How can I trust you at all?"

"Oh, honey, I would never do anything like this again. It just happened so fast. We were just at this party, and we started kissing, and—"

"For Christ's sake, stop it!" His words thundered throughout the condo, echoing off the gleaming granite of the countertops, the sparkling marble in the bathroom, the polished wood floors. "I believe you, Billy, but don't make me hear about it!"

"Okay, okay."

"Will you leave me alone? Please," he said, his voice lower. "I need some time."

"I'll sleep on the couch tonight." Another cliché, and somehow I knew he wouldn't agree.

His eyes were more tired and raw than I'd ever seen them. His lids were heavy, as if they might snap shut at any moment. But his jaw was a sharp line. "I don't want to hurt you, but I can't even look at you right now." He stared past me, over my shoulder. "I'll just go somewhere."

I started to cry then at the sight of Chris, my husband, with his jaw set straight, his eyes filling with tears. When those eyes flicked to mine, they told me that he hated me a little.

"No, I'll go," I said. I couldn't make Chris do the leaving.

I went into the bedroom. Immediately, my eyes landed on the frog. It was perched atop two paperbacks, and it looked more smug than ever. I felt a churn of anger in my stomach and though, *You nasty little shit. It's all your fault.*

But I knew that wasn't true. I'd gotten what I wanted, and then I'd made my choices. This was, decidedly, my responsibility.

I dragged my eyes away from the frog and stood helplessly.

I couldn't figure out what to pack, what bag I should pack in. I had to work the rest of the week, so that meant work clothes, but what did any of that matter? And where was I supposed to go? Tess lived in Wilmette with her kids. She didn't even have a guest room. For a second, I thought of Evan in his big lakefront condo, but then I hated myself all the more for even momentarily considering it. Alexa flickered in my mind, but we weren't that kind of friends, and there certainly was no room in her apartment. A hotel? It seemed too spare, too lonely, too…awful.

Finally, I thought of the person who used to come to my mind first. I picked up the phone. "Mom," I said, my voice breaking a little. "Can I come over?"

chapter thirteen

I knocked on my mother's huge mahogany door. She opened it almost immediately. She was barefoot, wearing a navy blue track suit and a white, cloth headband around her dyed-black hair.

"Baby doll," she said, hugging me. I drooped against her. I let go. What is it about my mother's arms that can always make me sob?

She led me into "my" bedroom, one of the six in this huge house she and Jan had built during their marriage. Jan's two children had been married and long out of the house when they met, but because my sisters and I were still college age, or just graduated, Jan, in his sweet way, insisted that we each have our own room. The fact was that Dustin and Hadley had rarely stayed in theirs.

Mine was wallpapered with salmon and white toile and decorated with white furniture. It was a space that calmed me whenever I entered it, but it was a room to visit, not a room to live in. It usually signaled a short vacation. Except that now I was on an indefinite vacation from my marriage.

"You didn't say anything on the phone. What's wrong?" my mom said, sitting on the bed next to me.

"Chris," I said simply. "He asked me to leave."

"Oh, Billy." She covered her mouth. Her delicate fingernails were painted the color of pink tulips. "Why?"

I shrugged.

"What happened?" she asked.

"I messed it up. I've messed up a lot of things."

"Come here, honey," she said, making a shushing sound. She pulled me back into an embrace, causing me to cry again. This was why I'd come. To receive comfort, surely, and, not unimportantly, a roof over my cheating head, but I'd come to get my mother back, the one I'd had before she was a jet-setting, bridge-playing, independent social maven.

In the morning, I realized that the maven was still very much alive.

"Sweetie," my mother said, cracking my door. "I'm off. Will you be all right?"

I glanced at the nightstand clock—7:30. Shit, I'd be late for work. *Way* late by the time I showered and dressed and joined the throngs of traffic on the inbound expressway. But then I realized I didn't care.

I looked back at my mom. She was dressed in pink and tan plaid slacks, a white golf shirt and a jaunty pink cap.

"Where are you off to?" I asked.

"Golf. I play twice a week with Richard and Betsy."

"Richard and Betsy?"

"I'm sure you know them."

I was sure I didn't. "When will you be home?" I asked,

trying not to sound needy. I'd wanted her to have her own life, after all. I still wanted that.

"Hmm. Two-ish, probably, because we'll have lunch at the club. Come meet us!"

"No, thanks."

"Off to work then?"

"No," I said, deciding in that moment I could not bear the thought of the office.

"What will you do?"

Take an overdose of ibuprofen? Find one of Jan's hunting rifles? "I'm not sure, but I'll figure it out."

"Well, the house is yours," she said, grandly sweeping an arm, as if a Willy Wonka treasure trove of delights awaited me. "You're welcome to be here as long as you need."

"Thanks."

She blew me an air kiss and turned away, leaving me to wonder why I didn't feel so welcome at all.

I lay in bed for an hour, unable to drag my mind's eye away from a memory—a scene I could see with perfect, laserlike clarity. Chris and me. Not the fight from the other night, not his pained face, although that image threatened to intrude every so often. No, the memory that played itself on a loop was the night he asked me to marry him.

It had surprised both of us, the intensity of our affection, the swift movement from strangers to people who shared their lives together. And our passion was a force to be reckoned with, too. Something that could, and did, strike without warning, forcing us together into theater bathrooms and coat closets during parties.

And so there we were on a Tuesday night in Chris's apartment. I sat like a grand poobah on Chris's big chair, a glass of wine on the arm, a small plate of Parrana cheese Chris had sliced for me.

I was content and calm and in love when, about a half hour later, Chris called me into the kitchen. There was a small table in the corner, where we usually sat, but the kitchen was drastically different. There was the scent of something nutty and warm in the air, mixing with a hint of pungent garlic, but that wasn't it. The kitchen was lit up with honey-white lights, making me think of snowy Lincoln Park at Christmas. Chris had strung lights around the two tall windows and over the top of the cabinets. White candles flickered from every surface—the counters, the stove, the windowsills. Dinner was set at the table, his grandmother's silver candelabra in the center.

"Chris?" I said, turning to him.

He was wearing a blue oxford that night, which made his eyes appear the color of the Caribbean Sea. He smiled big. It was his nervous grin. "Billy," he said formally. He gestured to the table. I saw his hand tremble a bit.

"What's all this?"

Chris was always doing the sweetest things for me. I reveled in his pampering, and I tried to treat him equally as well—shopping for him during my lunch hour, sending him e-mail cards and leaving little notes in his briefcase.

"It's a special dinner. Sit."

At the table, Chris brought me a pastry baked golden brown and stuffed with porcini mushrooms.

"Mmm," I said, practically moaning with the first bite. "This is amazing."

"I can't wait," Chris said. And suddenly, he was on his knees next to my chair.

"What are you—" I started to say.

"Shh." He put a gentle finger to my lips. "Do you know what you are to me?"

I laughed nervously. Suddenly, the moment carried a weight of something life-altering. "I'm your girlfriend?"

"Yes. Thank God." He laughed. "But you're also..." His words died off. He looked down. He took a deep breath. He let it out and raised his eyes to me again. "You, Billy Tremont, are my most treasured and favorite person in the world."

I blinked back tears that had quickly formed. His words repeated themselves in my ears—*favorite person*. No one had ever said such a thing to me before, not my mother, certainly not my father, not my sisters or a friend.

"You, too," I said. "You're the best person I've ever met."

"I had a speech planned," Chris said, "but I don't think I can do it."

He reached in his pants pocket and pulled out a box, which was covered with black taffeta. He opened it, and there it was—a dainty platinum band studded with diamonds, with a round, sparkling diamond that sat above the others like a queen.

"Will you marry me?" Chris said. "Billy, will you be my favorite person for the rest of my life?"

I did start crying then. Hard, fast tears that choked me, filled my chest with a crushing force. "Yes!" I screamed. "Yes, yes, yes." I tackled him with a hug. Chris fell to the floor.

We never ate dinner that night.

This was the scene that looped in my mind as I lay in bed in the quiet of my mother's house. The memory of our engagement reminded me of how I had utterly failed Chris. How would it feel to have the most important person in your life, your *favorite* person, disregard their duties and betray you, casually, quickly, as if those titles meant nothing? This ripped me apart because his words had meant something that night. His proclamation that I was his favorite person had carried more significance than a ring or a wedding.

I rolled over and buried my face in the sheets, realizing that I was no longer anyone's favorite person.

"Lizbeth, it's Billy."

"Morning. You on your way in?"

"Not exactly." I was, exactly, still in my pajamas, standing at my mother's taupe-tiled kitchen counter, nursing a cup of green tea, hoping that the antioxidants claimed on the box would rid me of the pollution in my world. Despite the charge of motivation I'd gotten from Odette last night, I had few ideas on how to start doing something now. What I *had* done—talking to Chris—I had fucked up royally.

"I don't feel so good," I said to Lizbeth. True enough. Emotionally, I felt like crap.

"Oh, it's that spring flu, right?" Lizbeth said. "I know five people who have that. You have to be really careful or it could turn into pneumonia."

"I'll be careful. Thanks. I'm sure I'll feel better tomorrow."

"Great, well, Roslyn has been looking for you, so let me transfer you."

I clenched my teeth together. Roslyn had an ultrastrong bullshit detector.

"Billy," she said, coming on the phone. "I'm sorry to hear you're not feeling well."

I coughed for effect. I lowered my voice to a near whisper. "Yes, thanks."

There was a slight pause. Roslyn, I knew, equated sickness with personal weakness. As a result, everyone usually came to the office when they had colds and flus and tonsillitis, fighting through fevers and runny noses and getting everyone else sick in the process. Everyone except Roslyn, that is. The woman was never ill, never nervous, never much below or above her own personal flatline.

"Well, take care of yourself," she said with as much compassion as if she were ordering a hamburger. "But I wanted to talk to you briefly about the Teaken account."

I took a seat at my mother's breakfast bar, pulling the green tea toward me. "All right."

Twenty minutes later, the green tea was gone, and I was hunched over the breakfast bar, mumbling responses to Roslyn's exhaustive list of questions about the Teaken budget, the firm's P&L and the status of getting new prints to hang in the lobby, a task which had somehow fallen to me. The tedium of my job overwhelmed me. Where was the creative thinking about different story angles for our clients, different ways to write a press release, alternative media outlets? Those decisions, those queries were what I had always enjoyed about my job. My old job as a senior account exec. This new one was all business, all the time. Before the promotion, I hadn't thought of the work as business or boring or beneath me. I'd enjoyed it, except for those times I was obsessing about how I should be promoted, without ever stopping to think about what being a VP would entail.

At last, Roslyn wound down. "Well, we can figure out later which account exec to assign to the new Bulls benefit," she said.

Me! I wanted to scream. *Let me do it.* But I was a VP now. I worked on the big picture, not the individual accounts. "Sure," I said, listlessly.

"We'll talk about it when you get here tomorrow."

It wouldn't matter if I really did have pneumonia. Roslyn would expect me to get a chest X-ray and some powerful antibiotics and be back at my desk in a day.

I began dialing Evan's number almost as soon as I hung up with Roslyn. It was sheer habit—seeking out Evan's opinion about all things work. It was how our friendship had functioned for nearly eight years. But I'd blown that. We both had. I clicked the off button on my mom's phone, still sitting at the breakfast bar. I turned it on again in the next second. I couldn't avoid him forever. We had to talk about what happened. What there was to say, I wasn't sure, but *something* had to be said, acknowledged.

I dialed Evan's direct line. He answered on the second ring.

"Hey, it's me. Billy."

A slight pause. "Where are you? I just stopped by your office."

"Sick."

"Really?"

"No. Just sick in the head."

We both laughed lamely.

"You ever going to talk to me again?" Evan asked.

"Yeah. Sorry I've been avoiding you."

"Hey, I've been rejected by women before," he said in a teasing tone. "Not many, but…"

I tried another laugh, but it was forced, more of a groan than a giggle. Another pause, longer this time and more potent, since Evan and I rarely had the slightest break in our conversations.

"I'm sorry, Ev."

"For what?"

What should I say?—*I'm sorry I wished your lust into existence? I'm sorry I didn't have enough willpower to resist it?*

"The other night," I said finally.

"I'm not. Well, I'm sorry you're uncomfortable, and I'm sorry about Chris, because you know I like him." I flinched at the sound of my husband's name from Evan's mouth. "But I'm not sorry it happened."

I stood from the breakfast bar and opened the French doors to my mother's sun porch and her green manicured lawn. It was a decent spring day—slightly overcast and in the mid-sixties—but it might as well have been a blizzard in February. I couldn't appreciate it.

"It can't happen again," I said, relieved at my statement. That was doing something, as Odette had said, instead of avoiding the situation. I charged on, emboldened and motivated now. "I adore you, Ev, you know that, but this absolutely cannot happen. I love my husband. I'm just sorry I started down this road and brought you with me."

"We'll see," Evan said.

"No, we won't," I responded quickly. Evan's powers of persuasion were legendary—from clients to store clerks to the women he dated, he could talk anyone into anything. It would be even harder to successfully have this conversation face-to-face, so I plowed on. "Nothing can happen like that ever, ever again. You have to respect my decision."

He exhaled loudly. "When are you coming back to the office?"

"Tomorrow, I suppose, but that doesn't matter. I mean what I say."

"I'll see you then."

After I got off the phone with Evan, I washed my face, combed my hair and brushed my teeth, thinking some basic personal hygiene might make me feel better. Wrong. The phone call was sticking with me, and I felt guiltier and guiltier as each moment passed. Not only at the thought of Evan's hands on my skin in that bedroom, but at the phone call itself. Talking to him seemed, somehow, like cheating on Chris again.

And so back to the kitchen, back to my mother's phone, and without thinking about what I would say, I dialed Chris's work number. He was in a deposition, his secretary said, but he should be out in ten minutes and would call me back. I sat at the breakfast bar, not even trying to entertain myself. Ten minutes passed, then another. I dialed his number again.

"Still in there," his secretary said, but she sounded disingenuous this time. Or was I imagining it?

I hung up and pushed a few buttons to block my mom's number from appearing in Chris's phone. Then I dialed his number. He answered immediately, with a somber, "Chris Rendall."

"It's me."

Silence.

"I just wanted you to know that I'm at my mom's."

"Good. Thanks. Tell her hi."

The phrase "awkward pause" took on a whole new meaning.

"And I also wanted you to know," I rushed on, "that I love you more than anything, and I'm so sorry about all this, and I'll do anything I can to make it up to you."

Why, why, why was it so hard to come up with words unique to our situation, to Chris and me, to explain what I meant? Why did I once again sound like Hope talking to Bo in Salem?

"I need some time," Chris said.

"Right, sure. How much?"

"I don't know, Billy." There was a despondent weight in his voice that said *forever might not be enough time away from you.*

"What can I do?"

"Nothing. Just give me some time alone."

"Please, Chris. Tell me something I can do or tell you or…." There was so little it seemed I could do, really. I'd been honest with him, and now he was asking for time. So simple, and yet so complicated. "We've got to talk about this, Chris. About our marriage."

"Yes, we do," he said, with an eerie finality, "but not now. I'll call you. Bye."

In memory of Jan Lovell, who was loved, the plaque said. My mother had placed it on the side of the house, right by the barbecue where Jan died three years ago.

I'd been pacing the lawn, hoping the spring air would simultaneously calm me and then kick me in the ass and usher in a sense of purpose. A sense of anything. I'd thought about Chris, and the night of our engagement, for so long there was a thick layer of fuzz in my head, which insulated me from further rational thought. So I paced, feeling the occasional rays of sun strike my face, the new grass crimp under my bare feet, until I noticed the plaque. I hadn't paid attention to it recently, since we rarely came out here. This section of the lawn, with its two barbecues (one charcoal, one gas—they gave off different tastes, Jan always said) were Jan's domain. The grills still stood, like sentries, as if waiting for his return. And above them was the plaque. It made me think of an important gift I'd been given in my life. Not the engagement ring from Chris, but a high school graduation present from Jan.

He and my mom had been married for a year, and I was fond of him, but wary. I knew he could go the way of my father and bolt, so I kept my emotional distance. Holding back seemed smart, and I thought Jan wanted it that way, too.

On the night before the graduation ceremony, my mother threw a bash. She was inside, consulting with caterers and triple-checking that the house was in its usual pristine condition, while Jan and I began the barbecue process. This was an important series of actions for Jan, similar to a pilot's preflight checks. He made sure there was enough gas, he tried all the burners, he cleaned the grates, he readied the charcoal. I wasn't sure why he'd asked me to be with him, but I felt a mellow companionship, standing with him on the grass, which was still wet from an earlier rain shower, nursing a can of soda and watching the sun bruise the gray sky as it tried to fight its way through the clouds.

After oiling the hinges on one of the barbecue lids, Jan took a deep breath. "All right, Billy, that's done," he said in his deep, rough voice. He usually wore golf shirts and khaki pants—the uniform of the retired suburban male—but that night my mom had dressed his big, lumbering body in a starched white shirt. His gray crew cut had been trimmed as well, and he kept running his hand over his hair and then pulling at the collar, as if waiting for the time he could get out of it. "I wanted to give you something," he said.

"Okay," I said. "Do you want me to take the rag inside?" I pointed to the towel he'd used to clean the grill.

"No, no, doll." Since being married to my mom, he'd adopted a shortened version of my mother's "baby doll" term of endearment. Jan tilted his head and studied me. I felt a sudden nervousness. I wasn't used to being looked at. Four years of high school, and I still wasn't comfortable in my teenaged body. But when I gazed back at Jan, I relaxed. He was nodding, clearly on the verge of saying something. And he looked strangely emotional, his lips pushed together. He ran a hand over his gray hair.

I waited. I could hear my mother's tinkling voice calling

something to the caterers, something like, "Oh, dear, those are horrid!"

"Here's the thing," Jan said, reaching for the shelf next to one of his grills and lifting a small, yellowed envelope. "I want to give you a coin. Now, I know that doesn't sound like much, but this is special." From inside the envelope, he took out a copper-colored coin. His hands were like large mitts, and the coin seemed petite in comparison. He handed it to me.

"Thank you," I said, peering at it. On one side was a woman who appeared to be soaring through the air, her arms outstretched.

"She's called Flying Liberty," Jan said. "I got that coin and a couple others like it when I was in the service in Italy. I carried them in my pocket and whenever things got bad—and they did—I looked at the Flying Liberty. I always thought that she could go anywhere and do anything. She was freedom, and she gave me strength, you see?"

"Sure," I said, nearly tingling with the personal information. Jan was the kindest man—that was always apparent from his actions—but he was a man of few words. "And you want to give this to me?"

"That's right, Billy." He patted me on the shoulder with his big hand. "You're a flying liberty now. You're off on your own, and…" His voice died away a little. "Well, I'm going to miss you when you're at school."

"I'll miss you, too." Suddenly I felt trembly. Leaving high school, leaving my mom and going to college was a terrifying thought, one I'd pushed aside by searching for a summer job and pretending August was far, far away. "I can't believe you're giving me this," I said.

And then he uttered the sentence that changed everything for Jan and me. "I gave them to all my kids."

In that instant, I felt for the first time that I loved this man.

That he could think of me as one of his "kids" was a bigger gift than anything he could ever have handed me.

Now, I felt a swell of sadness staring at Jan's plaque, thinking of what my mom had lost when he died, of how intensely she must have missed him to have made this plaque and hung it on the side of the house, like a mini headstone. I thought of what I'd lost, too, after Jan died.

I spun around then, struck, at last, with a charge of motivation. I went into the study that had been Jan's. Photos of his extended family lined the walls. The desk was big and manly, the chair a rolling leather boat. It pleased me that the room was still here, still his. It meant that my mother hadn't rid herself of everything old in order to embrace her new life.

I had to boot up the computer and wipe off a thin sheen of dust. My mother didn't believe in e-mails—too impersonal, she said. She preferred to write notes on her pink personalized stationery with her name embossed in silver at the top. The only Internet access she had was through an old dial-up that took about five decades to connect. Once I was connected, I went immediately to Google.

I hesitated. I fiddled with Jan's silver Mont Blanc pen that stood in a leather holder on the desktop. *Do it,* I told myself.

I put the pen down, and I typed in *Brandon Tremont.* My father's name.

I'd done this years ago when the Internet contained only minimal information, and I'd found nothing except a family tree showing descendants of a particular Tremont family from Pelahatchie, Mississippi, and the mention of a man named Brandon Gunnison Tremont, born 1859. Decidedly not my father. I'd been strangely relieved at the dead end. My dad was nowhere to be found. I didn't have to deal with what-ifs. And yet my obsession, my curiosity about him, grew intensely over the years. Until a few weeks ago, that is, when such worries and thoughts had been miraculously erased from my mind. Yet that erasure had left me flat. My obsessing had been the way I'd kept myself connected to him. He was a ghost now. I wanted to say an official goodbye to the ghost and maybe get some answers to satisfy the child in me who'd wondered for so long.

Now, I sat back from the computer feeling as if I'd been slapped. There were 26,415 results for Brandon Tremont. I did the search again, putting his name in quotations so that it would only search for those two names together and in that order. Fourteen results this time. Could he be one of them?

I clicked on the first one. My finger on the mouse felt heavy, awkward. There was a Brandon Tremont Web site, apparently for a guy who was a computer graphics consultant. Did my father have his own Web site? Was he in computers now? Anything was possible. I wouldn't have been shocked to find out he was a circus performer. I clicked on the "biography" link of the site. And there was a picture of Brandon Tremont—a kid who looked about eighteen years old and had albino-white hair and terrible acne.

I went back to the Google site. The second and third results also concerned the acne-ridden Brandon, who had apparently been on his high school lacrosse team. The fourth and fifth were about some Brandon in Tampa, Florida—a black man, a photo revealed, so again, not my dad. I began to wonder whether this might require a private investigator. My father had hidden from my mother, from his responsibilities, for years. He might have easily changed his name.

I clicked on the sixth result. It seemed to be a misplaced link, a Web site for Cover to Cover, a bookstore in Telluride, Colorado. But then I noticed a section called "About the Owners," which I clicked on. My fingers felt light now, as if they were moving too fast, and for some reason, I wished I could reverse the click. Irrationally, I moved the mouse to the top of the screen, ready to hit the back button.

Too late. There he was.

An older version, of course. Silver hair now, instead of heavy, rich brown, lines stretching from his eyes. He had his arm around a woman with frizzy, honey-colored hair and tortoiseshell glasses. Below the picture, the caption read, *Brandon and Lillian Tremont, owners of Cover to Cover.*

Without taking my eyes off the picture, I lifted the phone next to Jan's desk and dialed United Airlines.

"I'd like to get a flight to Telluride, Colorado," I said. "Today."

chapter fourteen

"Can I get you something to drink before takeoff?" the flight attendant asked. They were so much nicer here in first class. This was the only seat left on the flight to Denver, and luckily I had a plethora of frequent flyer miles from business traveling. "Maybe a water or an orange juice?" she said.

"Chardonnay, please." It was only 3:45 in the afternoon, technically not happy hour, but it wouldn't have mattered to me if it were 7:30 a.m.

"Certainly," said the flight attendant, who was clearly familiar with daytime drinkers.

The Chardonnay came in a thimble disguised as a wineglass. I downed it in about three seconds while other passengers filed by, heading back to the coach section, where I usually sat.

"Another?" the attendant said.

"Please." I fought back the urge to beg for the bottle. This was all happening at lightning speed. And nothing, save my quick-moving relationship with Chris, had ever happened fast in my life. I was a planner, a watcher and, as I'd recently told Odette, a procrastinator. Not even twenty-four hours before, I'd been in Odette's basement office debating what to do with my life. Since then, I'd admitted near infidelity to my husband, moved out of the house, tracked down my father and gotten on a plane to find him.

The second glass of wine came, filled to the brim this time. I gave the attendant a grateful smile, which hopefully said, *Keep 'em coming,* because the fact was I'd only tracked down my father on the Internet. I hadn't called him. I hadn't even called Cover to Cover to find out if it was still open, let alone if he was still the owner or if he was even in town.

I saw my father as a skittish, delicate animal that could frighten easily. You had to sneak up on such an animal. This was a complete departure from the way I used to think of him when I was a child. He was a tall, strong man in a house of women. He was the person who lifted you up and threw you in the air until you screamed with laughter and my mother said, "Brandon," in a disapproving but laughing voice. He was the man who spoke two other languages—foreign, awkward-sounding words. He was the head of our family, the sun we all moved around. But he'd taken off, and my feelings about him had gone through wide, fluctuating metamorphoses—from pining for him, to hating him and denying his existence, to obsessing that somehow it was me, the last child, who had scared him out into the world alone.

He wasn't alone now, though. At least according to the Web site, he was married to Lillian of the frizzy hair. This made me oddly jealous and irritated. And his owning of a bookstore was perplexing. He'd never seemed the bookish type. But what did I know about him? Absolutely nothing.

I had a few more thimbles of wine once we were airborne, then managed to sleep for an hour or so. In the Denver airport during my layover, I went to the bathroom to wash the plane grime from my face. I had only a small bag with me, the one I'd brought to my mom's and then grabbed again after I'd hastily written her a note letting her know I'd call soon. As I went through the bag now, I realized I'd forgotten to pack my cleanser. I also didn't have my moisturizer, my blue hairbrush (the only one that could mildly control my waves), a change of socks, the cute Italian driving shoes I'd just bought or any decent shirts. I sank onto the tiled floor, fighting back the panicky feeling of being adrift and unprepared. An older woman walked into the bathroom and glared at the sight of me on the floor. I scrambled to my feet, staring enviously at her huge wheeled bag that probably contained everything she needed to survive for three years.

I left the bathroom and bought a few toiletries in a shop, feeling mildly comforted by the tiny bottles of shampoo and conditioner and moisturizer. In the next store, I bought two soft T-shirts, one in yellow, one pink. Spring colors. I had no idea what the weather would be like in Telluride—to be honest, I couldn't have found Telluride on a map if forced at gunpoint—but I knew it was mountainous, maybe cold, and so, channeling the woman with the massive suitcase, I bought a sweatshirt and a windbreaker. Lastly, I found a tan golf visor for Chris and quickly told the clerk to add it to my bill. It seemed pathetic, that visor—a small offering from a bad wife. But I felt driven to get him something. I wanted to carry something in my bag that showed me, in some way, that he was still with me.

The plane to Telluride was a tiny pop can of an aircraft. The whole thing rumbled and shook. About forty-five minutes into the flight, the pilot came over the intercom. "Those of you on the right can see the town of Telluride. We'll be landing momentarily."

I glanced out my window and saw the sun setting over a small hamlet, which looked like a box of candy—a jumble of brightly colored, shingled houses. The plane swooped to the left, leaving only a russet-red sky in my plane window, then began to descend.

The Cover to Cover bookstore wasn't closed. Instead, it glowed yellow next to two businesses now dark for the day. A few blocks down, a hotel called the New Sheridan seemed like a fairly hopping place—a few people pushing in and out of it, while shouts of laughter rang from the bar next door. I probably should have inquired earlier whether there were any rooms available. I probably should find lodging now since it was dark. But that bookstore shined too brightly.

I took a few halting steps toward it. I was as nervous as I'd ever been. I peered in the glass of the clothing store, right next to my father's shop, trying to make out my reflection between stacks of jeans and a mannequin wearing a flowered skirt. My hair was unkempt from sleeping on the plane. I had little makeup left. This shouldn't have mattered. A father shouldn't care what his daughter looks like, particularly if he hasn't seen her for over twenty years. But my father wasn't the average dad. He was someone who scared easily. So I swiped some lipstick across my mouth, patted powder on my cheeks and drew a comb through my hair.

The door to the bookstore was old, arched and wooden. It opened with a creak. The melodic sounds of Mozart or some other classical music piped through the store. The place looked historical—the walls at least fourteen feet high and lined with books, two library ladders on either side. In the center of the store were a few round tables piled high with books and little yellow rectangular signs proclaiming, *New in Paperback!* or *Memoir!* or *Historical Fiction!* I wondered if the exclamation marks were my father's idea or the influence of frizzy Lillian. The fact that I had absolutely no idea—no clue whatsoever—about what kind of person my dad was made me sad and exhausted and impatient to see him now.

A man with blond dreadlocks stood behind the desk to the left. "Excuse me?" I said, but the words came out choked. I cleared my throat. "Sorry," I said, wondering what I was apologizing for. "I'm looking for someone."

"Sure," he said, nice as can be, putting aside a paperback. "Who's that?"

"Bran—" I managed to say. "Bran—" I tried again. Why couldn't I say my father's name? Why did I sound like I was in a diner asking for a muffin?

"Brandon Tremont?" the guy said, seeming a little less friendly now and a little wary of me, the strange woman with the speech impediment.

"Yes, yes, that's right," I said, suddenly mimicking Roslyn and her efficient style. "Is he here, please?" *This was it, this was the moment I'd imagined for years.*

"No, I'm sorry. Gone for the day. Can I help you find something?"

My father, I felt like saying. *You can find my father, my family, my husband, my life. If you could just locate that for me and ring that up, that would be great.* Instead, I swallowed hard and said, "When will he be in?"

"He's usually here by 9:00 in the morning. Store opens at 10:00."

"And Lillian?" I'm not sure why I asked after her. Maybe

I was thinking she was in the back and would take me home for a Walton-family-type reunion.

"You know Lillian?" The blond guy leaned on the desk with a smile, his blond dreads sliding over his shoulders.

"Uh, no. No, I don't."

"Well, I'm her son."

This shocked me into momentary silence. Lillian's son got to work with her, live in the same town as her—as her husband, *my dad*—while Brandon Tremont's kids had no idea what he was like, what he was doing. Until a moment ago, I hadn't even known for certain if he was even alive. The unfairness of it squeezed my stomach, leaving me with a nauseous, resentful feeling that made my mouth suddenly taste like tin (although I suppose it could have been the eight thimbles of Chardonnay).

"You're her son," I said, only managing to repeat his words.

And then it hit me. He might be Brandon's son, too. He might be my brother. He looked a little younger than me. It could easily be the case.

He held out his hand and smiled wide. His teeth were crooked but white. "I'm Kenny."

I shook it. "Billy Rendall," I said. "And your last name?"

"Gilchrist."

I let out a huge breath I hadn't realized was stuck in my chest. "So you're not…"

Kenny tilted his head to the side, not understanding me.

"You're not Brandon's son?" I said.

"No, no. He's my stepdad."

Which makes you my stepbrother. For some reason, I wanted to vault over the desk and hug him. I thought about telling him who I was and what I was doing there, but my father might run for the hills if he knew I was in town. I wanted to meet him now, no matter what his story, no matter what an asshole he was. I wanted to see him and to tell him what he'd done to our family by leaving. I wanted to ask him why. And then I wanted to leave Telluride.

I missed Chris right then. I wished I had my husband next to me.

"Do you want to leave a message for Brandon?" Kenny asked.

"No, thanks," I said. "I'll stop back tomorrow."

As I approached the New Sheridan Hotel, two women walked past me, both pushing jogging strollers with sleeping toddlers inside. They were talking quietly and laughing.

I opened the hotel door and watched them disappear down the street, their heads inclined together. It made me think of Tess and how, before she'd had the kids, we'd done nearly everything together. We had lived only three blocks apart in Lakeview. We talked on the phone before work, we met up for lunch, we worked out together afterward, and we usually went carousing at night. But now we had such different lives and so little time for each other.

The desk clerk greeted me and announced that he had only a few rooms available. "You're lucky," he said. "If you'd come in next week, we would have been booked for the rest of the summer."

"I thought this was a ski town."

"Oh, it is, but summer is even better. We've got film festivals and jazz fests. What are you in town for? Just visiting?"

"That's right." *Visiting my father.*

When I got up to the room, I dropped my bags and immediately called Tess from my cell phone. Seeing those women had made me want to reconnect with her, even if it meant confessing my indiscretion with Evan.

"'Lo?" her son, Sammy answered. In the background, there

was a clatter, then a shriek that sounded like it came from Joy, Tess's youngest.

"Sammy, it's Aunt Billy. Is Mommy home?"

The phone was dropped on the floor, and I could hear Tess's exasperated voice saying something to Sammy.

"Hello?" she said, in a tired voice.

"It's Billy."

"Hi, hon, what's up?" She didn't sound too interested but I could hardly blame her.

"Bath time?"

"Yep. Sammy wants to wear his red pants in the tub, so I can't get him in and Joy doesn't want to get out, even though the water is about as cold as Lake Michigan."

"Oh, sweetie."

"Don't feel bad. This is par for the course. What's up with you?"

Oh, not much. Just left my husband and got on a plane to find my father.

"Well, this is kind of out of the blue," I said, "but—"

"Sammy!" Tess screamed. "Put that down! Billy, he's going for my curling iron. I forgot to unplug it. I gotta go. Call you later."

I sat in the silence of my hotel room, praying that the gods of electrocution would spare Sammy. I thought about calling Chris. I wanted to hear his kind voice and tell him where I was and what I was doing, but he'd made it very clear that he would call me when he was ready. I got out my PalmPilot and found Hadley's number in London. I dialed but there was no answer, just a message and the voice of her husband, Nigel, in his clipped, British accent, asking me to "kindly" leave a message. I tried Dustin in San Francisco. No one home there, either. I tried her cell phone. It went immediately to voice mail.

I flopped back on the bed, wanting desperately to talk to someone, to tell someone I was here. I thought of my mom. Until recently, she was often the person I turned to when I needed a chat. But what would she think if she knew I was looking for *him?* The note I'd left at her house simply said I'd call her soon. But I couldn't do that now; I felt like I was cheating on her. Yet I knew being here was right. Finding my father was something I needed to do.

Then I found myself sitting up, picking up the phone again and dialing a number I barely knew, finding the digits from somewhere in the haze of my brain.

"Hola," someone answered.

"Is Alexa there?"

"Un momento."

I stood and walked across the room, unsure what I was going to say to her, unsure why I was even calling except that I felt like talking to a friend, and she had appeared in my mind.

Alexa answered.

"Hi, it's Billy."

"Hey, Billy," she said, and she actually sounded pleased to hear from me. "I'm glad you called. You won't believe what I did today."

"What?"

"I started working on a business plan for the PR firm I want to start."

"That's wonderful!"

"Yeah, well, we'll see. After the last time I saw you, I decided to ask for help, and I found this woman here in my community who started her own law firm, so she's walking me through what needs to be done."

"Wow. I am so impressed." I held myself back from saying that I was proud, too. Proud of Alexa and the way she was turning her firing into something better for her life. It was exactly was I was trying to do. Take what the frog had brought into my life and make the best of it.

Alexa and I talked for twenty minutes about her business plan and ideas, her fear that she would never find capital to start the thing, but how she was happier working on this than she'd ever been.

"There's just so much that has to happen if this is going to work," she said.

"You'll do it."

"I don't know, but I'm going to try. Enough about me. What's up with you?"

"I'm actually in Colorado."

I gave Alexa an abbreviated version of my decision to look for my dad, leaving out the fact that Chris had tossed me out of the house.

"My God," Alexa said. "This is huge for you. Shit, I've never even met my father."

"You're kidding?"

"Nah, he was some white guy my mom dated many moons ago. When he found out she was pregnant, he took off."

"Have you ever wanted to look for him?"

"No. He's not my father—not in any true sense. My mother and my aunt and these kids over here are my family. But you grew up with your dad, right?"

"For seven years." Seven very short years. Years that were decades ago now. Suddenly, this seemed a very rash, bad idea to be in this town.

"Billy, you've got to give it a shot," Alexa said, as if sensing my doubts. "You've obviously been wondering for a very long time, and now you're there. It's what you've got to do."

Her words reminded me of Odette's. And they were both right. It was time for me to take some action.

chapter fifteen

The next morning, I called work and asked for Lizbeth. "I won't be in again today," I said. "And I'm not sure about tomorrow either." I was supposed to fly home the next morning, and wasn't sure what time I could make it to work.

"Still sick?" Lizbeth asked.

"Mmm," I murmured.

"Well, Roslyn wants to talk to you."

I coughed. "Lizbeth, I can't right now. Can you just let her know I'll try to be in there by tomorrow afternoon? Thanks."

I hung up before she could say much else, and looked at my watch—9:50 a.m. My father should be at the store now, and Cover to Cover would be open in ten minutes.

At five minutes after ten, I pushed open the door of Cover to Cover with shaking hands. Just like last night, the door creaked and then a lilting strain of classical music washed over me. But this time, Kenny wasn't standing at the desk to the left. This time, it was my father.

★ ★ ★

He looked even older than he had in the picture on his Web site. His hair was thinner and more gray. His chest looked slightly sunken, and he was shorter than I'd remembered. But his clothes were youthful—jeans and a brown T-shirt. His skin was tan.

He was studying something at the countertop computer, a pair of reading glasses perched on his nose. "Morning," he said, still looking at the screen. Then he looked up, directly at me.

"Good morning," I said. I felt ridiculous, wishing my own father a formal good day.

"Can I…" But his words died away. He took off the reading glasses.

The classical music came to the end of the song, and silence filled the store. It was the loudest silence I'd ever heard. I struggled to find words to speak. My father seemed to be having the same problem.

"Billy?" He said my name quietly, with a question mark at the end, but there it was. I felt jolted. How did the asshole who'd taken off recognize his youngest, the girl he hadn't seen since she was seven?

I nodded.

"Come in. Please." He hurried around the counter toward me. I drew back in surprise.

He halted. "I'm sorry."

I was still too shocked to say anything.

A door slammed at the back of the store, and a woman came into the front room. Lillian. Her hair wasn't as frizzy as I'd thought. She also wore jeans over her wide hips and a thin, light blue sweater. "Brandon, we need to fix that sink again," she said. "Oh, hello there," she called when she saw me.

"Good morning." These seemed to be the only words I knew how to utter.

Lillian looked from Brandon to me and back again.

"Lil," he said. "This is my daughter, Billy."

Outside the store, in the back, there was a small cement courtyard occupied by an iron table painted mint-green and a overabundance of flowers and plants.

"Lillian loves gardening," my father said. He gestured to the table.

I nodded. I was still having trouble finding words. I hadn't expected him to be so welcoming. I didn't think I would have the odd desire to fall into his arms and ask why he left. The courtyard was shaded and cool, the sky sunny and bright blue above us. The place was calming, and that made the entire experience come into sharper focus—*this is my father, my dad, he's right here.*

We both sat. I pushed my chair back from the table a few inches. At last, my mind started working again. "How did you recognize me?"

He smiled. It was a rueful smile that sent deep creases from his eyes, down his tanned cheeks. "I wish I could tell you I'd always know one of my girls."

I bristled at the term "my girls." How dare he?

"But," he continued, "the truth is that I've kept my eyes on you all."

"Your eyes?" I crossed my legs, and wrapped my arms tight around my body.

"Years ago, I paid someone to find you."

"Do you mean you had someone watch us? Like a detective or something?"

He nodded.

I huffed. "I can't believe you. You take off, you don't

give my mother a cent of money, and yet you had us watched?"

His eyes roamed my face. He opened his mouth to speak, but right then Lillian came outside with two tea-cups on saucers. They were mismatched, and one of the saucers was chipped. The saucer rattled as she placed one cup in front of me.

"Do you take sugar?" Lillian said. Her voice seemed a lit-tle high, and I realized she was nervous for her husband.

"No, thank you."

Lillian sent my father a tight, optimistic smile.

He met her eyes. "Thanks, Lil."

"I'll just be in the shop." She gestured toward the store.

The screened door slapped as she went inside, a summer sound. I took a sip of the tea. *Soothing Chamomile,* it said on the tag attached to the tea bag. I hoped it worked like gangbusters.

"I really had no right to keep tabs on you girls," my fa-ther said.

"No, you didn't."

He grimaced. "It wasn't until about eight years ago that I did it. I'd just married Lillian, and she had changed my life." He smiled a little now. "She changed me for the better. But I knew I couldn't contact you three. I'd given up that chance a long time ago. I felt like I had no right. And yet I had to know if you were okay. So I had someone find you and let me know. And I got to see how you looked now that you'd grown up."

"You had them take pictures of us?"

He gave a short, chagrined nod. He leaned back as if afraid of a blow.

I shuddered a little and looked away from him. I couldn't help but wonder where such pictures had been taken. Eight years ago, I was spending most of my time trolling the bars and nursing hangovers. Possibly, there was a photo of me coming out of a drugstore with a massive bottle of Advil. Or maybe later, one of Chris and me. I got a pang of regret with the thought. I wished desperately that he was here with me now, helping me navigate this conversation with this strange man who was responsible for my existence.

"I apologize," my father said. "I shouldn't have invaded your privacy. It's unforgivable, but I just needed to make sure you were all right. I knew I didn't deserve to ever talk to you girls or be a part of your life, but I had to know. Can you understand that?"

Like I had to know about you, I thought. But I wouldn't give him the satisfaction. "Not when you didn't care whether we were all right for so long," I said.

"I always cared."

I barked out a disbelieving laugh.

"Billy, it's true. I was an ungrateful shit. I was a lousy husband and father, but I always, always cared."

I opened my mouth, ready to let him have it.

He held up his hand as if to stop my protests. "Please. I know it didn't seem like it, but that's really true."

I crossed my arms. "You have a very odd way of showing it."

My father pushed his teacup away, and leaned forward with his elbows on his knees. His eyes searched my face again. "You've grown up beautifully. Your mother did an excellent job."

Something about the softness of his voice put a hard feeling in my throat that I had to swallow down. "Why did you leave?" I said, my tone just as soft.

He sighed. He looked down. After a long moment, he spoke again. "I was having a very difficult time after your mother and I got married. We hadn't planned to get married, but she was pregnant." He paused and sat back. "I'm sorry, did you know that?"

"Did I know that you got married because she was pregnant with Dustin? Yes, I did. And if you think I'm going to feel sorry for you…" I trailed off, shaking my head.

"No, absolutely not, but you asked, so I want to tell you why I did what I did." He took a deep breath. "I wasn't ready to get married. I was just starting out in my family's business, and I was living in downtown Chicago and enjoying it tremendously. When your mom got pregnant with Dustin, that all screeched to a halt. I wanted to embrace our new life in the suburbs, but being the shallow person I was, I was always wishing I was somewhere else."

"Then why did you have more kids?"

"Your mother wanted to. And I did, too. I loved Dustin, and I thought if we had more kids, maybe I would get used to being a family man and become content."

I thought of the male names he'd given us all. "You were hoping for boys."

He nodded. "I was a ridiculous fool, but yes. I was."

"So you got two more girls, and then you decided to take off."

He shook his head. "It wasn't like that. I felt like I was doing nothing but making everyone miserable. Your mother wasn't happy because I wasn't happy. One day, I snapped. I just really snapped. I'd started drinking too much, and your mother complained about it, and…" He shook his head as if reliving the situation and still finding it hard to believe. "I was on my fifth whiskey of the night. Your mother asked me to stop. She was always very polite." He made a wry laugh. "She was standing over me while I sat in front of the TV."

I thought of the blue recliner that no one used but my

father. It had sat there after he left, reminding us all of him. Finally, when we moved to the apartment by the hospital my mother gave it away.

"I was so angry at her," my father continued. "I knew she was right, but I wanted the whiskey to take away the hard edges. I just wanted her to get away from me. So I stood and grabbed her. I screamed at her. I shook her. I wanted to hit her." His words had been coming faster, but now he paused, and his shoulders dropped. "I knew that night that I had to leave. I thought if I left, she could be happy with someone else. She could move on."

"You left her with no money!" I said this loudly, breaking the calm of the courtyard. I thought of my mother peering out windows, waiting for my father's car. I thought of our move from the white house with the columns to that crappy apartment.

"I didn't mean to do that," he said. "I went to L.A." He waved a hand, as if that part of his life was hard to explain. "I always meant to support you girls, but I lost a lot of money and led too high a lifestyle. There were other women. A lot of them."

"You abandoned us. That's nice. You were...what? Maybe doing drugs and partying with the gals, while we were scraping pennies together?"

He nodded again. "I—" his voice seemed to break. He cleared his throat. "It's inconceivable to me now, that I acted how I did. I was such a mess. And after a while, I just erased the thoughts of my old life. I would hardly let myself think of you girls or your mom."

"That's it? You *erased* us?"

A gust of wind swept through the courtyard, ruffling his hair. "I'm not explaining this well. Probably because there is no good explanation for my behavior."

"Apparently not."

We sat, both of us staring at the table. My father drank from his teacup.

I lifted my face and looked at him. "Did I have anything to do with it?"

His gaze met mine; his eyebrows drew close together. "What do you mean?"

"I don't know. I was the last child, and I've always wondered if I somehow pushed you over the edge."

"Oh, hell, Billy. No. Absolutely not. You were a wonderful, amazing little girl. You seem to be an amazing woman. It was me who was the problem. I hated myself back then. I hated myself when I left, too. In my own eyes, nothing could redeem me. I was horrible and I knew it, and I knew without a doubt that you girls were better off without me. Or at least I convinced myself that that was the case. It was only when I met Lillian about ten years ago that I stopped the booze and I stopped running through life. I was able to look at what I'd done, what I'd been like."

"She seems nice," I said grudgingly.

"She's wonderful. She was my massage therapist in Los Angeles. That's how we met." He chuckled. "She got me to see what a jerk I was. She got me sober, which wasn't easy. We moved out here six years ago, and opened up this store the next year…." His words died away. "I have to say this to you." He paused and looked at me intently. "Billy, I am sorry. I'm truly sorry."

I said nothing.

"An apology doesn't help, does it?" he said.

"Not much." I paused. "Maybe a little."

I took a sip of tea, and I noticed him glancing at my hands. "You're married, right?" he asked.

The teacup rattled as I set it down. "I don't know anymore."

★ ★ ★

Somehow, someway, I ended up telling my father about Evan and that night at the party. The tale rushed from my mouth. Other than Chris, I'd told no one what I'd done, but I realized now that I needed a confessor. That such a person would be my deadbeat father was beyond bizarre and yet somehow strangely right.

He nodded while I talked, his expression one of rapt attention, but his face lacked judgment, which kept me talking.

"I can't believe I did it," I said, as I came to the end. "I'm so ashamed."

"Shame and regret," he said shaking his head a little. "They're the most insidious of emotions. I know them all too well. And what I've learned is that eventually they'll devour you if you let them."

"I want to be devoured by them."

"You want to be punished?"

I nodded.

"Oh, sweetheart." His voice was filled with sadness. "Did you tell your husband?"

I nodded again.

"Well, then you're being punished, I would guess."

"I deserve it."

He didn't respond at first. Then he said, "Do you want your marriage to work?"

"Yes." My voice cracked a little. "God, yes. He's such a good man. And I love him. I really do."

"You'll have to fight for it. I wish I had."

I met his eyes. They were brown, like mine. "Were you having an affair when you left us?"

"I was having an affair with myself. I was a selfish bastard. But I wasn't involved with another woman until I moved to L.A."

I took a sip of the tea that had grown cool. There seemed to be nothing else to say just then. A breeze rustled the fronds of a large plant next to the table. A few birds flew overhead, chirping.

"Do you like music?" my father asked.

"What do you mean?"

"Live music. Do you like seeing live music?"

I felt a burst of something like hope in my chest. "I do. I love it."

He grinned. "Me, too. There's a great acoustic guitarist playing tonight down the street. Will you stay? Maybe meet Lil and me?"

"I'd like that."

I left Cover to Cover with a lilt in my step, glancing around the town. Brick-front clothing shops, cafés and stores pushed tight together. A few moms with kids ambled down the street. A jogger trotted by. I smiled at everyone, feeling lighter than I had before and more clear-headed, as if the skies had opened above me for the first time in months. It had been only four weeks since Blinda had given me the frog, and yet I'd been through what seemed like a few years of changes. Now, after finding my dad and hearing him say he was sorry, I felt like I'd knocked something off a large emotional checklist. And we were going out for music that night! I was seeing my father.

My delight at the situation slowed my steps. That I should be so excited about this potential relationship struck me as pathetic. After all, this was a man who had abandoned a wife and three daughters. Why was I letting him off the hook so easy?

Weighted now rather than light, I trudged back to my room at the New Sheridan Hotel. It had a large, carved Victorian bed and a red velvet Victorian-style chair. I dragged the chair to the window, bringing my cell phone with me. Outside my window, the mountains looked like hunks of gleaming gray granite with occasional outcroppings of green and a few snowcaps up high. A beautiful vista, but maybe my time in this town was over. Maybe it was time to go home.

I lifted up the phone and dialed the airlines.

I gave my reservation number and mentioned the fact that my flight to O'Hare wasn't leaving until the next morning. "But I'd like to get a flight today," I said.

"Okay, let's see what we have," the agent said. "Hmm, it doesn't look good. You could try standby on the two flights left to Denver, but they're already overbooked. You're better off going tomorrow."

I hung up the phone, wondering what to do. I stood and went to the small writing desk. In the top drawer was a book detailing activities in Telluride. I couldn't leave until tomorrow, and I had hours before I was supposed to meet my father, something I wasn't even sure I wanted to do now. I'd found him and I'd spoken to him. I'd gone so far as to ask him why he'd left. I'd done what I came to do. What was the point of making nice and seeing him again? He would probably never be a part of my life.

I flipped through the Telluride book some more, deciding that I would do what I often did at home when I was confused—I would find a museum.

A half hour later, I entered the Telluride Historical Society, housed in a large, red brick building with white gabled roofs. Immediately, I lost myself in the history of the place, learning it had once been a hospital and that it had been destroyed a few times before being restored. I turned to the photographs, which showed the hardworking inhabitants of what had once been a thriving mining town and, before that, a summer camp for Indians. I read about how the railroad came into town, and how the wealth of Telluride had attracted Butch Cassidy and his gang.

I stopped at the materials about Butch Cassidy, thinking that Chris should be here. He'd always been fascinated by Cassidy's "Wild Bunch." But more importantly, I wished he could meet my father. I had made the trip to Telluride for me, but I wished my husband was at my side.

I left the museum and walked until I found a park. Sinking onto a shady patch of grass, I dialed Chris's work number.

His secretary answered and said he was out to lunch. My heart dipped. "Do you know when he'll be back?"

"Mmm, not sure. Maybe… Oh there he is! One sec, Billy." I was put on hold. It took Chris, by my watch, three minutes and five seconds to pick up the phone, and by that time I'd gone from missing him to being pissed off at him.

"Hi, Billy," he said, his tone lifeless.

"Took you quite a while to get to the phone, hmm?"

"Yeah, I'm working here."

"Yes, work is always important to you," I said. We were both quiet. "But you've got other work to do. We both do. Our marriage is falling apart, Chris."

There was a thud on his end. He'd pushed his office door closed. "Thanks to you," he said.

"Excuse me?"

"Well, you're the one who decided to mess around with Evan."

"We did *not* mess around."

"It depends on your definition, I suppose. Call it whatever you want, but this thing was your doing."

"And for the two years before that when we barely spoke or fooled around? Whose doing was that?"

Chris said nothing.

"It was both of us, Chris. And that's why we both need to work on this now."

"If we want the marriage to work, you mean."

I felt chilly with fear, and I stood up and began to pace on the green lawn. "Don't you?" I asked.

"I'm not sure."

"Please don't say that."

"I don't know, Billy. I hate this. I'm in agony here. But I just don't know."

I began to tremble inside at his words. I could feel the sands of our marriage slipping through our fingers.

"I should go," Chris said.

"No! Don't."

"I can't talk about this now."

"Okay, well...let's talk about something else."

"What else is there?"

I glanced up and took in the main street of Telluride with its brick storefronts and sunny sidewalks. "I've got a topic," I said. "I'm in Telluride, Colorado."

"What? What are you doing there?"

"I met my dad."

"Are you kidding?"

"Nope."

"Holy shit, Billy. How'd that happen?"

I sat back down, this time in a pool of sun that had splayed itself across the green grass, and I started talking to my husband.

chapter sixteen

Kenny, Lillian's son, was at the bar when I walked in that night, his blond dreadlocks pulled back from his face.

He smiled when he saw me. "Buy you a beer?"

"Sure, thanks."

He caught the bartender's eye and gestured. "I hear we're related," he said.

"Almost. We're stepbrothers. Or sisters." I shook my head. "Something like that."

He handed me a beer. "Stepsiblings, I think would be the proper term. And I hear there are two more of you."

"Yes. Two sisters." I felt like mentioning that neither Dustin nor Hadley were like me at all, but I held back.

Earlier in the day, after Chris had listened so intently about my trip to Colorado, I'd made the mistake of calling Dustin in San Francisco. We were in nearly the same time zone for once, and I wanted to talk to someone else about meeting my father—*our* father.

Dustin hadn't answered at her office, but she called me back ten minutes later. "How's Chicago?" she asked.

"Actually, I'm in Colorado."

There was the briefest of pauses. "Where in Colorado?"

"Telluride."

Now the silence was longer. "Are you seeing Dad?"

I felt a zing of shock. "Did you know Dad lived here?"

"Yeah. I had someone locate him."

"When?"

"A few years ago," she said simply.

"Why didn't you tell me?"

"I didn't tell anyone."

"Then why'd you find him?"

"I wanted to find out where he was and what he was doing. And I learned that he's married and has a son. He left us and got a whole new family."

I sat up on the lawn outside the Telluride museum. "That's not exactly right. He didn't meet Lillian, his wife, until eight years ago, and Kenny is Lillian's son."

She gave a short laugh. "So you're chummy with the whole clan, huh?"

"I met them," I said defensively. "Did you?"

"God, no. I found out what I needed—that he's still a bastard who doesn't deserve us."

No amount of explanation could convince Dustin that I should give our father any more of my time. After our phone call, I had lain back on the grassy lawn and debated what to do—see my father or not. But I couldn't leave for O'Hare until the next day, and it seemed ridiculous to be in the same tiny town and not meet him. I'd finally, grudgingly, gotten up from the lawn and gone to take a shower.

Now, at the bar, I told Kenny generalities about Dustin and

Hadley, leaving out the part that they'd probably want to torch this place if they knew our father was about to walk in.

"What about you?" I asked Kenny. "Any brothers or sisters?"

"Nope, just you."

We smiled at each other.

"I'm pretty happy you showed up," Kenny said. "I always thought I could use a sister."

"Oh." I tucked a lock of hair behind my ear, feeling embarrassed but pleased. "I suppose… Um, I suppose I could use a brother, too."

Lillian came in the bar then, trailed by my father. I watched him, trying to see him the way Dustin and Hadley might. They would look for signs that he was ready to run again. They would search for indications of his cold nature. But all I saw was his face breaking into a grin when he spotted Kenny and me. He took his wife's arm gently and pointed us out, then walked behind her like a gentleman, guiding her with a hand on her back.

"Hello, Billy," Lillian said shyly when they'd reached us.

My father patted me awkwardly on the shoulder. "I'm so glad you came."

I was, too.

The bar was filled with dark wood and mirrors browned with age. The ceiling was tin, stamped with tiny diamond shapes. We sat on a few huddled bar stools and watched a man with long hair and a scruffy beard play an engaging set of music—Allman Brothers, Grateful Dead, Clapton, some blues. Soon Kenny drifted away to friends he saw near the door and Lillian got up to speak with a woman next to us. My father and I stayed put, one stool separating us. He had rolled up the cuffs of his navy blue shirt, and he looked very much in his element in this small-town bar. Although I was the out-of-towner, I noticed something similar about my father and me. We both swayed minutely to the music; we both closed our eyes once in a while when we heard a lyric or a note that touched us.

The singer broke into a new song—"I Looked Away" by Derek & the Dominoes.

My father leaned toward me. "I liked Clapton better when he was with these guys." He gestured to the singer.

"No way," I said. "He's written much better stuff since then."

"I absolutely disagree," my dad said, but he said it with a small, pleased smile as if he was proud of me for being able to have this conversation, as if he was proud of himself for being with me right then.

"Let me ask you this," he said. "Old Santana or new?"

"Old," I answered without hesitation.

"That's right." He nodded. "And what do you think about Jagger these days?"

"What about him?"

"Is he past his prime?"

"Oh, no. He's just as good."

A grin of paternal delight spread across my father's features. For a moment, it filled me with happiness. I'd made my father proud! But then I crashed back to reality. He had no reason to be proud of me. He'd had nothing to do with me or who I'd become.

I set my beer down on the bar. "Look, Brandon," I said, making sure to use his first name. "Let's make sure we both understand something. This…" I gestured back and forth between him and me. "This is not going to be some Hallmark card, father-daughter relationship. You made sure of that a long, long time ago."

Out of the corner of my eye, I saw Lillian turn her head.

My father looked at me for a while, then averted his gaze. "I understand," he said.

I felt horrible. Logically, I wanted to hurt him, some way, somehow, for what he'd done all those years ago, or what he'd failed to do. But now, I just felt cruel.

I stood up. "Excuse me. I have to use the restroom."

The bathroom had two stalls, plus a sink and a wooden chair in the corner. I took a seat and looked at the rose-colored fabric that papered the walls and the tiny black tiles on the floor. I sat, listening to a few strains of music seep inside. The bathroom seemed the loneliest place on the planet.

A few long and quiet moments later, the door creaked open. Lillian stuck her head in, her long mess of golden hair practically preceding her. "Can I come in?"

"Of course," I said in an even tone.

She walked inside and leaned against the sink. She had a beer in her hand, but she'd barely drunk any of it. "Brandon feels awful."

"For taking off when I was seven, or for acting now like he didn't?"

She blinked. A pained expression moved fleetingly over her face.

"I'm sorry to be harsh," I said, "but—"

"No, that's all right. He did a very terrible thing back then. And he lived a life of guilt and disgrace for many years."

"Until he met you," I said. "You saved him. That's what he says."

"Men." Lillian shrugged and laughed lightly. But the laugh faded. "Finding Brandon was the best part of my life, too. I always flitted from one thing to the next. I was a waitress, a dental hygienist, an actress, a teacher and a massage therapist. But Brandon forced me to find what I really wanted to do, which was to work with books. He was the one who got us here and found the space for the store. He made me realize that people can start over."

Starting over. It was exactly what I'd been trying to do—start over with my father. Soon, I had to go home soon and start over with my mom and Evan and my job. And especially with Chris.

"Billy," Lillian said, "he might deserve your anger, maybe even hatred, but if you're here to punish him, I'm going to ask you to leave."

I felt a grudging admiration. "You must really love him."

She put her beer down on the counter. "I love that man more than anything. And I think part of my job as a wife is to protect him. I'd love to see him get to know you girls, but not if it's like this." She waved a hand in my general direction. "I know you think he deserves it, but I think he's served his time."

We sat wordlessly for a few seconds. "I just want to move on," I said at last.

"Will it help you move on if you're spiteful to him?"

I thought about it. "No. It will make it worse."

She stood from the sink and touched my arm briefly. "I'll see you out there."

When I came out of the bathroom, Lillian and my father were holding hands, listening to the music. I gave a tentative smile, which they both returned. The three of us spent the next twenty minutes quietly, the music pardoning us from constant conversation. When the singer took a break, Lillian excused herself. She gave me a long look, as if giving me one more chance.

Without the strum of the guitar to fill the bar, the silence between my father and me was weighty. He cleared his throat. He ordered an iced tea and another beer for me.

"Would you like a glass?" he asked formally.

"No, thank you," I said.

Another painful quiet while the bartender opened my beer.

"I have to ask," my father said. "How are Dustin and Hadley?"

I bit the inside of my mouth. I held myself back from saying *Why don't you ask them yourself?* But I felt as if I'd given Lillian a silent promise to be nice. "I thought you knew how my sisters were since…you know, since you had us followed or whatever."

"That only tells me the hard facts—where you live, who you live with. I want to know how you all *really* are. Are your sisters happy?"

Quite the question. Who could answer it except themselves? I told my father about Dustin's husband and her job. I described the slanted street in San Fran where they lived, where Dustin herself had ripped out walls and put in new drywall. I told him how Hadley wanted kids, but I left out how hard she'd been trying. I tried to offer him a few details of their lives without giving too much. That would be for them to do someday, if they chose.

He asked me about my job. I explained what I did, what I used to like about it and what I disliked about my new position, the position I'd dreamed of for so long.

"Sometimes you have to know when to double back," my dad said.

"What do you mean?"

"There's no shame in going home. I wish I'd realized that a long time ago."

I wasn't sure if he was referring to my job or our family, or both. But his statement held a kernel of truth. And in that instant, I saw something else we had in common. We tended to run from our challenges. My father had done so physically, while I usually made the jog mentally. But hopefully we were both learning to fight that inclination.

We watched as the guitarist took his seat again. The moment of quiet was somehow comfortable now.

My father turned to me. "I hope you'll come back again. We've got a great jazz festival in August."

I heard his words over and over—*I hope you'll come back.* An influx of emotions filled in around them—pride that my father wanted to see me again, disgust at my own reaction, and somewhere, way back in the mix, a sliver of hope.

"This has to be enough," I said. "For now."

He grinned, the motion making creases in his tanned cheeks. "That's fine. It really is."

I nodded. I realized this day had been enough for me. I'd found him. I'd met him. I'd learned something about why he left. I knew he hadn't left because of me. I liked him a little.

I slipped off my stool and hugged him. I had expected him to smell like my stepdad, Jan—like a golf course, like a barbecue grill—but my father had his own soft scent of paper and spicy soap.

A moment later, I was walking back to my hotel, down the main street of Telluride. Above me, the sky was bright with stars.

chapter seventeen

The flight home from Colorado was a blur of blue airline seats and the run from one gate to the next and eventually the skyline of Chicago as we landed. The entire time, I'd been in another world, reliving the time with my father the way I used to relive my first dates with Chris, and then shifting my thoughts to my husband, our relationship and the concept of marriage in general.

Getting married, I decided, was like being handed a pair of tiny, precious packages, each with a Fragile sticker on the side. Both persons had to carry their package carefully. If one person mistreated or dropped theirs, as I'd done recently, as Chris had done early in our marriage, the packages began to deteriorate, causing both people to wonder whether they needed, or wanted, them at all.

But I knew I wanted to brush off our precious packages and tape up any rips. I wanted a second shot at carrying mine every day.

At O'Hare airport, I called Chris.

"He's in court until 1:00," his secretary said, "then he's going straight to a deposition."

I squeezed my eyes shut. "When do you expect him?"

"About 5:00. Maybe a little later."

"Thanks. I'll call him then."

Still standing in the arrivals terminal, I dialed my mom's number in Barrington. Miraculously, she was home.

"Baby doll, are you all right?" she said. "I've been worried about you."

My heart leaped. "You have?"

"Well, of course. You simply took off a few days ago."

"Oh, well I—"

"Look, darling, I'm having a few people over for lunch," she said, quickly leaving the original topic. "Why don't you join us?"

I looked at my watch—12:00. I could spend an hour or two at my mother's and still get to the office later in the afternoon, something I desperately needed to do for more than one reason. But I also needed to talk to my mom, to tell her I'd met Brandon. I said I'd get a cab and be there in thirty minutes.

Telling Chris I'd kissed Evan was agonizing. Now, as I sat in the back of a taxi, heading toward my mother's house, I felt like I had to come clean all over again. I'd have to explain how I'd gone to Colorado to track down the husband who'd abandoned her and her children.

In some strange way, I wanted to shock her with my announcement that I'd found Brandon Tremont. Like electric shock therapy, maybe it would startle her back to the way she used to be without scaring away the good parts of the new person she'd become.

There were four cars in the driveway, all Mercedes and BMWs. Inside, the house was sunny and bright. Piano music tinkled from the stereo. The French doors were open to the patio, and I could see people chatting, enjoying the new, weighty summer air. My mother was in the kitchen with a pink sweater tied around her shoulders.

"Baby doll!" she exclaimed when she saw me. She rushed around the counter to hug me. "I was cutting the cake. You're just in time for dessert."

"Who's here?"

"Oh, just people from the club. They're delightful. Come meet them." She wiped her hands on a towel and led me by the hand to the patio.

"Everyone," she said, putting her arm tight around my shoulders, "this is my daughter, Billy." She introduced me to three couples and a woman named Blythe.

I shook hands, and my mother checked her guests' drinks and announced that dessert would be served soon.

"Billy, honey," my mom said, when the introductions were over, "you simply must hear about our golf game this morning. There was the most unbelievable wind."

The whole crowd burst out laughing. "It was absurd!" my mother continued, everyone's eyes on her. "Marg nearly killed one of the caddies when the wind took her ball."

"Yes, right," said Richard, who was Marg's husband. "The *wind* was what happened to that drive."

They all laughed again, and my mother continued with the story of their game. Her eyes shone bright, as she spoke, letting her gaze move from one of her friends to the next, then back to me. These people clearly adored her, and she them. It was the happiest I'd seen my mother since Jan died. And that alone made me happy.

Eventually, my mother brought dessert out to the porch and she and her guests told more stories about a dinner they'd all been to a few nights before. The conversation ran effortlessly, my mother at ease in her role as friend and hostess.

A half hour later, her friends were saying their goodbyes. I helped my mother bring the plates into the kitchen and load the dishwasher. Now was the time, it seemed.

But how to tell her about my father? Meanwhile, my thoughts kept straying to Chris, still in his deposition, and to Harper Frankwell. I had work to do at the office, and it didn't involve a budget.

In the kitchen, my mother polished her tiny cordial glasses with a white cloth, all the while talking animatedly about the unbelievable putt Richard had made and the fabulous golf pants Blythe had purchased.

I tried once or twice to steer the topic toward my father, or toward her and me, but her chatter was too hard to derail. In some ways, I didn't want to stop her. She seemed so happy chugging away in her kitchen, and I didn't want to tear her from her new life. Yet I needed, at least, to find some part of the woman she used to be. I thought of the way my father had run from his problems, and how I'd vowed not to do the same thing any longer, not mentally or otherwise.

"Mom," I said interrupting her. I took the glass from her hand. "I have to talk to you about something."

"Of course, dear. As soon I get this done." She picked up the glass again and held it to the light, peering at it with a jeweler's cunning eye.

"I'd like to talk now, if that's okay."

"Flawless," she declared the glass, ignoring the pleading tone in my voice. "Now, let's cover up that cake." She bustled over to the cake plate, whistling an aimless tune.

I hated to do it, but there was one dose of electric shock coming up. "I *have* to talk to you." My voice was loud, something my mother disliked, and she pursed her lips, giving me a slightly stern stare.

"Mom," I said, putting my hand on her arm. "Please stop moving for a moment. *Please*. Mom, I need you."

She blinked a few times.

Before I could tell her that there was no immediate crisis, and that I needed her in a general sense, she'd pushed the cake plate away and took me by the shoulders. "Oh, sweetie, I'm sorry." She gave me a quick, tight hug. "Are you all right? And how are things with Chris? I got so caught up in my little gathering that I didn't think. Forgive me."

I sensed her there—my mother of old.

"No, it's fine," I said. "I was glad to meet your friends, and I love to see you enjoying yourself."

"Still, it's not right." She shook her head. "I really don't know how I could have forgotten to ask you. Tell me what's happening. How is Chris?" She led me to the breakfast table tucked into bay windows.

"I'm not sure," I said, settling onto a padded bench next to her. "We haven't talked much since the other night."

"Oh, Billy, don't let this go too long. You can lose each other when you do that."

Now it was my turn to blink a few times. This *was* my mother of old, the one who told me honestly when she thought I was angry or in denial about something. I'd gotten tired of that, of her constant involvement, but now, seeing her thrive, I craved that part of her again.

"You're right," I said. "There's been something wrong for a while, and we've been pushing it away."

"It's like your father and me."

At the mention of my father, I flinched internally. I worked up my courage and began to think of how to tell her I'd met him, but then her statement sank in. "What do you mean it's like you and dad?"

"Oh, I don't know. I guess I knew he was unhappy. It was hard to miss really, with his drinking and his moods, but I didn't do anything about it."

I turned toward her on the bench. "Mom, you did nothing wrong. He was the one who left out of the blue."

She put her hand over mine. "Nothing really happens out of the blue, and rarely is someone completely blameless. I know I'm not."

"That's ridiculous."

"No, it's not."

"You didn't do anything," I said.

"That's the whole point, baby doll. I didn't *do* anything. You know how my family was."

I nodded. My mother had been raised on the North Shore. She'd been "trained," as she put it, to be a perfect country club wife. She hated it, but she learned how to set the perfect table, how to iron her husband's shirts with precisely the right amount of starch, how to make witty banter with the neighbors she disliked. She met my father at a jazz club, where she'd gone on a whim, and she realized immediately he wouldn't be the husband her family wished for her. He was a playboy with a mysterious importing job that involved lots of overseas travel. But they fell in love, and she got pregnant. She said she felt alive for the first time. But that excitement didn't last long. She was busy with the quick succession of three children, and before she knew it, her husband had left her.

"Your father was rarely happy in our marriage," she said.

Like Chris, I thought.

"But I didn't want to see it," she continued. "Oh, it was obvious in many ways, as I said, but I tried to ignore it. I thought if I were the ideal wife, he would eventually settle into this new life and he'd love it."

"It still wasn't your fault, Mom. He was the one who ran away."

She shrugged, rearranging her pink sweater around her shoulders. "I don't think in terms of fault anymore, although as I said, I know I'm not blameless. I should have faced things head on, long before he thought to leave. That's why my marriage with Jan was so much better. I didn't look the other way anymore, not about his problems or mine."

"That's how I want it to be with Chris," I said. "Starting today, in fact." Chris had asked for time alone, but I'd decided that he'd had enough time. Not because I didn't respect his need for privacy, but because I'd started to see how entirely too much time had passed without me addressing our distance. In some ways, I think I had expected it, some subliminal part of my psyche telling me that all men left—physically or emotionally—at some point. I was hoping Chris hadn't entirely taken off yet.

"Good luck, sweetie." My mother's dark eyes searched my face. "And if you don't get it right the first time, try again."

I felt a swell of emotion in my throat. "Thanks."

"And let me know if I can help you," she said. "I'm not sure why but I've been a little…" She shook her head, a slightly puzzled expression on her face. "Well, I've been a little different lately. Really, I've been having such a good time." She gave a breezy laugh. "But I want you to know that I love you, Billy, and I'm always available for you. *Always.*"

"I'm here for you, too."

"I know."

I smiled at her, at my mom who had been there all along. I wouldn't have to shock her with the news of meeting my father. I would tell her eventually, but there was no need to bruise her with it. Instead, I would talk to her about Chris. I would ask her more about how she felt about Jan's death, and how she felt now about her friends and her new life.

I caught a glimpse of fresh potential in my relationship with my mother. We might not be able to get back to the way we'd been before the frog. But we might be better.

Late in the afternoon, I took a cab downtown. When it reached my condo, I asked the driver to wait. It was 3:30, which meant I could still get to the office before Roslyn left. I wanted to drop off my bag and change clothes first.

In the condo, it was quiet, a stale scent in the air. Had Chris been staying somewhere else? I went to our room and checked the master bath. A damp towel lay on the floor from this morning, and his contacts case and solution were lying haphazardly by his sink, the way he always left them when he was in a rush. The rest of the house was similarly disorganized. My usually structured husband must have had a rough week. He must have never opened the windows to let in fresh air. The thought made me incredibly sad, then optimistic. He was upset, true, but that meant there was still something between us that could shake him. Which meant, I decided to believe, that I might be right about my instincts. We might carry those packages again.

I went to my closet. I considered light pants and a summer sweater, the kind of outfit many people at Harper Frankwell would be wearing on a Friday, but I had important business. I put on my sage-green suit with a white blouse and black spectator pumps. I opened every window before I left.

During the drive to Michigan Avenue, I noticed the trees were full and vividly green. People crowded the streets and sat outside at cafés. It was early June, and it was officially summer in Chicago, the start of a new season.

Once inside, I said hello to the receptionist and went to my office. I stood in the doorway, resisting the urge to sink into the butter-yellow seat. I looked at the stack of budgets to the right of my desk and the notes about prices for the new prints that might decorate the foyer. Then I looked behind my desk to the credenza where Odette's cookbook stood, along with my old orange notebook, where I used to keep all my random ideas for press releases. I thought about my father's words, *Sometimes you have to know when to double back.*

I turned and walked the gray carpeted hallway toward Roslyn's office, half praying she was there, half fearing. But I knew I could find her somewhere in the building, since Roslyn was rarely anywhere else. This job at Harper Frankwell was her life. Her whole life. I wanted the job, too—one I enjoyed—but I wanted the other parts of me to flourish as well.

My heart rate picked up as I neared her office. The suit I was wearing suddenly felt stifling. I blew my bangs away from my forehead with a puff of air. I tried to clear my mind and think of how to say what I knew I had to say.

Roslyn was at her desk. "Hello, Billy," she said when she saw me. "Nice of you to come in."

"Can I have a minute?"

"I'd like that. I think we need to talk."

I closed her door. "So do I."

She took off her glasses that were affixed to a silver cord and let them fall onto her chest. She tilted her head a little and said, "I think we both know that you weren't sick the last two days."

I coughed, not to fake illness, but because she'd surprised me. I hadn't expected her to call me on it so quickly. Yet I was glad. I wanted to be honest with her, and she'd just opened the door. Wide.

"I'm sorry, Roslyn." I said, "You're right. I wasn't sick. I had some…family matters to attend to. And I have something to discuss with you."

She gave me her patented tight-lipped, raised-eyebrow smile, which said, *This better be good.*

I swallowed hard. I sat up straighter. "I want you to demote me. I'd like my old job back."

Roslyn sat back in her chair so quickly that her breath seemed to have been shoved out of her lungs, causing her to make a loud "humpph" sound.

I enjoyed a childish moment of triumph. I'd shocked the unshockable Roslyn.

"You want to be *demoted?*" she asked. She began to laugh. Admittedly, being scornfully laughed at was not as fun as shocking her.

"Yes," I said with force in my voice. "I'd like to be an account exec again."

Roslyn got her mirth under control and sat forward, elbows on her desk. "Billy, you've been a VP for how long now?"

About four weeks, I wanted to say, since *Blinda gave me that frog.* But I remembered that first morning, when everyone thought I'd been a vice president for a whole lot longer. "Well, geez," I said, deciding to bat the question back to her, "how long has it been?"

Roslyn opened her mouth to speak, but nothing came out. She clamped her mouth closed. "Hmm," she said. "I can't remember. Troubling." She shook her head, her perfectly styled hair never moving. "Anyway, the point I was trying to make was that you've been in this position for a while, so why in the world would you want to backslide and become a—" she shuddered "—an account exec?" She said "account exec" the way others might say "child molester."

"Let me ask you something. Do you think I'm a good vice president?"

She pursed her lips. "Well, I wanted to talk to you because I think there are definite areas that require improvement."

"Exactly. I'm really not great as a VP. But did you think I was a good account exec?"

More pursing of lips. "You weren't bringing in the big clients."

"But bringing in the big clients is only important if you want to be a vice president, right?"

"I suppose that's true. You did have your own cadre of small-time clients, and you handled them quite well."

"And I did a good job on other people's projects, right?"

"Yes, you're an excellent team member, but—"

"I'm sorry to interrupt, Roslyn, but I think you see my point. I am better suited to be an account exec than a VP."

"But Billy," she said in a chiding tone. "How embarrassing. To be demoted? It's unthinkable."

It would have been unthinkable to me in the past. Back then, I was all about forward motion, at least in my mind. I wanted to get a job, get engaged, get promoted, get married, keep moving, keep achieving. What I'd forgotten to do was stop and look for the quality, the satisfaction in each station. I'd also forgotten to actually *decide* what direction I wanted to take next. I'd been walking a scripted path, never halting to ask whether it was the right path for me. Not everyone needed to be an officer of a company. Accomplishment, I'd realized, needn't always come in the form of a raise or a title. Instead, I would find accomplishment in giving the best performance I could in a job I loved.

"You demoted Scott Billingham last year," I pointed out to Roslyn.

"Well, he was horrible. He deserved it."

"I deserve this. I *want* it."

Roslyn gazed at me with a perplexed expression. "What would we tell people?"

"I'll handle it. I'll send out the memos and explain to everyone that we both thought it was best."

She gave me a wry smile. "Now you're acting like a VP."

I smiled back.

"Well," she said, "we are still looking to fill Alexa's position, so your timing couldn't be better."

My stomach cramped. "Oh, no, I couldn't step into her job." How could I possibly take Alexa's space when I'd so unfairly axed her?

Roslyn shrugged. "That's what's available, Billy. Take it or leave it."

"What about *my* old position? The one that was vacated when I was promoted?"

Roslyn scoffed. "That was filled eons ago."

"By who?"

Again, she cocked her head. "I can't remember now. Good Lord, what's wrong with me? But it doesn't matter, that position is long gone. You'll have to take Alexa's spot."

"Couldn't we rehire her? I know I asked before, but really, she's such an asset." I'd send myself to the street if it meant getting Alexa her job back.

Roslyn gave me a queer look. "You're right, we have discussed this, and as I said then, this company does not rehire people who were terminated for cause. End of discussion. You'll be taking her position. Effective Monday."

My arms quivered as I walked the hallway, trying to shrug off my jacket. It felt as heavy and hot as armor. In my head, my overachieving sisters sang a chorus—*What have you done? What have you done? You've given up an officer's position!* They were loud and hitting lots of high notes, which made my body tremble more. I'd just willingly tossed away the position I'd strived toward for over a decade. I heard my father's voice—much weaker—chime in with, *Sometimes you have to know when to double back.*

I got a flash of what it would be like to come in Monday morning—quizzical, pitying looks from coworkers, packing of my office and retreating to a tiny cubicle, attempts to explain it (a lame, "I thought this would be best for me"), receiving of assignments from people *I'd* been ordering around lately. I began to sweat.

I took off my jacket and rolled my shoulders to release the tension, reminding myself that it didn't matter how this would look to others, it only mattered how it felt to me. And the truth was, when I peered around my panic and examined the rest of my mind, I spied sheer relief.

Except for one thing. I had to talk to Alexa and soon, before she got wind of this. I wasn't even sure if Alexa still spoke to anyone from Harper Frankwell, other than myself, but I knew it had to be me who told her. And this was a conversation that had to take place in person, I decided. In a strange way, I'd come to enjoy Alexa's friendship, and she deserved face-to-face honesty. I looked at my watch—4:15. I stopped at an empty cubicle and dialed Chris's number. His secretary said that she thought his dep would last at least another two hours. Just enough time for me to stop by Alexa's.

I hustled toward the elevator, tossing my jacket over my arm, but a voice made me stop.

"Getting ready for me?" Evan said.

I turned, and there he was, all blond hair and dimples, smiling a private smile. "Excuse me?" I said politely.

He gestured with his chin toward the coat I'd stripped off, and gave me a wicked raise of one eyebrow.

"Ev," I said.

He took a few steps until we were only an inch apart. "I missed you," he said in that low voice.

I took in the tanned skin of his face and the brown flecks in his green eyes. I glanced at those lips, the lower one pillowy and much larger than the top. But instead of feeling thrilled and stirred inside, I felt ill with remorse, and now I started noticing everything Chris had that Evan didn't. Chris's eyes were kind while Evan's, at least to me, were blatantly sexual. Chris's mouth was generous, waiting to tell stories about Shakespeare's myth and his own hunt for the perfect Raclette cheese, ready to smile at me or kiss me on the forehead, while Evan's mouth was ready only for laughs and raw pleasure.

I had outgrown my crush.

"Can I talk to you privately?" I said.

The eyebrow shot higher. "Anytime."

I turned and walked toward my office. Might as well use it one more time. I closed the door behind us and leaned my back against the door. Evan perched on the desk.

"I thought I explained on the phone," I said. "I asked you to respect me and my marriage. None of this—" I waved my hand between him and me "—can happen again."

His cocky grin fled his face, and he looked at me pensively. "I did listen to you. I'm leaving Harper Frankwell."

"What?" I stepped away from the door, toward him, thinking now of Evan only as my friend, my one friend in this firm.

"I'm going to New York. To Norwich & Towney. I just accepted the job five minutes ago."

Right when I was demoting myself. "You can't leave Harper. You've been here forever."

"Exactly. Time to move on." He loosened the collar of his blue and white checked shirt. "And like you said, I had to respect your decision. With me gone, nothing will happen."

"Oh, God, Ev. I've made such a mess of this." I covered my face with my hands. I'd wished for Evan to be interested in me. More than interested—I'd hoped for him to lust after me. I'd gotten the interest, I'd gotten the lust, and I'd made such a spectacular muddle of it Evan felt he had to leave.

"You didn't do anything," Evan said. "I've been thinking about New York anyway."

I raised my face. "You were?"

"Hell, yeah. I've dated all the women in Chicago, right? Greener pastures and all that."

We both laughed, but they were small, weak laughs.

"You're sure?" I said.

"I'm positive. Two weeks, baby, and I'm living on Spring Street."

"When will you tell Roslyn?"

"Right now."

"I don't know if now is a good time, especially after the conversation I just had with her."

"What conversation is that?"

"I demoted myself."

He scoffed. "C'mon."

"I'm serious. I asked for my job back as an account exec."

His mouth dropped open a little. "Are you kidding? Why?"

"I'm no good at being a VP."

"You were good enough. You just didn't like it."

I thought about that for a moment. "You could tell?"

"Of course I could tell. We grew up together around here."

We were both silent.

"You know, Ev," I said, breaking the silence. "Roslyn is going to ask you to leave immediately."

"I know."

I thought about the first time I'd seen Evan—standing at the receptionist's desk with his brand-new briefcase. I thought of our closed-door meetings in his office where we'd gossip about coworkers, and I thought about our lunches discussing dates and families and career paths. Now those paths had diverged. Our lives were heading for opposite ports. Hopefully, like friends from the past, we'd always remember the exceptional moments spent together.

"I'll miss you," I said. "I'll miss our friendship."

He touched me on the shoulder, then took his hand away, leaving a cold spot. "We'll always be friends," he said. But it sounded like a greeting card designed for high school graduation, and I knew the situation was probably the same. We promised to be close forever; we'd mean it. But new friends and daily routines would get in the way.

"I should talk to Roslyn," he said. "You know, give her time to forge a warpath to my desk and set fire to it."

"Right," I said. "Make you an example for others."

"Exactly."

I opened the door and stepped back to let him pass. I wanted to hug him, but it no longer seemed an option. We'd gone past the point of friendly embraces.

"See you," I said.

He grinned. "Yeah, see you."

I knew we were both lying.

At Alexa's building, I asked the cabbie to wait.

"Make it quick," he grumbled.

The warm weather had brought everyone to their cement stoops, and I had to pick my way past four teenaged guys to get to the buzzer. They stopped their conversation. They eyed me predatorily, as if I was holding the latest video game that featured mass killing.

"Hello, sweetheart," one of them said under his breath. The others giggled—snide sounds.

"Hello," I said, with all the primness of an English governess.

I hit the buzzer for Alexa's apartment, trying to appear efficient and nonchalant, but fear and dread grew inside. I glanced at the cab. I could get to it in ten steps if need be. God, was this what Alexa went through every day?

"Hola," someone said through the buzzer.

"Hi, uh, it's Billy Rendall, I'm here to see Alexa, if you could just buzz me in…" I spoke the words so fast, I wasn't sure anyone could decipher them, but the buzzer sounded. I pushed the door hard, slamming it closed behind me, still under the watchful eyes of the teenagers.

I took the stairs quickly.

Alexa opened the door. "Billy! How are you?" She gave me a quick embrace, which left me flustered and flattered. "Come in, come in," she said, as if I always stopped by. "I have to show you something."

The place was much as I'd seen it last time—old, mismatched furniture, a TV with rabbit-ear antennae, toys scattered throughout. The kitchen, viewed from the living room, was tidy, but the Formica tops were yellowed, the linoleum floor cracking.

"Look," Alexa said proudly. She held out her arm, gesturing toward the corner of the living room, where an old door had been laid across two stacks of blue milk crates. On top of the door, sat a host of papers and pens and, in the middle, a silver cell phone.

"What's this?" I said, taking a step closer.

"It's my desk!" Alexa was beaming, as if she'd said, *It's my new Porsche!*

"Wow, great." But I was ashamed. What I had in my life, both before and after the frog, could easily be termed an "embarrassment of riches." I hadn't worried about money

in years. Alexa, on the other hand, was scraping by, supporting an entire family, and was thrilled about a desk made from
a door.

"So you're working from home?" I asked her.

"I know it isn't much, but I'm determined to open my
own firm, like I told you on the phone, so here…" She
moved behind the makeshift desk. "Let me show you." She
picked up one stack of papers after another, displaying them
for me. "Here's my application for a small business loan, and
here's a lease on this tiny office I found if I get the loan. Say
a prayer."

"This is great," I said.

She held up a two typed sheets of paper. "Then here's a
list of potential clients, and this is a list of people who might
give me capital, like Carlos Ortega. Do you know him?"

I shook my head no.

"Well, he's big-time around here. He used to be an alder-
man, now he's into venture capital and real estate. I'm too
small-fry for him, but you gotta aim high, right?"

"Absolutely," I said. "You amaze me, Alexa."

"Oh, it's nothing." But she smiled as she placed the papers
onto neat stacks already on her desk.

I couldn't help but think of Alexa's clean cubicle, the one
I'd inhabit on Monday. "Look," I said, "I have to tell you
something."

She looked at me. "Of course. God, I've been going on
and on, and you didn't come here to see my paperwork. Hey,
what happened with your dad?"

"It was really… Well, it was wonderful for what it was.
Thanks for asking. But that's not what I have to talk to you
about."

"What's up?"

"I demoted myself today."

"What?" Her eyes went big.

"Yeah, I know it sounds weird, but I asked Roslyn to take away my VP position and give me my old account exec job back."

Alexa surprised me by hooting and clapping her hands. "Holy shit! Roslyn must have lost it!"

"She was pretty good, all things considered, but there is something else." I took a deep breath, and plunged ahead. "She said I'd have to take *your* job. It's the only opening."

Alexa's head snapped a little as if someone had startled her.

"But you know what?" I said, rushing in with my words. "I don't think I can do it. I told her I would, but now…"

She watched me closely. "Now what?"

"I like you, Alexa. I like hanging out with you." I paused. She remained stoic. "And I don't want to ruin that by taking your old position. So forget it. I'm just going to have to look for a new job. I can't take yours."

She shook her head. "No, that's ridiculous. There are no jobs in this town, remember?"

"I know, but—"

"Look, Billy…" She smiled briefly. "What I said on the phone a few days ago was true. I think you did me a favor by firing me. I am going to get that PR firm of my own. I don't know how and I don't know when, but I've realized how much I want it since I left Harper. So let me do you a favor in return. Take my job. Enjoy it. *Really* enjoy it, you know?"

That was exactly what I wanted—to take pleasure in my job without the mental machinations of how to slide into a VP spot. "You're sure?" I asked.

She stood and reached out her tiny hand, squeezing mine. "I'm positive."

We stood there a moment, our hands touching, and I recognized something in Alexa right then. Here was a friend.

"Hey," Alexa said, "how about a beer? It's almost five."

I shook my head. "I'd love it," I said, "but I'm hoping I have plans with my husband."

chapter eighteen

I saw Chris appear at the edge of Grant Park's green lawn. He turned his head this way and that. Finally, he seemed to notice me, sitting cross-legged on a blanket, our picnic basket next to me. He paused. He was too far away for me to read the expression on his face, but that pause scared me. I sat up taller and waved. Another pause. I gestured for him to come to me. His body was still.

"Chris," I called out, waving again.

It felt suddenly as if I were in a bad dream, one where I could feel Chris, I could see him, but he couldn't, or wouldn't, see me.

At last, Chris raised his hand slightly. That hand floated up to his chest and sank again. It made an arc in the sunlight. Then he took a step onto the green.

"What's all this?" he said when he reached me.

"A picnic. It's a beautiful Friday evening, and I thought we could use it."

He nodded.

"Sit, please," I said.

He sank on his knees onto the green tartan blanket.

"I got all your favorites," I said. I flipped the latch of the wicker picnic basket. I took out the items I'd picked up just a half hour ago—a creamy Tomme de Chevre cheese, delicate rice crackers, star fruit, a long, thin loaf of French bread.

"Nice. Thank you," Chris said. The formality between us was killing me.

I pulled a bottle of Merlot from the basket and handed it to Chris with a corkscrew. He went to work on the wine, while I set out glasses and plates for the food. I'd purposely brought the silver wine goblets we used as toasting glasses during our wedding. Chris noticed, his eyes locking on them, then rising to meet mine. He gave me a slight grin. He took the wrapper off the cheese. I slid the bread from its paper sleeve. We did this all in quiet preparation for what we both knew wouldn't be a whimsical, easy picnic in Grant Park. This was a summit meeting.

Once we each had a glass of wine, and I'd set out the food, there was nothing else to busy our hands.

"Chris," I said, and again my voice sounded formal, even ominous.

He looked at me. There was something sad in his eyes.

I couldn't think of how to start. There were too many things to say, none of them the right jumping-off point.

Chris saved me. "Tell me about the rest of your time with your dad."

I smiled gratefully. He gave me a small lift of his mouth in return.

"Well, it was interesting," I said. I told Chris everything about the night with my dad and Lillian and Kenny. I told him how I'd been cruel to my father, and how it had felt both good and horrible. I told him how kind and wise I thought

Lillian was. I told him about my conversation with Dustin, and how, despite my sister's warnings, I was glad I'd found our father.

"And I came to some realizations while I was out there," I said.

"Like what?"

"I realized that I don't know what a great marriage looks like. I was only around my mom and Jan for a year before I went to college, and obviously my mom and dad didn't help me out. In some ways, in my mind, I think I set us up to fail. I was afraid you'd do the same thing as my dad."

I'd been playing with my glass, but now I looked up at Chris. He nodded at me to continue.

"We may not have a perfect marriage, Chris, but we have so much. We have money and our health and an amazing home and families who love us."

Chris watched me, his eyes intent on mine.

I took a gulp of air. "But more importantly," I said, "we have something special between you and me. It's love. I don't just mean that I love you like I love my mom. *I am in love with you,* Chris. And I think that's a big distinction. I nearly forgot that after we first got married. I forgot it recently with the whole…" I couldn't bring myself to say Evan's name.

Chris winced a little. "Go on."

"What I'm trying to say is we can't blow this. We can't take this gift for granted." I got a catch in my throat. I willed myself to plow forward. "Look, I know what happened at the beginning, from my point of view anyway. I expected you to run, and in a way you did, but I need to know why. You said something the other night about how during the wedding I cared more about place settings than I did about us. And you said that afterward I cared more about work. Then you shut down. Is that really what you felt?"

Chris took a sip of his wine and looked across the park. A pack of joggers ran by. A lone biker rode past. But on the patch of lawn, we were alone. Now it was my turn to stay silent.

"I don't know how to describe it," Chris said, "and this is going to sound, well…silly. But I felt left out during the wedding. You and your mom were the fearsome twosome. You were planning that event for the whole year, and I rarely got consulted. I started to wonder whether you wanted to marry me, or whether you just wanted to get married."

"That's crazy. I've never been one of those girls who was just looking for a ring."

"I know, I know. But I started to wonder. I felt so isolated from you during that time."

"I didn't think you wanted to be that involved. I had no idea you felt left out. Why didn't you say anything?"

He shrugged. "What guy wants to get all worked up about flowers and tablecloths? I can see now that I should have talked to you, but I thought I'd wait it out. I just wanted to be married so things could get back to the way they were before."

"But they never did get back that way. You stayed distant."

He took a bite of cheese, his jaws moved sharply as he chewed. "Not always."

"No, you're right, not always, but…"

"I know what you mean," he said. "I was…what's the word? Removed. A lot of the time. It was kind of easy to be that way. You were working your butt off to make VP."

"And you were working your butt off to make partner."

"I know. We didn't put our marriage first."

I looked down at my glass. I thought of my mother's words about lack of blame. "No, I guess we didn't."

"I held myself back from you more and more," Chris said. "I hated it, but I didn't know how to change it. And I missed you, Billy. I mean I really missed you, even though you were right there."

I nodded. I knew what he meant.

"The days slipped by," he said. "It's such a lame excuse, but I got used to acting that way."

"We should have talked about this before," I said, mastering the world of understatement.

He nodded.

"Do you think it's too late?" I had to ask.

Chris stared at Lake Michigan, then turned toward me. "Do you?"

In his brown eyes, I saw memories. The blind date when we met, with Tess and her husband smiling proudly across the table. The walk home down Sheffield Avenue, when Chris loosened his yellow tie and stopped me on the sidewalk, saying, "Can I please, please kiss you?" Chris with his shirtsleeves rolled up, making me sea bass and salad in our condo. The times when we'd lie nose to nose in bed, talking about our day.

"No," I said. "I want to try."

His hand slid across the blanket and touched mine. "Me, too."

"Would you go to therapy?" I said this quietly. I'd brought up the topic before, but he was always reluctant.

"Yes," Chris said without hesitation.

I gripped his hand. "You would?"

"Yeah," Chris said. "You're my wife."

Those words—*my wife*—sent me soaring to the sky.

Chris and I had enjoyed the picnic in the park, but now we had to clean up. Literally and emotionally, there were dishes to be scraped, food to be thrown away, the blanket to be folded and stowed. And none of it was neat. Crumbs were everywhere, the blanket had grass sticking to it, and spilt wine made it all sticky.

The rest of Friday evening was beautiful, as if Chris and I were lit by candlelight. Saturday morning, however, brought harsh sunlight.

"Why can't you put this stuff away?" Chris said through the open door of the bathroom. I was still in bed, stretching like a cat and ready for our pasts to be over, for the rest of our life to start.

I blinked at the irritated tone of his words and pushed myself up on my elbows. The first thing I noticed was the frog, still on my nightstand. I looked past the frog to Chris and saw that he was holding a white bottle of face cleanser I'd left near my side of the vanity. "I always leave that out," I said.

"I know. And it bugs me." He made a big show of opening the maple medicine chest and placing the bottle firmly on a shelf. He closed the cabinet with something nearing a slam.

I flipped the covers back and went into the bathroom, slipping my arm around his waist. "What's up?"

His body was tense. "Nothing."

"C'mon."

"Nothing."

I turned him to face me. "Chris, we decided yesterday that we wouldn't say nothing's wrong if it is, and I know it's not my face soap. So tell me."

His eyes roamed my face. "It really is nothing. Nothing specific. I just think it's going to take some time to get over everything."

I felt a sinking of my spirits, then the familiar desire to hide. Or run from what we had right in front of us. Instead, I paused and thought about the concept of time and what Chris had said. "I get it, okay? You need to trust me again, and that'll take time. In some ways, I feel the same. It's going to take me a little while to accept the fact that you withdrew from me years ago and didn't tell me why. And I have to get over that I didn't do anything about it."

His face was impassive.

"We're in this together," I said. "That's the whole point. We have to start from right now."

"It's not going to be easy."

"I know."

His eyes studied mine, then something in his face relaxed. He put his arms around me and pulled me into his chest. "I fucking love you," he said into my hair.

At that moment, I realized that our relationship, if we could get it to work, would never be as perfect as when we were first dating. But then I was also coming to recognize that our life back then probably hadn't been perfect either. I'd just wanted to see it that way.

And since I was redefining words and concepts, like "marriage" and "accomplishment," maybe I needed to redefine "perfect" too. "Perfect," in the context of our relationship, didn't have to mean a marriage free of conflict or tension. But it would, hopefully, mean a marriage free of apathy and of deception. It would mean a relationship heavy on trust and affection.

Something made me turn and glance at the frog then, and I could swear I saw it wink.

chapter nineteen

Sunday afternoon was muggy, but the early evening was willow-tree cool. With Chris napping on the couch, I put on my running shoes, left the condo, and walked and walked and walked. I wasn't sure what had drawn me outside. I had nowhere to be, no errands I needed to run.

As I crossed LaSalle Street, I figured it out. I couldn't help but glance at the brick three-flat across the street. Blinda's place. I'd walked by a number of times since she left on her trip, and her basement unit was always dark, the shades pulled tight. Now, the drapes were open and there was lamplight from within. I fought the urge to head straight to her door and pound on it. Instead, I hurried home. Chris was still asleep. I went into our bedroom and lifted the frog from my nightstand.

I looked at its little face, which I'd grown oddly fond of. I studied its legs that appeared ready to leap.

"Time to say goodbye," I whispered.

I rushed back to LaSalle Street and crossed the road, hitting the buzzer for Blinda's apartment.

"Hello?" came Blinda's melodic voice through the intercom.

"Blinda, it's Billy Rendall. Sorry to just stop by on a Sunday, but I saw your light was on and—"

The buzzer sounded. The door clicked open. I pushed it and moved to her inside door. And there she was, looking just like she always had. Her long blond hair was in need of a good brushing. She wore a flowing pink skirt in some kind of crinkly cotton material and a navy blue top with spaghetti straps.

"Billy," she said kindly, waving a hand inside. "I'm so pleased to see you." She made it sound as if she'd been calling me for weeks, instead of the other way around. "Sit, sit," she said, gesturing to her woolly red and orange couch. The place looked the same, too—yellow candles flickering from the bamboo side tables, boxes of Kleenex at the ready.

"How was Africa?" I said to be polite. What I wanted to say was, *Where have you been? How could you give me that frog and then disappear?*

"Africa was surreal and sublime and heartbreaking," she said. "It always is."

"Good," I said. "Well, I think that's good, right?"

She smiled beatifically. "It was good. And you, Billy? How are you?"

"Huh. Well." Where to begin? "About the frog."

She took a seat across from me. "Yes, the frog."

"Why did you give it to me?"

"Why don't you tell me what happened first?" Her green-blue eyes widened and she leaned forward, as if waiting for my answer with great interest.

I thought about demanding that she tell *me* everything first, everything she knew about the frog and why I'd received it, but I was struck with the thought that none of it really mattered. The fact was she'd given it to me, it had changed me and eventually I'd dealt with that change.

So I started talking. I told Blinda how everything had been altered after that one night. I told her about the last month and what I'd done after I couldn't get rid of the frog—how I'd gotten my life back to the way I wanted it at this moment.

"Sounds like you've got it under control," Blinda said.

"For now."

She laughed, nodding. "I'm glad you realize that. Life is always a balancing act. There's no goal line."

I reached for my purse and removed the frog at the bottom. "Is that what you were trying to teach me when you gave me this? Were you trying to show me that no matter what you want or what goals you have, there will always be something to deal with when you reach those goals? Were you trying to show me that no one's life is ever perfect?"

"I've been told everyone learns their own message from the frog," she said.

"What do you mean 'everyone'?"

"Everyone who's had him."

"So other people have had this frog and been changed by it?"

She nodded. "That's what I've been told. I was one of them."

"Oh." I stared at her, stumped. I wanted to ask, *What happened to you? Tell me your story.* But somehow I knew Blinda would only smile peacefully and ask me a question in return. "Well, look, I've got to give the frog back."

She shook her head. "No, no. You have to give it to someone else."

"What? Says who?"

"That's just how it works."

"I already tried to give it to a museum."

Blinda cocked her head a little. "What happened?"

"It came back."

"I've heard that would happen if you weren't truly done with it. Now that you are, you have to pass it on to someone else. An individual who needs it."

"But I can't give this thing to someone else." I glanced at the frog. His eyes bulged up at mine. His slash of a mouth seemed to deepen in a grin. "He brought me hell."

Blinda gave me a patient smile. "Is that really true?"

I looked at the thing again. I rubbed the little bumps on his back, letting the last month swirl through my head. "It hasn't been all bad. The things I wanted were legitimate. But after I got what I wanted, some things, like my job, weren't how I imagined they would be. And others—" I frowned "—like having Evan flirt with me and my mom get her own life. Well, they just brought their own issues. Mostly, I wanted to feel like I had some part in the course my life was taking."

"But you did in the end, didn't you?" Blinda asked. "You've created the world you've got now."

I nodded.

"So, now you've got to pass him on," Blinda said. "That's how it works."

Three weeks later, Alexa and I met for coffee at a diner on Lincoln Avenue; in fact, we met regularly for coffee or tea now, discussing Alexa's dream of opening her own firm, filling her in on the gossip from Harper Frankwell. I'd also been going to the suburbs one night a week to see Tess and the kids, but it was nice to have a girlfriend in the city.

At each of the get-togethers with Alexa, I carried the frog with me, looking for the right opportunity to carry out Blinda's mandate. Whenever I saw one, though, I began fretting—*Could I do it? Should I do it?* It seemed reckless. Who knew what havoc the frog could wreak? And yet when I called Blinda, she asked me to look around and see what the frog had brought me. And what I saw was a life that fit and a husband to share it with. I wanted that for Alexa, too. Or whatever her version of happiness entailed.

"I'm just nervous," Alexa said now. "It's nearly impossible to get money to start a business, you know?"

I nodded.

"I was turned down again for a small business loan. And of course, I never heard from that Carlos Ortega guy I was hitting up for capital." She shook her head sadly. Her hair was loose around her face. She wore white Capri jeans and a white blouse.

"I'm so sorry," I said.

"I am, too."

"It'll come together."

"So why is nothing happening? I'm getting scared." Her eyes darted to mine, then back down. She seemed slightly embarrassed by her confession. She rushed on. "And it's not just professionally. I mean, I'm tired of living with my family. I'm tired of dating these neighborhood boys my mother keeps setting me up with."

"Alexa, you're an awesome person, and let's face it, you're gorgeous. You're going to find someone."

She blew on her coffee. "Someone like your Chris, huh?"

"Exactly." Chris and I had been working hard to be honest with each other, to make time for each other. We'd begun to carry the packages of our marriage more carefully again. It was sometimes uncomfortable and foreign, but it was imbued with the low light of optimism, bringing our home a whole new kind of feeling. "You'll find a Chris for you," I said to Alexa.

"I'm starting to doubt that." She stared at the white mug of coffee in front of her, her eyes flat, her mouth downturned.

"Hey, look at me."

She glanced up, her eyes still emotionless.

"I think you're going to get everything you want," I said. "And I mean *everything*. It just might not be an easy road. Can you handle that?"

Her eyes flickered with passion now. "Are you kidding? I've never had an easy road in my life. I just want something to happen. *Now.*"

I sucked in a chestful of air, biting my lip. "I want to give you something."

"A loaded handgun?"

"No," I said, chuckling. I reached in my bag and found the frog, my hand closing over it. I looked up to meet her eyes, nervous. "Here you go." I held out the frog, a scrap of jade in my pale hand.

Alexa took it. "That's really nice of you."

I could tell she was underimpressed, and I couldn't blame her. I remembered my own less than wondrous reaction when Blinda gave it to me.

"It's sort of a…" I said. How to put this? "It's a charm."

"What kind?" Alexa turned it around and studied it.

"Trust me on this." I closed her hand around the frog and gripped her fist in mine. "It's a good luck charm."

epilogue

Alexa Villa moved through the darkened apartment. This was her favorite time, when the place was silent. When her mother, her aunt and all the kids were asleep. The apartment was never truly dark, due to the blazing streetlights outside, but with the blinds closed like now, those lights gave a yellow radiance she found comforting.

She found her purse on the kitchen counter, next to a stack of dishes crusted with macaroni and cheese. Ignoring the dishes, she brought the purse back to her single bed. Across the room, in the other twin bed, two of her nieces slept soundly, their dark hair mingling on the white of the sheets.

Alexa switched on the tiny, bedside lamp and dug in her purse for her notebook. She'd just had an idea about a Hispanic university dean who might give her some work. Her fingers brushed past pens and lipsticks and her checkbook. The notebook seemed to be missing. But what did it matter? He probably wouldn't want her PR services. Probably no one would. She didn't have an office yet or any capital to get one. The doubts about this path she'd chosen got bigger and bigger. She lay back against the headboard, feeling overwhelmed with a sense of futility.

Think positive, she told herself, but it was tough. Listlessly, she reached for the purse again and pushed her hand deeper inside, her fingers closing over something small and cool and smooth.

She sat up and took it out. She held it under the lamp's circle of soft light. The frog Billy had given her. An odd present.

She looked at it closer, she saw that it glittered in the lamplight, as if it was made from polished stone. Something about the frog struck her as charming. She studied it some more, turning it around in her hand.

Then she set it on her nightstand, right next to the lamp. Forgetting about her notebook, she turned off the light.

The next morning, Alexa helped get the kids ready for school and out the door. Once the place was quiet, she sat at her makeshift desk. She took a few deep breaths and rolled her head from side to side. It was getting harder and harder to get herself going in the morning.

After a few more neck stretches, she reached in the milk crate to the side of the desk and took out a few files. She lifted her cell phone and switched it on. As she did so, it sprung to life in her hand, the screen lighting up pink then green then purple, the ringer chiming loudly through the apartment.

It was probably the second bank she'd applied to, telling her she'd been rejected for a loan. She sighed as she hit the answer button. She reminded herself of her internal promise to be professional, no matter what. "Alexa Villa," she said. "Good morning."

"*Buenos dias.* This is Carlos Ortega. I'd like to talk to you about your business proposal."

Book Club Questions
for *The Night I Got Lucky*

Would you want to get everything you wished for overnight? What are those things you would ask for?

If all your wishes were granted, do you see any problems that would arise? Are all your desires realistic? Do they fit your personality and your life?

Why do we so often think the grass is greener on the other side? Have you, or someone you know, gotten what they wished for and found the grass wasn't so green? How did they handle the situation?

Do you know anyone who, like Billy, feels as if they're trying to make things happen in their life but who is actually rather passive?

For Billy, the price of wish fulfillment was the feeling that no one in her life had free will. Would you want your wishes granted if the players in your life had no say in it?

What did you think about Billy's unresolved feelings for her absentee father? Do you believe that abandonment like that in one's childhood can affect the adult?

For this dyed-in-the-wool city mom,
life in the country is no walk in the park…

Wonderboy
Fiona Gibson
On sale September 2005

Urbanite parents Ro and Marcus are trading in life in
London's fast lane for a quiet country life in Chetsley.
As Ro struggles to adjust to the "simple life" though,
she learns that her husband's reasons for moving may
not have been so simple, and Ro must make a decision
that may change her and her son's life for good.

RED DRESS INK
™

www.RedDressInk.com

RDIFG532TR